THE HUNT FOR THE RAJPUT PRINCESS

Also by OSCAR Z. HUTSON

SEE YOU IN HELL

MUGHAL GOLD

THE FLIGHT OF THE WHITE DOVE

OSCAR Z. HUTSON

THE HUNT FOR THE RAJPUT PRINCESS

Chapter One

The small turbo-prop plane touched down at the small rustic airport on the outskirts of Jullundur, India. Elijah Davenport looked out his window and saw several planes parked on the tarmac with ramps near their open doors. Passengers were boarding one of them. A cloud of dust whirled by, making many on the ground shield their faces with their hands. He looked further into the distance and saw range after range of purple mountains. Excitement shot through him. He had seen them before. It was the mighty Himalayas. The plane coasted to a stop. He picked up his briefcase and walked down the aisle, stopping to thank the airhostesses. They smiled at him. They had gotten to know this clean-shaven young man with the sculpted features and easy smile. As he stepped onto the ramp, the familiar smells of India carried on the morning air, triggered pleasant childhood memories.

In the busy airport terminal a man in a dark suit stepped forward.

"Mister Davenport?"

"Yes," said Elijah.

"I'm Lalji Patel," said the man, extending his hand, "from Jullundur Machines. I'm very pleased to meet you."

"How do you do?" said Elijah, shaking his hand.

"I hope your flight was pleasant? We have made reservations for you at Hotel Nirmal. I shall take you there now, if that's all right with you."

It was six p.m. and the flight from Chicago to London with a stop-over, and from there to Delhi and then to Jullundur had been long and arduous. Resting to get an early start the next day was exactly what Elijah had in mind. "That sounds perfect. Thanks for meeting me."

"It's my pleasure. We're all excited about your presence in Jullundur. "

They went to the baggage claim and picked up his two suitcases. A porter carried them to the waiting car, a new Ambassador. Patel took the wheel and Elijah eased his six-foot, two-hundred-pound frame carefully into the passenger seat.

The Hunt for the Rajput Princess

As Patel drove, the isolated airport disappeared behind them. They passed through a hilly countryside with poplars along the road, while higher areas were dotted with pines. A few clouds hung in the blue sky, and in the north the snow-covered foothills of the Himalayas rose exultantly. Elijah had been here before and if he remembered right, their present elevation should be about ten thousand feet. These ranges were snow-covered even though it was early May. He surveyed the areas they passed. Jullundur was just as beautiful as he could recall. He asked Patel, "How is business doing? Is the factory running at capacity?"

"Yes," said Patel, "we are quite busy. And may I offer you my condolences, Mister Davenport? We shall all miss your uncle very much. He was an exceptional man, well liked and a very good engineer and businessman."

"Thank you," Elijah said, "I'll miss him too, even though it's been years since I last saw him." His uncle, Joe Fernandoe had owned Jullundur Machines and left it to Elijah in his will. Elijah had traveled to Jullundur to sign the paperwork, inspect the business and make some decisions about his inheritance.

They reached the city, *Jullundur City: Population: 500,630.* Someone had added the symbols, plus or minus. Pedestrians threaded their way through the streets, walking fast in both directions, deftly maneuvering their way without crashing into each other. The few vehicles on the road used their horns to get through.

On the sidewalks, Elijah recognized kebab stands selling pani puri and other 'stuff' he had enjoyed as a youngster. "When I was a boy, my friends and I used to spend the little money we had at those kebab stands."

"Would you like to stop and have some kebabs now?" asked Patel.

As Elijah watched, a bicyclist distracted by the sight of a group of young girls crashed into a kebab stand. Elijah laughed. "Did you see that?" he asked. He turned and watched as the vendor, swore and frantically brushed the hot coals from his clothes while the cyclist quickly got up and pushed his cycle away from the scene.

They left the crowded streets of the city and the landscape changed to farmland again. A Ford Mustang sped up and passed them in the right lane and slid back smoothly in front of them, matching their speed. The Ford started slowing down and Patel had to brake heavily.

"What the hell is he doing?" he yelled. Elijah had his hand on the dashboard, wondering the same thing.

Patel glanced in his rear view mirror and gasped, "Where did he come from?"

Elijah turned in his seat and looked back. A Jeep with four men holding rifles appeared a little too close. He wondered if these were highway thieves and slipped his wallet into the glove compartment. The car in front slowed even further, down to a crawl, then stopped. They were now hemmed in and Patel had to stop.

"What do they want?" asked Elijah, as he felt his pleasant welcome to India slowly unravel.

"I don't know," said Patel, nervous as sweat broke out on his forehead. Two men got out of the front car and walked towards them. Elijah glanced back and the three men with their guns drawn advanced from the rear.

"This is a fine welcoming committee," said Elijah.

The passenger door flew open, a hand grabbed him by the collar and yanked him bodily out of the car. He vaguely saw Patel being handled in the same way.

The man holding Elijah wore Muslim garb of a dark jacket and white pantaloons.

"You American, come with me," he said in a heavy Arabic accent, as he pulled Elijah along. The gun in his other hand kept Elijah from his natural instinct to fight back. Elijah turned and looked at Patel, who had his arms raised, while one of the men shot out all four tires of the brand new Ambassador.

They left Patel standing by his car, while the three men got back into the Jeep and drove around the disabled vehicle.

The man pushed Elijah into the rear seat of the Ford and the second man who had man-handled Patel out of the car slipped in beside him. He had a dark beard and piercing eyes. The large man climbed into the passenger seat and the driver took off followed by the Jeep. Elijah looked back again to see the forlorn figure of Patel standing by his car. He saw him turn and trudge back the way they had come. Elijah was thankful that these thugs hadn't hurt Patel. They had made no attempt to search the vehicle for valuables. They can't be thieves, he thought.

"How do you know I'm American?" asked Elijah. "I could be English or Dutch or even Indian."

"We know," said the man in the passenger seat. "You remember 9/11? Those were some of my friends who hijacked those planes. They are now in Paradise."

Oh, yeah, thought Elijah, with twenty-one virgins. "But I thought they were mostly Saudis."

"So am I. We move around."

Oh, God, thought Elijah, I'm in the lion's den. "What do you want from me?"

"Have you heard of ISIS? They need another American as a hostage so they can make deals with the coalition that's attacking them."

"What does ISIS mean?" asked Elijah.

"It means, the Islamic State of Iraq and Syria." He smiled and added, "But before we hand you over to them, our leader may have a job for you. Consider this time you will have as a reprieve."

"What job?" asked Elijah.

"No more talk," he said and turned around.

Elijah studied the man seated next to him. He looked young, about twenty-two. with a mustache and a beard. His turban, long straight nose and rugged features suggested an Afghan lineage. An ammunition belt ran across his chest and shoulder. He gripped his rifle tightly. Elijah guessed it was an AK-47 from the little he knew of weapons.

As the sun disappeared behind the mountains, the landscape they passed through grew harder for Elijah to discern.

"Who is your chief?" asked Elijah, speaking in Pushtu.

"Our leader is Abdul Rehman," the man answered. "How do you know Pushtu?"

"I learned long ago."

Before Elijah could ask more questions, their car came to a stop on an asphalted parking area next to a dilapidated warehouse. On either side of the building, recently tilled fields stretched to nearby hills. Behind stood a small orchard, heavy with spring blossoms. Two empty Jeeps waited in the parking lot. The Saudi opened the door and ushered him to the warehouse. They stopped him and one man ran his hand over his clothes searching for weapons. Inside the dimly lit room, several men milled about, holding the familiar AK-47s. Someone pointed out a chair and gestured for him to sit.

The leader of the group stood apart. He wore a shalwar with a black silk jacket and a black turban. He stared at Elijah and said, "You are American, no?" Elijah nodded. "My name is Abdul Rehman. We are members of a Fundamentalist Muslim group. There are many groups like us."

Elijah wondered what kind of job they had in mind for him. He looked at the other men in the room. He looked into their eyes and thought, what did I do to earn such hostility? One man kept raising his rifle and pointing it at Elijah. Rehman turned around and raised his hand. The man lowered his rifle and looked down.

Rehman's eyes glittered. The room got quiet.

"As you can see," he said, "my men don't like you."

Rehman had the broad-shouldered stature of a wrestler. His muscles were easy to discern beneath the folds of his garments. His features were those of an Afghan, whose forebears descended from conquerors like Alexander the Great and Ghenghis Khan. He had a presence about him that marked him indelibly as a chieftain. He looked like a man of character who would deal fairly with you. Looks can be deceiving, thought Elijah, I know nothing about this man.

As he strode back and forth with the ease of an athlete, Rehman said, "The Jullundur papers said that an American engineer was coming here. We thought we could use you. It would also raise our status among the other militants. You're primarily taken as a hostage for ISIS. But before we send you to Syria, we need the services of an engineer in some of our villages. You will co-operate, of course."

"What are your ties to ISIS?" asked Elijah, trying to figure out the connection.

"I don't like Americans," said Rehman. "And ISIS are my heroes. I want to help them."

"And what do you want me to do in your villages?" asked Elijah.

"These are poor villages. They have no funds for hiring engineers and installing machines. But I will let you know the details soon. For now you are our guest." Finished with him, Rehman motioned to the others. As they filed for the door, Rehman turned back, "You cannot escape. There will be guards outside."

On his way out, one of the men threw Elijah a blanket. Elijah rose and walked around the small office to take stock of his surroundings. His wallet was in Patel's car. A dim light bulb cast a yellow glow downwards. Through the windows Elijah saw two guards outside, sitting on makeshift chairs. A bathroom stood in the far corner which he checked out and looked for any means of escape. He went back into the office and sat down again, trying to think.

They seemed to know all about him from the local papers. What kind of work did they need in the villages? His palms grew sweaty and his heart quickened as he contemplated plans of escape. So I'm just a hostage who can get his head chopped off by these people who call themselves ISIS. Not if I can help it.

Chapter Two

In a remote campground in the hills of northern Pakistan stood a Ford truck and two tents. Three men tended a fire. Darkness had settled and they were preparing the evening meal when a Jeep and a Mustang rolled in. Rehman and his men got out, the men walked to a large tent pitched among the shade of the trees, and Rehman to a smaller tent set apart. He pushed aside the flaps, bent his head to clear the hanging canvass and stepped in. He sat down on the carpet laid on the floor, thinking about the day's events.

Rehman had one objective in life after his parents were killed in an air raid by the Americans in Kabul. He wanted to strike back at the people who had caused him such grief. He was away at the time in Uzbekistan where he worked as a mechanic in one of the many oil refineries. On his return, he walked through the village, alarmed at the destruction all around, until he ran the last hundred yards to find his home in ruins. Several neighbors came forward and hugged him with words of solace and regret over what had happened. They took him to the graves of his parents.

In the depths of his anguish grew a slow hatred for the people who were responsible. He became a militant with a mission to destroy everything American. He formed his own group, wanting no one to tell him what to do. He did not have money or property to finance his efforts, but the Taliban heard of him and welcomed him. He soon got financing from various Taliban groups while he stayed in control of his men. Large amounts of money were laid at his disposal including checking accounts in various banks in many countries, for services rendered against a common enemy.

Rehman made some notes in a pad he carried with him. He had a job for the engineer in two villages. After the job was done? Who knows? We'll see. His plan would also boost the image of his Fundamentalist Muslims with the people of the Afghan villages.

He put his notebook away and joined his men at the campfire. "We have information that he may be CIA," he said, as the men nodded. "But I would like to put him to work in a couple of our villages. So don't go swinging your swords as yet."

"That's fine with me," said Iqbal, the driver of one of the Jeeps. He had gray eyes and a beard and his turban covered a balding head.

"I would like to be the one to wield the scimitar on his neck, when the time comes," said Farook, a bearded dark man of forty. "I was in America in the south, in Louisiana. They treated me like they treat the blacks there. I would like to give them a dose of their own medicine. The bastards. One of them even called me a descendant of a slave." The hatred still shone in his eyes. He had not forgotten the humiliation and the disrespect he had endured. "Even the police had been of no help," he added.

"Some of them call themselves 'skinheads,'" said Rehman, getting into the prevailing mood. "They think they're superior to the dark-skinned people. Let them come here; we'll take the skin off their heads, all right. They want war, we'll give them war."

Rehman set the box he was carrying on the ground and took out two cell phones. He gave one to Iqbal, saying, "I picked these up in Jullundur. You can call me on this number to keep in touch." Iqbal took the phone and studied it. He asked Rehman to show him how to operate it. Once he was sure of the right buttons, he put it away in his tunic pocket.

*   *   *

As Elijah sat in the room vacated by his captors, his thoughts went back to three weeks ago. He had been sitting at his desk in his home office in Portland, Oregon, working on a design for a new production machine.

Derek sat reclining in a chair and reading a book, a cup of coffee at his elbow on the side table. He and Bob Winter had a habit of dropping by on Saturday mornings.

Elijah had graduated from MIT as a mechanical engineer. His apprenticeship was in a firm in Florida as a junior design engineer. At engineering seminars through the years, he made acquaintances from around the country. He designed and built special purpose machines for clients, needing to automate their production systems.

An old friend invited him to join their team and he moved to Portland, Oregon which had a number of lumber companies that boasted of being highly mechanized. After a few years he saw many sawmills in the area closing down. He mentioned it to his partners, but they didn't think it was serious. Elijah decided to break away and formed his own company.

The first two years he had to rely on work from the lumber companies. But he gradually began to build a clientele not tied to wood products. He was in a strong position when all kinds of problems started taking a toll on the lumber mills. Now that he had diversified his product line, he was glad he was out of the loop.

Derek Robson was a good friend of his from his days at MIT. Elijah brought him on board as an employee when a firm that catered to the lumber industry laid him off. Derek was an innovative engineer, with hands-on experience. Like Elijah, he was good at all facets of the business. Electrical, mechanical and machinery start up. If a problem cropped up they would help each other out.

Someone knocked on the door and walked in. Elijah looked up. "Hi, Bob," he said.

"Here's your mail." He laid a bundle of letters on Elijah's desk.

Elijah sorted through the various bills and junk mail and paused as he came to an envelope with foreign postage. He slit it open and read. "I don't believe this."

Both Derek and Bob looked up. "What?" asked Derek.

"It's a letter from an attorney in Jullundur in India. It seems I'm the sole beneficiary of my Uncle Joe's estate. He owns a factory and other property in the area. I'm supposed to go down there and sign some papers."

"Does India allow foreigners to own property in their country?" asked Derek.

"I don't know," said Elijah. "But since I'm related the rules of inheritance apply."

"Did you know this uncle of yours? Doesn't he have children of his own?" asked Bob.

"Yes, I knew him well. He's -- he was my mother's brother; he never married. When we were young, my brother and I spent many vacations at his estate. We lived in India at the time."

"What do you intend to do? Go back and settle down there, or become the absentee owner of a factory producing shoddy goods?" asked Bob.

Elijah didn't know if the goods produced were shoddy or not. In fact he did not even know what they made.

"I don't know," he said, "I have my own commitments here."

"You could sell the factory and the property and transfer the cash back here," said Bob

"I don't think so," said Derek, "the Indian Government allows you to take out only twenty thousand rupees, but I'm sure all this property is worth a lot more than that."

Derek, sitting across from Elijah, glanced up from the magazine he was reading. "If you're going to be driving in an unfamiliar area I'd suggest you take this GPS system with you. It also comes with a tracking device which is similar to the collars they use on the wolves introduced into Yellowstone Park. I'll get it for you as a going away present."

"And what am I supposed to do with it?" asked Elijah.

"Put it in your pocket and turn it on and look at the monitor and it gives the exact co-ordinates of where you are. Something to pass your time with in that remote wilderness that's India."

"You still think of it as a land of tigers and elephants, don't you?" said Elijah with a smile.

After brooding over the letter for a few days, Elijah called for a meeting with Derek, Bob, Bill Hancock, the foreman and his secretary Alice Johnson. "You're all aware of the letter I received. I think if we made some adjustments, I could make the trip, and call it a vacation. It will take two or three weeks to update my passport and get a visa. We have three projects in the works. Derek, Bill and Bob, you know which ones they are. That's enough work to keep the shop busy for nine months. There are more projects on the drawing board."

"The three projects in the shop are on schedule," said Bill, "everything else looks good. I think you should go enjoy that vacation in India."

"I understand Simla is close to where you're going," said Derek. "I'd take my skis if I were you."

"I don't ski," said Elijah, and shrugged.

A week later after he sent his visa application a curious thing happened. Elijah got a call from the CIA. "We understand that you're making a trip to Northern India. Could we meet with you to discuss some security measures?"

"But I'm just a civilian with no training in these matters," said a surprised Elijah.

"We'll give you a crash course. You still have a few weeks before you get your visa."

He met with one man in a downtown Portland motel room, most probably registered under an assumed name.

"Have a seat, Mr. Davenport," said the agent, Bill McCloskley, while he pulled up a chair near the table. He opened a briefcase and took out some papers.

"We do this all the time," said McCloskley. "If we can get a person to cooperate when making a trip to places of interest to us, we give him an assignment. You will be paid handsomely if you get us what we want. Now here's what we want you to do." He spread a map on the table and circled key areas with a red felt pen, while explaining what Elijah's involvement would be. "You would have to take pictures of hideouts and faces on a sight-seeing trip into Pakistan and then we give you a secret assignment."

Elijah shook his head. "That's too dangerous. If I'm found out, they will kill me. You have men trained to do this. Send one of them."

"Yes. But they are people just like you. Anyone within the CIA is easy to spot if you have the database that the terrorists in that area seem to have. We will train you for these three weeks. Target practice and other activities that will help you. You seem to be in good physical shape, which is a plus."

Elijah was reluctant, but it appeared easy enough on the face of it.

"We will provide you back-up at all times. Equipment and weapons will be made available to you. How and when will be relayed to you."

With great mind searching, he finally agreed. They parted with a handshake.

Three weeks later when Elijah was packing, he noticed the GPS monitor and the tracking device. He tossed it into his suitcase. He had much more sophisticated equipment from the CIA and he shuddered to think about what he had got into.

The flight from Chicago to London had been almost ten hours. Elijah decided to relax and enjoy the journey. He sipped a glass of wine and looked at his hands. They were callused from his weight lifting routine at the gym.

The plane landed at Heathrow Airport and then flew on to New Delhi.

After a tedious two-hour wait in the sweltering heat of New Delhi, he was glad when they finally took off for Jullundur.

Though his uncle had meant well, Elijah hadn't expected it to turn out like this. There was still the CIA assignment to contend with, if he escaped.

Chapter Three

As Elijah sat thinking, the door opened and a cold gust blew in along with the two guards. "It's cold out there," said one man in Pushtu. The second man leaned his rifle against the wall, then pulled out a chair and sat. He draped his blanket around his shoulders. The first guard walked around the room, ignoring Elijah. He too finally sat on one of the chairs across from Elijah.

You are interrupting my escape agenda, thought Elijah who had already formulated a plan of action. He spread his blanket on the floor and lay down. After an hour of feigned sleep he sat up and looked at the guards. Both of them grabbed their rifles. Elijah stood and pointed to the bathroom. One of them nodded.

Elijah walked slowly. Once inside, he locked the door and moved swiftly. He turned on the light and kept the water faucet running. He had noticed earlier that the ceiling was made up of Styrofoam panels.

Standing on the toilet seat he reached up and pushed his fingers into the two by three-foot soft foam panel and lifted it out and dropped it on the floor. It landed with a soft plop. Bending his knees he leaped up and grabbed a joist and hauled himself up and crawled forward to lie across three joists. All that weight training at the gym had developed his arms and his fingers. Dust got into his eyes and nostrils and mouth, almost choking him. He kept count in seconds, it had taken a minute. He pushed up and stood on the framework of the wood structure that made up the office and bathroom. With one hand holding on he pushed aside the insulation that kept clinging to him. Carefully, he walked on the joists to the edge where the wall met the ceiling. He crawled on all fours and slid his legs along the outside of the wall and dropped lightly into the dark warehouse. He heard rats scurry away. The smell of mice and bat droppings almost stifled him. Holding his breath to keep from inhaling the foul air he waited for his eyes to adjust to the darkness. He ran, hoping he wouldn't trip over anything. It had been two minutes since he had entered the bathroom. At the farthermost point from the office structure he groped along the wall until he found a doorknob. Slowly he inched it open. Hope there's no alarm connected, he thought and hesitated. Nothing happened. The cool night air chilled his sweating body as he picked his way through the darkness. With his heart thumping madly, he ran as fast as he could.

*   *   *

The two guards stared at the bathroom door. After three minutes they looked at each other then jumped up, ran with their rifles to the door. The first man yanked at the door-knob. It was locked. One of them kicked it open. Looking up they saw the large hole in the ceiling. They both raised their weapons and unleashed a barrage of shots. The ceiling soon became pock marked with holes and chunks of foam fell out. One of the bullets hit an electrical wire and the lights went out. They ran back into the office cursing loudly and tried the door to the warehouse. It was locked. They shot it off the door. The impenetrable darkness in the warehouse made them wary. They had no idea where the light switches were located.

"Rehman will kill us," one of them shouted. "You search the outside. I'll try looking here."

After half an hour they met outside. Their prisoner had melted into thin air.

"The son of a bitch," spat out one of them vehemently.

"May he die a thousand deaths," said the other

"I don't think I'll wait for Rehman," said the older of the two. "I'm just going to disappear back to Afghanistan."

"I think I'll do the same."

They hid their rifles in some bushes along the way. The weapons could draw attention to them especially since they were on foot.

"That damn American. We should have killed him when we first got him.

*   *   *

A hundred yards away, Elijah heard the shots fired in the warehouse. He kept running, his breath growing ragged. The unfamiliar landscape slowed him down. In the darkness he stumbled over shrubs and almost collided with small trees as they loomed in his path like giant arms with fingers clawing at him. He grew breathless and slowed to a walk when he located a dirt road. Safety lay to the left or right? He had to make a decision. He turned right and continued as fast as his tired legs would allow, fear still giving him the impetus to keep going. When he had gone about a mile he noticed a crossroad, and there he spotted a *goda ghadi* (horse carriage), clip clopping along at a walk. He hailed the driver, who brought the horse to a stop. In fluent Hindi he told the driver, "Take me to Hotel Nirmal."

While riding in the carriage, he wondered if it were safe to go to the hotel. The kidnappers knew his name and his connection to the factory. When they found him missing in the morning, will they may go to the factory or the hotel? If he could make it through the night he might come up with a plan. Could the police be trusted? He couldn't take a chance.

It was one-thirty a.m. when they reached the hotel. "Wait here," he said to the driver in Hindi. He walked over to the clerk on duty, "I'm Elijah Davenport, I believe, I have a reservation."

The clerk checked his register and said, "Yes sir, room 103. You are very late." Apparently news of the kidnapping had not reached him.

Elijah didn't have his wallet. "Can I use the bathroom please?"

"Yes, over there to your left."

In the bathroom, Elijah pulled out his shirt revealing a flat purse attached to his belt. He eased it up from its secure place against his waist. The purse held two hundred dollars and another credit card. He took out the credit card and put it in his shirt pocket, then put everything back in place and walked back to the lobby.

He took the credit card from his pocket and gave it to the clerk, "Give me a hundred rupees, please." With the money in his hand he walked out and gave half of it to the carriage driver.

"Shukria," said the godawallah.

Back with the check-in clerk, Elijah said, "If anyone comes looking for me, tell them that you haven't seen me." He placed the remaining wad of notes into his hand. The clerk looked surprised. He pocketed the money and nodded. Elijah continued, "Would you also put me in another room? But don't change it in your register."

The clerk nodded again, "Yes sir, you can have room 112, which is on the eastside of the building. Here's your key."

He went up to his room, filled the bathtub and sank into the warm water with a grateful sigh. His jet lag was nothing compared to the kidnapping. Life would never be the same after this.

"Patel should have made it back to the factory. He has my bags and my wallet."

After a half-hour of soaking, he felt the kinks in his muscles had unraveled. Stepping out of the water he dried himself and put on a hotel bathrobe. He sat down at the desk and made a list of things he had to do in the morning. He looked at his watch. It was three a.m. They were twelve hours ahead of where Derek was in Portland, Oregon, so it must be three p.m. over there. He put in a call to Derek and quickly described what had happened. Derek, sounding incredulous, blurted out, "You better get the hell out of there. Try to get the next flight back. Do you know what ISIS does to foreign captives?"

"Calm down, Derek," said Elijah, "I just need a few hours in the morning and then I'll be on my way back home. I will meet with the lawyer and have the papers signed. That's it."

"Maybe you should get a gun," said Derek.

"You remember the GPS unit you gave me?"

"Yes."

"Well, those people were going to take me to Syria. If that happens you will never know where I am. If this happens again, what do I have to do? Strap the monitor to my leg and turn it on? Will that tell you where I am?"

"Yes, but it only has a transmission radius of a few miles."

"If I fly back tomorrow I won't need it." He didn't tell him that he couldn't leave yet. He had another mission to complete.

After his conversation with Derek, he sank into the inviting bed and almost drifted off to sleep. He sat up with a start. They could easily find me here. Grabbing a blanket and wrapping it around his shoulders he went looking for a storage room. Maybe I could hide there. All the doors he considered as storage areas were locked. Finally he walked down a stairway outside and found a wooded lot. Scouting in all directions to be hidden from view he wrapped himself in the blanket and sat with his back against a tree and fell immediately into a sleep full of nightmares. Waking suddenly, his watch indicated it was only four a.m. and he dozed off again.

When he woke again the time was seven thirty. In the early morning light he found he was all alone. Wrapped in the blanket, he walked back to the hotel, went up to his room. He called the front desk and could tell it was a different clerk on duty. "Did anyone come looking for me?" he asked.

"No, sir," said the clerk. "Not since I came on duty this morning. The night-shift man didn't mention anything unusual, sir."

"Thank you," said Elijah with a sigh of relief. Better to be safe than sorry, he thought remembering the uncomfortable night he had spent. "Oh, do you know of a store where I can buy some clothes?" he added, "I lost my baggage yesterday."

"Yes sir," answered the clerk, "there's one just down the road from here."

Elijah thanked him. Dusting off his shirt, now worn and dirty, he patted the hidden purse attached to his belt. He remembered the time he first started wearing it when he was on vacation in Paris.

He found the store and bought a set of clothes and a few essentials.

Back at the hotel he changed into his new clothes. He looked at his reflection in the mirror. "Why the long face?" he asked loudly trying to cheer himself up. He checked out, walked into the street and hailed a taxi, giving the cab driver the address to the factory.

*   *   *

The morning after Elijah's capture, two Jeeps drove up to the warehouse. The first thing Rehman noticed was the absence of the guards. His aides ran for the door. Rehman shouted in Pushtu. "Dharwaja kolo. (Open the door.)"

The men pushed the door open and they all strode in. A blanket lay on the floor. There was no one in the room and it was dark but for the light coming in from the windows. The bathroom door stood open. Men crowded into the bathroom. They could see perforations in the ceiling and the large hole from a missing panel. With lots of shouting, they ran to the warehouse door and found it open. They could hardly see in the darkened warehouse. It smelled musty and dank. They frantically searched for the light switches. When they finally found the switch and had the entire warehouse lit up, the men ran looking for clues. The door on the far side stood ajar. With rifles on the alert, they scoured the outside area for a long time before giving up. There will be hell to pay, thought Iqbal, the driver. Elijah and the two guards had vanished without a trace.

Rehman watched his men running around like so many incompetent fools. His anger rose but he controlled himself, breathing deeply. The man is clever, thought Rehman. All the more reason I need him for a project. We will find him. He stands out in a crowd. Unless he decided to run home, like a coward. Where are my two guards? He walked out of the warehouse into the sunshine. His four men were searching the outside now. One of them came towards him with two rifles.

"We found these in some bushes, sir. They belong to the two guards who are missing." He stared uneasily at Rehman.

Although Rehman carried no rifle, he did pack a Czech-made M52 automatic in his waistband. His men had seen him hit a bulls-eye repeatedly at twenty-five yards during practice sessions.

"They must be on their way back to Afghanistan," said Rehman. "All right, get your men together. We are now on a mission to find this American."

"Yes, sir."

"I want you to hide your weapons and move through the streets," said Rehman. "Keep an eye on the hotels here and on the factory and follow his movements. I don't want him killed. We want him alive. Is that understood?" He paused for the proper effect. "We will meet at our camp in the hills in the evening."

"But, sir," said one of the men, "we are only four people now."

"I will get two replacements." Rehman pulled out his new cell phone and made a call. He nodded to them and they fell out. All four climbed into one Jeep, leaving the other for Rehman and drove back to the city.

"ISIS will get their hostage," said Rehman as he climbed into the Jeep.

Chapter Four

The taxi dropped Elijah off and he looked at the massive structure before him. He estimated it to be thirty feet high and two hundred and fifty feet wide by four hundred and fifty feet long. The lettering of the words, Jullundur Machines Ltd, stood out twelve inches high on the front of the building. Its chrome-plated relief caught the rays of the morning sun reflecting as though neon lighted against the grey background that formed the top part of the painted exterior. The lower half contrasted in a light sandstone color.

As soon as the legal papers were signed, he would be the owner of this factory. He looked around to make sure he hadn't been followed but saw nothing to alarm him.

He walked into a spacious office. The walls were sand colored. A couple of sofas upholstered in red velvet and a few chairs made of dark teak stood near a glass-topped coffee table also made of teak. Industrial magazines arranged neatly sat on the table. The quiet room smelled of roses though he didn't see any. The receptionist sat at a desk with a pair of earphones and a miniature microphone attached to her head set.

"Can I help you?" she asked, with a smile.

Elijah introduced himself. She dialed a number and spoke softly into the mike. "The Secretary to the directors will be with you shortly," she said to Elijah.

A very elegant lady dressed in a sapphire blue *shalwar* with a silk shawl draped around her neck and shoulders walked in. She was light skinned, with striking features. In spite of being pre-occupied he thought, Wow! She is pretty.

"I'm Sonia Chatterjee." She smiled and extended her hand.

Elijah shook her hand and explained who he was. She led him to a chair and they sat down.

Sonia gazed, wide-eyed; "Mr. Patel told us about your abduction. He was greatly distressed. Now that you're here, he'll be most relieved and happy. How did you get away?"

"It's a long story," said Elijah, "I'll tell you later. Right now I want you to introduce me to the senior members of the office staff and set up a meeting. Also, call the attorney, Mr. Deshpande, to attend the meeting."

"I'll be right back," she said, leaving her seat. She spoke briefly with the receptionist, and then walked out. She returned shortly with a middle-aged gentleman. "This is Mr. Tom D'Souza, vice president and Technical Director of the company." Then looking towards Elijah, "and this is Mr. Elijah Davenport." They shook hands.

Mr. D'Souza was in his late forties, with an oval face and a muscular neck. He must have been a wrestler in his youth, thought Elijah. He had a receding hairline of black hair. His clean-shaven face broke into a smile. He had kindly brown eyes. He wore a tie and a white shirt, but no jacket.

"I understand you've had a harrowing experience," said D'Souza. "Please sit down."

"Yes," said Elijah, finding a chair. "I'm glad Patel made it back OK."

"Terrorism is moving all over. You are still very vulnerable. I recommend you return to the U.S. as soon as possible."

"You're right, that's why I'd like to sign the papers and disappear from here."

Elijah could sense what D'Souza was thinking. This man is a target and he could bring unwelcome attention to the company.

"Would you like me to show you the factory while we wait for Mr. Deshpande?" asked D'Souza.

"That would be wonderful," said Elijah. But before they could make a move, Sonia, walking fast, met them with a distressed face. Now what? thought Elijah.

"Mr. Deshpande is missing," said Sonia, "his secretary says he hasn't come in to work today."

Both Elijah and D'Souza sat down. "It might be wise to get some sort of security around the place," said Elijah, "round the clock, until we're sure this isn't related to any militants."

D'Souza nodded and picked up the phone on the table and started talking in Hindi. Sonia went back to her office. They don't want the papers to be signed to transfer ownership to me, thought Elijah. Is this related to the kidnapping?

When D'Souza was off the phone, Elijah told him, "Come with me. We have to get to the bottom of why Deshpande is missing."

They went out to the parking lot and found D'Souza's Toyota Camry, and drove off to Deshpande's office.

As they drove off, Elijah stared into the distance, his mind far away. Who are these militants to dictate to me what I can and can't do? he thought. On the other hand if they hand me over to ISIS it will be the end. Yes, it might be wisest to leave as soon as possible. But what about my secret mission? I guess it will have to wait. But if I stayed and blended into the background I wouldn't be a target. Maybe getting a disguise will buy me some time while I take care of business. His thoughts flickered to Sonia. Perhaps she could help.

The Camry turned a corner and Elijah spotted a Jeep parked by the side of the road. Two occupants of the vehicle looked familiar. They were part of the gang that had captured him. A knot formed in his stomach. He took a deep breath and made a mental note of where they were parked. He was sure they had recognized him. D'Souza and Elijah reached Deshpande's office. The police had arrived ahead of them.

The Inspector walked towards them, "Your presence here has started a lot of problems for me, Mister...." his voice trailed off.

"Davenport," said Elijah.

"Yes Mr. Davenport, I'm Superintendent of Police, Amrit Singh."

They shook hands. "I have a lot of questions for you," said Singh. "First of all, I thought you were taken hostage. When and how did you escape? Why didn't you report or contact the police after your escape?"

"I'm sorry about that last part. I should have contacted you, but I'm not sure whom to trust. I've been hiding most of the time."

"My city is a peaceful place. Now people are being kidnapped and another is missing."

"Surely, Mister Deshpande is not dead, is he?"

"I don't think so. But we don't know where he is. We have put out an APB on his car. I would suggest that you keep a very low profile for the time being and I would not go back to your hotel tonight. It might be under surveillance by whoever is behind these incidents."

"They did tell me they were Fundamentalist Muslims."

"They are in my city now?" wailed the superintendent. "All the more reason that you stay out of sight."

Amrit Singh was tall with a turban like most Sikhs wore. His dark beard and mustache were well groomed. He had gray eyes and was light skinned. "Tell me more about these people who kidnapped you. How many were they? Did their leader have a name?"

"There were six of them," said Elijah, "their leader's name was Abdul Rehman. Five of them had rifles and they had two Jeeps."

"It's a common name. Can you describe him?"

"He was tall and well built and he looked and dressed like an Afghan. I'm not sure I can describe him in more detail. Oh, yes, one of the men said he was a Saudi."

"It's a start," said superintendent Singh. "It's been one thing after another. In terms of safety have you considered going back to the U.S.?"

"Yes, that seems to be the consensus. I feel like an unwelcome guest. If Mister Deshpande were here, I could leave today. Oh, I did see one of the Jeeps parked near the factory. I recognized two of the men and I think they knew me."

"Really? I'll send my men to pick them up."

*   *   *

Elijah and D'Souza drove back to the factory in silence. D'Souza made no offer to put him up for the night. Elijah thought, I don't blame him; he probably has a family and doesn't want to endanger them. I feel like a modern day Jonah.

They passed the Jeep, still parked in the same spot, Elijah noted. Those bastards, he thought. Mr. Singh has your number.

Back at the office, D'Souza turned to Elijah. "You are the new owner of this factory. Make yourself at home. Let me know if there is anything I can help you with."

"Thank you, Mr. D'Souza. I'm fine right now."

As Elijah sat in the conference room, Sonia came in and gave him a message from Derek.

"Thank you," said Elijah, "could you spare a few moments please?"

"Yes."

"Could you close the door?" When she was seated, he said, "The militants are still out there. I saw a Jeep parked nearby with two of them in it. I think the only way I can survive would be if I could disguise myself. Can you help me?"

Sonia stared wide-eyed in amazement. "Yes, I can think of a few things we can do. I would have to go to a store and make some purchases. What size shirt do you wear?"

"Large," said Elijah, "forty chest."

"All right, I shall tell Mr. D'Souza what I'm going to do and be back in about half an hour."

"I appreciate your help and I admit I am scared." For the first time Elijah noticed her fine features, and such beautiful eyes and eyelashes. He took in the details of what Sonia wore as she stood before him. The sapphire blue pantaloons of the *shalwar* were tight around her ankles. She wore high-heeled shoes that added to her elegant walk. The long sleeved blue *shalwar* descended to below her knees, gripping her narrow waist and followed the contours of her hips. It had a V shaped neckline, embroidered in gold. A silken shawl was draped around her neck and over her shoulders. Her hair was brown and straight and shone with a luster, tied in a ponytail.

"Also could you ask Mr. Patel to bring my suitcase up here? I would like to meet him again after our harrowing experience together."

"Yes, I'll send him," she said and left.

Patel walked into the conference room a few minutes later with Elijah's luggage. Elijah looked up and said, "Mr. Patel! How are you?"

"Mr. Davenport," said Patel, with a smile breaking across his face. "Am I glad to see you, Sir. I thank God for your safe return. This is indeed a happy moment for me." He lay the suitcase on the floor near the table and shook Elijah's hand with the fervor of a lost brother now joining the family.

Elijah smiled and said, "Sit, we'll exchange our experiences with the militants in great detail."

They talked for an hour with Patel gaining a new respect for the intrepid Elijah's adventure. They never touched on the possibility of how close he had come to losing his life.

"And here's your wallet," said Patel, taking it out of his pocket.

"Great, all my money and credit cards survived."

"Well, you have to be careful. The militants are still around, I'm sure."

"I'm trying to do that. When you next see me, you may not recognize me. Miss Chatterjee is helping me with a disguise."

"Really? That should allow you to move around the city. But I would still be very careful." He rose and shook hands again with Elijah.

Elijah checked his wallet and put it away. He placed the suitcase on the table and opened it. He probed through the contents until he came across the GPS monitor. This would have to be given to someone he trusted. He felt he could give it to Sonia or Patel or Mr. D'Souza. They were the only people he knew in Jullundur.

He wondered what kind of a disguise Sonia would come up with. He thought of the Godfather movie and of the cheek pads that Marlon Brando had worn. That wouldn't be comfortable.

After what seemed like an hour, Sonia walked in with two large bags and set them on the table. She locked the door and showed him the items she had bought. A pair of loose pantaloons specifically designed for men, a loose shirt and a black velvet sleeveless jacket and a white turban. From another bag she took out a small bottle of waterproof glue, a roll of two-centimeter wide cloth tape and a small bottle of rubberized glue.

"You cut some of your hair and you know what a mustache should look like. Use the waterproof glue to stick it to the tape. When it's dry, put some of this glue on the bare side of the tape. When that dries, you stick it on."

Elijah looked at her in wonder. "You thought of all this?"

"Don't you think I do this all the time?" said Sonia, laughing. "I just put my imagination to work."

She pulled out a pair of scissors. He sat at the table and waited while Sonia cut small lengths of his hair and laid it on a paper napkin.

Soon Elijah had a decent looking mustache waiting to dry before he could try it on. "I'll leave you now," said Sonia.

"When you're ready give me a call on my extension." She walked out locking the door after her.

Elijah changed into the clothes, hanging his own pants and shirt on the back of a chair. Finally he stuck his mustache in place. She had bought a hand mirror. He unlatched the door, called Sonia's extension and waited. She came in took a look and put her hand to her mouth and chuckled. He smiled and said, "You think it's funny?"

"No, but you do look different."

She reached for the turban. Folding the cloth into a long sash, she then wrapped it around and around his head making adjustments here and there until it looked right and tucked in the loose ends.

The sandals were another matter. He preferred his boots. But the sandals changed his appearance completely. Even my mother won't recognize me, he thought.

"You look good," said Sonia.

"Thank you Sonia. I'll put my clothes and my boots in those bags for now. I hope Mr. D'Souza doesn't faint." Sonia left the room.

Elijah found D'Souza in his office. "I'll take that tour of the shop now if you have the time."

D'Souza looked up and gasped. "You look absolutely different. Where have I seen you before?" He laughed.

He led the way, opening doors until they were in the main floor of the production area. The loud hum of machinery made talking difficult. Elijah heard the sudden squeal of the start of a lathe, increasing in pitch to a whine, the decelerating moan of another lathe as it slowed down to a stop. The stutter of a milling cutter biting into the metal, the grind as a drill bit punched through, all added to the familiar noise of a busy shop. Elijah loved it.

D'Souza raised his voice to be heard above the din and explained the process at each group of machinery. The smell of machine oil and hot metal hung heavy in the air. Elijah was impressed with the array of machine tools and the operators attending them. The place was well laid out for flow of production, and he was sure no "shoddy products" were being manufactured here. He'd have to take that up with Bob when he got back home.

Mounted to the floor stood six automatic lathes in one cell. Material in the form of Aluminum castings were fed by an overhead conveyor line on one side and the finished product put in crates were loaded onto another conveyor line on the opposite side. Wide yellow lines marked the safety aisles in between. A group of eight milling machines formed the next cell. Each machine had automatic hydraulic clamping fixtures. One operator handled four machines. The same conveyor lines moved incoming and finished product only in reverse. The output of one cell became the input to the next cell. Automatic scanners rejected any items that did not meet specs. Elijah saw no forklifts here. Still further down stood a battery of drilling machines. All of them had automatic feeds. Some of the drill presses had multiple spindle attachments. One operator handled three machines. Elijah had never seen a system like this before. He surmised this would reduce the labor cost considerably. Moving down the line four men operated the assembly stations and induction heated heading machines. He could spend days here studying each process and enjoying it.

"What are they making?" asked Elijah.

"It varies from job to job. Right here, those castings being machined are aluminum pistons for your Ambassador car. Over there are bicycle parts."

They walked back to the conference room. D'Souza went to his own office.

Elijah had some ideas to automate an assembly line. It was second nature to him to think along those lines. He sat at the table with a pad and pen borrowed from Sonia. Self-consciously he pressed his mustache, as he made sketches wishing he had his CAD – computer aided design – system.

Elijah noted it was three p.m. by his watch and called the Superintendent of Police. Amrit Singh came on the line. "Mr. Elijah, what can I do for you?"

"What happened about the Jeep I mentioned this morning?"

"They are in custody, Mr. Davenport. However I can only hold them until morning without specific charges."

"The charges are kidnapping. Isn't that an offence according to your legal system?"

"Yes, it is. But you'll have to come down and file some paperwork."

Elijah thought about it. He was now in disguise and didn't want to move around without it.

"Hold them as long as you can," he said. "It does put a gap in their surveillance. Thank you very much." He hung up.

He called Sonia and asked her to rent a car for him for the rest of the week.

He was so absorbed in his sketches and notes that he hardly realized it was five p.m. Sensing someone in the room he looked up and found Sonia standing in front of him. "They dropped off a Toyota Corolla for you," she said. "You could stay at my apartment for the night if you wish. It may be safer if you followed me later. Here's my address and directions. I'll fix something to eat."

He felt confident that in his disguise he wouldn't be targeted as "The American." She would no longer be in jeopardy by associating with me, he thought.

"OK," he said, "why don't we make a game of it, I'll knock three times, a pause, two knocks. How's that for a code?"

She smiled, and agreed. "I'll tell the guard at the gate that a new manager will be using the Toyota parked here," she said, as she left

Elijah saw her through the large glass windows, stop at the gate and talk to the guard.

A half-hour after she left Elijah strode out, adjusted his turban, getting used to his sandals and loose pantaloons. He left the quiet factory in the Toyota. The armed Ghurka at the gate saluted him. He drove to the parking lot of a store and waited a while longer, giving Sonia enough time to arrive at her apartment. He locked the car, walked to the street and hailed a taxi and gave the driver Sonia's address. On arrival, he walked into the shadows and waited, looking around to see if he had been followed. Assured that it was safe, he moved to the gate. A guard asked him for identification. Elijah explained who he was. Sonia had told the guard she was expecting him.

The guard directed him to the second floor apartment where he did his coded knock on the door. Sonia let him in. It was a modest flat, well appointed with comfortable furniture. The dining area had a table with four chairs, crafted from Rosewood, with carvings of paisleys and curved leaves. The living room had three armchairs and a sofa covered in fabric with a design of flowers in pink with an ivory background. The side tables beside each armchair had lamps with carved wooden stands.

The lighting had been dimmed and the table was set for two, with a bottle of Chardonnay in the center. With a twinge of regret, he wished he had brought the bottle of wine.

On the table sat plates with Tandori chicken and parathas and somosas. Sonia said, "I bought them, I didn't make any of this. I hope you like it."

Of course she bought them, thought Elijah. Where's the time to cook.

They sat down and Elijah poured the wine.

"To your success," she said, raising her glass.

"To a beautiful lady," said Elijah. She smiled, and he continued, "Were you born here in Jullundur?"

"No," said Sonia, "I was born in Calcutta. My parents still live there, however my mother is a Rajput from Jaipur. I have a brother. He's an engineer just like you. He works at Chitranjan, where they make locomotives." She paused, "What about your family Elijah?"

"My parents live in Portland, Oregon. I have a brother too and he's an electrical engineer. He lives in Chicago."

"Are you married?"

"No. Just haven't met the right girl." He seemed at a loss for a right answer.

"Are your standards very high?" she asked, smiling.

"No," he said, not at ease. "Just have been busy with my work."

She didn't pursue it any further and he relaxed.

After dinner, he helped her with the dishes. They went back to the living room and Elijah noticed framed pictures on the walls of scenes from Indian life. Two of the pictures showed women in Bharatnataya dance poses.

They sat on the sofa and discussed the events of the day. "I feel safe with this disguise," said Elijah. "Thanks for all your help. I'm indebted to you for the rest of my life."

"It has been an interesting day."

She finally stood, went into the bedroom and came back with a couple of pillows and a blanket. "You don't mind sleeping on the couch, do you?" she asked, smiling.

"Not at all," he said, standing and taking the items from her. "I really want to thank you for your hospitality."

Standing in front of her, he realized she was just a few inches shorter than he was. She looked into his eyes and smiled, "We have a long day before us tomorrow."

She backed away slowly and left him with the blanket in his hand. Something about her was like a magnet. He wanted to look at her again and again. Oh well, he thought and made himself as comfortable as he could, on the couch.

He woke up at dawn and wondered where he was. Then he heard Sonia moving around in the kitchen. The living room where he had slept was still dark. The drawn curtains hardly let in any light. He walked towards the sounds in a sleepy haze, and found Sonia all dressed and had breakfast ready at the table. He excused himself and went into the bathroom, shaved and showered and was back in a short time.

She joined him at the breakfast table. "Where's your Toyota?" she asked.

"I took the extra precaution of not associating the car from the office with you. I parked it somewhere and took a taxi. I'll do the reverse when I come to the office this morning." Soon she was ready to leave. "I'll see you at work," she said, leaving Elijah behind.

He watched through the window as she walked towards an Ambassador. This seemed to be a popular car in India.

Back at the office, Elijah showed D'Souza his sketches of the design for the assembly line.

D'Souza studied the sketches with interest and soon was caught up with the idea. He finally said, "This is interesting. Why didn't we think along those lines? This could increase production considerably. We'll have to do a study. I'll pass these on to our engineers to make working drawings. Thank you, Mister Davenport."

Sonia knocked on the open door to the conference room and said, "Excuse me, Mr. Davenport and Mr. D'Souza, I've just had a call. They have located Mr. Deshpande and he will be coming in this afternoon. Apparently he had some kind of misadventure. He will tell you all about it himself." She sat in one of the chairs with her pad before her.

"That's good to hear," said Elijah.

"That's more like it," said D'Souza. "We were due for some good news."

D'Souza bundled up the sketches and left, saying, "I'll take these over to engineering."

"If we get these legal papers taken care of this afternoon," said Elijah, "I'd like to take a short vacation. Isn't Simla near this area?"

"Yes," said Sonia, "I could make reservations at a lodge there. How long would you wish to stay?"

"This Saturday and Sunday," said Elijah, and then added, "Would you come with me?"

Sonia looked most disconcerted. "Hush, Mister Davenport, what will people say if they heard you? Office romances are frowned upon over here." She smiled, however, as she said it.

Elijah looked at her and smiled. She was right, of course. Sonia went back to her office.

He stood and started walking around the room, deep in thought. Even with his disguise, he wondered, would the Fundamentalist Muslims tie me to Sonia? I haven't been seen in her company outside the office. I should leave this evening soon after Deshpande arrives. Forget about Simla. But there's still that other project for the CIA.

Chapter Five

Elijah, dressed in his Punjabi clothes, sat deep in thought, when Sonia came back from her office, "Before I make reservations for you in Simla," she said, "I thought you might like to join my friends and me on a short trip around Jullundur and Ludhianna. We planned this a while back and we leave tomorrow morning."

"That would be wonderful," said Elijah. "I'll pay for the gas and the motel costs. How's that?"

"We'll talk about that later."

"How long will we be on this trip?"

"About a week."

"A week?" His brow crinkled in a frown. "Do you mind if I think about this for a moment?"

"Yes, of course. You let me know what you decide." She went back to her office, her high heels clicking on the hard parquet floor.

The plot thickens, thought Elijah. I was thinking of two days, now it's nine days. And what about the safety of the others in the group and Sonia?

He called Sonia's extension and waited.

When Sonia came back, he waved her to a seat. She looked at him with raised eyebrows.

"Although I'm disguised, I would be tempting fate to go unrecognized for such a long time. Are you sure you and your friends are all right about my joining you?"

"Yes, you no longer look like an American. With your disguise and your mustache, I could say you're my husband," she said and laughed.

"Or I could just pack my bags and leave for the U.S. as soon as the papers are signed."

"It's up to you."

"I'd like to see Simla. You still have to ask your friends if they want me to come along."

"I will talk to them and see how they feel. I'll make reservations at Hotel Daulath in Simla for next Saturday and

Sunday, after our trip together. We can always cancel it if our plans change. You can still stay at my place tonight."

"Yes, I'll get the wine this time."

Sonia came back a few minutes later. "Your package from Derek just arrived. It's a large box, about yay big." She indicated a size with her hands.

"Could you possibly have someone put it in your car? I'll unload it when I come over this evening. There are some items I must show you. You're the only one I trust just now," Elijah confessed.

"What?" asked Sonia.

"I'll explain later."

Because he was the new owner, he felt obliged to ease the tension that may exist with management with so recent a change in ownership.

He went down to D'Souza's office and knocked. He could hear the rumble of the machines in the shop.

"Come in."

Elijah looked in and said, "If it's OK with you I'd like to walk through the shop once again. I won't trouble you, I think I know my way."

"That's fine."

He spent the rest of the morning observing each work cell, making notes on a pad, then moving on to the next group of machines.

The men in the shop hardly noticed that this was a man in disguise. All they saw was one of their own doing a time study and they were used to that. Elijah could still pass for one of the engineers, he thought, as long as I have this turban and mustache. I must remember to refrain from talking. He wore ear-plugs which were required in the shop with the level of noise of the operating machinery.

D'Souza, Elijah and Sonia met at two p.m. in the conference room with Mister Deshpande. Deshpande had been in an automobile accident the previous evening and was forced to spend the night in a hospital for a dislocated shoulder and bruised nose. For some reason, no one including himself had bothered to call his office.

"I'm all right now. I have the legal papers and the last will and testament of Joe Fernandoe. The property consists of the factory and its contents and the adjoining parcel of three acres of land. Mister Elijah Davenport has been designated as the sole beneficiary." He paused and took a sip of water from a glass in front of him.

"There are a few stipulations that Mister Fernandoe has made. One, the factory should continue operating in its present location. Two, all pensions and benefits will continue for all employees with tenure. Three, Mister Davenport will assume all responsibilities as CEO."

The papers were signed and witnessed. Deshpande took his leave.

After he left, Elijah asked D'Souza and Sonia to stay. In his position as CEO, he was making certain changes, he told them both. "Sonia, if you will make a record of the minutes. Mister D'Souza will continue as Technical Director and also have the title of General Manager. Sonia will be Vice President of Marketing and continue with her present responsibilities."

Elijah would live in the U.S. but would make quarterly trips to Jullundur. He'd always be available by phone or email. He shook hands with both of them.

Sonia left early, and so did D'Souza. Elijah once again drove to the parking lot and then took a taxi. He bought a bottle of Merlot and headed for Sonia's apartment.

*   *   *

Rehman's men were back on the job. They kept an eye on the factory, but no American could be found entering or leaving the premises.

"Has he left the country?" asked Rehman.

"We are only six people, sir," said his main officer. "We cannot watch the factory, the hotels and the airport. If he is that important they should send us more men."

"Stay with the factory and the hotels. He's bound to turn up." Rehman wasn't giving up as yet.

*   *   *

Elijah and Sonia sat down to dinner. Elijah noticed that tonight's dishes were different and looked delicious: creamed spinach in a spicy sauce, batta bhaji (cubed cooked potatoes sautéed in roasted mustard seed and yellowed with turmeric), kheema (curried ground beef), and naan bread.

"These are best eaten with your fingers," said Sonia.

"I remember," said Elijah, though he watched how she broke off a piece of naan and used a fork to get the kheema. He followed suit. It smelled and tasted delicious.

"It's very good," said Elijah. He poured the wine and sipping on his glass, asked, "I remember you saying that your mother's from Jaipur. Is that here?"

"No, that's in Rajastan, but my father is Bengali."

"So you could be called a Rajput Princess?" asked Elijah seriously.

Sonia laughed, "My mother is descended from a line of rajas, but there are rajas and their families living in Jaipur, Jodhpur and Udaipur to mention a few and they live quite comfortably by putting up most of their palaces to be viewed by tourists. You should make a trip down there."

"I was right. You are a Rajput Princess."

"If I am, it means nothing to me anymore," she said with a sigh.

Elijah felt he was treading on personal turf and tried to change the subject. He told her a joke he had read somewhere recently, making it sound real. It was about a teenage girl who went into the bathroom during a flight when they hit an air pocket. She came out looking pale and asked the air-hostess if she had punched the wrong button.

Sonia broke into laughter; "You are making this up?"

After they put away the dishes, Sonia wished him good night and he once again slept on the couch in the living room. He smelled her perfume as she walked away.

When he woke up Sonia was fixing breakfast. He smelled fried potatoes and samosas. "Good morning, Sonia."

"Good morning. You look rested," she said. "I did talk to Roy and Leela about your disguise and why you were wearing it. They thought it was exciting and still want you to come along."

Elijah sat at the table, wondering if all this trouble was worth it. He picked up his cup of tea and breathed the aroma in. It had a delicate scent of oranges and roses.

"I love your tea. It has such a pleasant aroma."

"That's Darjeeling tea," said Sonia, "it has its own flavor. I like it."

"Those things you wear in your hair and your ears. They're beautiful."

"These? They are gifts from my mother. Most Rajput women wear them."

She studied Elijah in his make-up. He kept pressing his mustache. He had done a good job with the turban. "You're getting used to the turban," she said, smiling her approval.

"Nothing to it," he said straightening up. "But I do take them off when I go to bed."

"We should hurry, Leela and her husband Roy will be waiting."

*   *   *

Soon they were at Leela and Roy Chakramony's apartment. Sonia knocked on the door and Leela opened it. "Sonia," she squealed with delight, as they hugged.

"How are you, Sonia?" said Roy from somewhere inside.

Sonia took Elijah's hand and drew him into the room. "This is Mister Elijah Davenport from the U.S. He is here on business." Looking at Roy, she said, "And this is Roy Chakramony and his wife Leela."

Roy looked startled at Elijah's appearance. "This is no American," he said.

"How do you do," said Roy, shaking Elijah's hand.

"Pleased to meet you," said Elijah, and then turning to Leela and shaking her hand,

"Pleased to meet you, Mrs. Chakramony."

Leela was in her early thirties, medium height and slim with brown eyes, brown hair and light brown skin. She wore a colorful sari. The jewelry she wore – matching gold earrings and gold bangles – enhanced her good looks. She wore low-heeled shoes.

"His accent is definitely American," said Roy, still staring at Elijah. "Would any of you like a cup of tea?"

"No, no," said Sonia, "let's go or we'll get a late start."

They all trooped out and Roy said, "We'll take my station wagon, it has a little more room than Sonia's Ambassador."

"He's very proud of his station wagon," said Sonia.

"Stop it you two," said Leela, all smiles.

Roy was in his early thirties. He was a shade darker than Leela. Dark brown hair well trimmed and clean-shaven. He had a straight nose and a receding chin. His eyes constantly lit up as though he was about to tell you a joke. With his wife besides him, Sonia and Elijah climbed in the rear of the station wagon. The interior smelled of new leather.

Leela turned her head and asked in Hindi, "How are your parents?"

"*Sub teak hi.* (They are well)," said Sonia

"Are they coming to visit soon?"

"No, not right now. You know Mister Davenport speaks Hindi, don't you, Elijah?"

"*Kooch kooch* (a little)," said Elijah.

"Let's make our first stop at the Hero Bicycle Factory. Mister Davenport will like a tour of the shop, since he's an engineer," said Roy.

"That's fine with us," said Leela.

"Yes," said Sonia, "I would like to see it too. I've heard so much about them – they're one of our clients -- we make some parts for them."

Even though reassured with his disguise, Elijah felt uneasy. With the safety of the group in mind, he kept a vigilant eye, looking at all the people they passed, if they were carrying rifles. Many were dressed as Muslims and some looked like Afghans. Maybe getting a gun wouldn't be such a bad idea, he thought. At least I can fight back. By the time Roy pulled into the factory parking lot, Elijah felt emotionally drained.

A tour guide brought them ID tags which they pinned to their garments.

"Please do not talk to any of the operators and stay within the yellow lines," said the guide.

Elijah stayed by Sonia's side as they followed the various stages of the manufacture of bicycles. When they descended a series of steps, he held out his hand to her.

He watched fascinated by the various processes. The steel tubes being cut at one station, being put into fixtures and welded by robots, the stamping presses and the assembly stations. He was tempted to turn to Sonia and explain things, but the guide was doing a good job. He smiled and looked away. Sonia bent her gaze sideways and smiled. She had noted his excitement as he observed the machines.

He felt self-conscious and uncomfortable walking in his Punjabi clothes. The new sandals took a degree of getting familiar with, using his toes to get a grip as he walked. It put a dent in his usually easy gait.

After the tour they were back in the parking lot. Roy presided, "It's lunch time. I'm in the mood for some South Indian cooking. How about Masala Dosa?"

"South Indian food up here in the north?" asked Elijah.

"Oh, yes," said Roy, "there's a restaurant called Anjulie, nearby. When we get tired of our own dishes, we try something different."

They climbed in and Elijah turned to Sonia and said, "Masala Dosa," with an emphasis on the "D" in Dosa. His American accent with the word amused Sonia, and she giggled, her laughter sounding like bells tinkling

The restaurant was clean, crowded and loud with the babble of people talking. The waiters balanced five or six platters in each hand, maneuvering their way between tables. The delicious smell of mouth-watering dishes was everywhere.

Once seated, Elijah couldn't believe the train of waiters as they arrived with the food. Large stainless steel plates with sixteen inch diameter golden brown, wafer thin crepes that were crispy and folded in the center. Inside was the Masala, a combination of curried potatoes and peas made yellow with spices. Along with each platter were bowls of Sambar and a red sauce, a green coriander sauce and a white coconut sauce. Elijah knew how to handle this and broke a piece with his fingers, dipping it in the sambar. It was delicious and made his tongue tingle. He kept wiping his mustache with his napkin, it seemed to get in the way of his food.

Roy ordered "*Limbu pani*" for everyone – iced and sweetened limejuice.

Elijah paid the bill and they stepped out into the noonday sun. He made a quick survey up and down the street. No signs of Fundamentalist Muslims.

"There's a textile mill nearby," said Roy. "We'll make our next stop there."

"We planned this trip months ago," said Leela, "but everything seems designed for Mister Davenport."

"Don't you want to see how your sari is made?" asked Roy.

"Yes, yes, I'm just joking. Sonia is falling asleep back there."

Elijah glanced at Sonia and marveled at her composed face.

They had reservations at a hotel and with the light fading, it seemed prudent to hurry to the *Hotel Araam.* Roy decided they would take a common room with four beds and two attached baths. The beds were arranged in a row. Sonia, next Leela, then Roy and Elijah.

It was a large room with four beds in a row with a gap of four feet between each bed.

Roy looked at the layout and pointed to the two cots at the end. "Maybe we should move these two together, so Leela can be close to me," he said, with a smile.

"He is very adventurous," Leela said and laughed.

Elijah helped Roy push the beds which squealed on the hard floor as they moved together.

"We have no privacy at all," said Sonia.

"I promise not to look," said Elijah, as Sonia turned away. Soon it was lights off and everyone was sound asleep in a few minutes.

When Elijah woke, the two ladies were dressed and ready. Sonia had on a skirt, wide at the bottom with the hem curled upwards and a blouse that exposed her midriff. The gypsies must have come from this part of the world thought Elijah. Leela, equally well dressed, was no comparison to the way Sonia filled those clothes. Sonia's face, with her straight nose and curved eyebrows, was something you only saw in Indian movies.

"And what do you call the outfit you're wearing today?" asked Elijah of Sonia.

"It's called a Gagra," said Sonia.

After breakfast, they decided to see a temple. Roy drove aimlessly for a while and finally admitted he was lost. They saw a village in the distance, and he made his way towards it and parked near the entrance. Women and children moved around doing their chores, but stopped when they saw the vehicle approaching. Roy got out and looked for an adult to ask for directions.

"I feel cramped," said Sonia, getting out of the car. The young boys and girls were already moving towards the car when they saw her. A shout went up, "Actress, actress."

Leela got out too. Soon they had a crowd around them. Elijah, who had also stepped out, looked on amused. Apparently these villages had on occasion seen film crews shooting scenes for Indian movies and Sonia definitely looked like an actress.

He looked at Sonia. She just smiled at her fans. Nothing shook her equanimity. She could take adulation in stride. What an amazing woman, he thought.

Roy elbowed his way in and pushed the crowd back away from the two women. Elijah stood at the rear of the car and watched the fun. Roy had to shout to be heard above the din. "*Mandir kaha hi* (Where is the temple)?" he asked.

A woman pointed to a road. "You take that road. It is nearby."

"*Shukria* (thank you)," said Roy. They climbed back into the station wagon. The women and children moved back and Roy made his way to the main road.

Elijah looked at Sonia. "So they think you're an actress."

"It must be this jewelry," she said with a smile.

Elijah extended his left hand and touched Sonia on her upper arm. She looked at him inquiringly. "I just want to touch an actress," he said with a smile.

She burst out laughing, and covered her face with her hands.

Leela looked back. "What's going on there?"

"Nothing," said Sonia, "this Elijah is just being silly."

"Leela, you qualified as an actress too," said Elijah.

Leela turned to Roy. "Did you hear that? Me too."

They found the temple. Elijah noticed many stone carvings of women with very large round breasts in various dance poses. He said to Sonia, "They're definitely women."

Sonia struck a dance pose just like the statue, with one arm at her hip and the other above her head.

"What are you doing?" asked Roy.

"She is posing for Mister Davenport," said Leela.

"I should have brought my camera," said Elijah.

The days went by quickly. All four of them seemed to be enjoying their short vacation. A certain familiarity had crept into the relationship between Elijah and Sonia. They felt comfortable in each other's company. Elijah, who had seldom dated the same girl twice, was finding himself drawn to the energy and vitality of this Rajput beauty.

The danger of the Fundamentalist Muslims still lingered at the back of his mind. He kept a wary eye, not trusting anyone on the streets.

Roy pointed to a large building complex in Ludhianna. "That's the Christian Medical College. It's a very famous medical research center."

"Is that right?" asked Elijah, genuinely impressed. Compared to Jullundur, he noted that Ludhianna was a larger city, with much more industry.

All too soon the vacation came to an end. Roy took them back to his and Leela's apartment on Friday evening.

"I'm sorry this fun trip is over," said Roy.

"Me too," said Leela, looking very sad.

"Thank you very much," said Elijah, shaking Roy's hand.

"Thank you," he said, turning to Leela with his arms outstretched for a hug. Leela gave him a hug, and they walked to Sonia's car.

"Bye," said Sonia.

"See you soon," said Roy and Leela.

On their way, Elijah said, "Can we stop at a store so I can get a bottle of wine and something to eat?"

"Yes," said Sonia. The stores were near each other. While Sonia bought take out dinner, Elijah got a bottle of Merlot.

Chapter Six

When they got to Sonia's apartment, she gave a sigh of relief. "Am I glad to be home," she said. She moved to the kitchen table and set down the food she had bought with another sigh. Elijah looked at her with concern, placing the wine bottle next to it.

"I'm going for a shower," said Sonia.

Elijah relaxed on the sofa; he could hear the shower running and his mind wandered with images of her. After about fifteen minutes, he looked up and there she stood framed in the doorway with the light falling on her face. She had taken off her jewelry, but she was dressed in a sari. Her hair, though combed, looked damp and hung loosely to her waist. It made her look exotic. Her beauty stunned Elijah. He stood and she walked towards him. He caught her gaze and his heart beat faster. Her dark arched eyebrows and her brown almond shaped eyes crowned by long lashes emphasized her fine features.

She smiled at him. He had seen her smile before, but this was different, like an invitation to a dance. So like a Greek goddess, he thought, and I haven't even had any wine yet. Her high heels lent a certain grace in her stride with her long legs draped in the sari, beating a rhythmic cadence as she walked towards him. As she came closer he smelt her perfume, the scent of lavender, not powerful but like a gentle breeze. He held out his hand and she put her hand in his, her touch warm and soft like velvet. He squeezed it gently as he pulled her to him. He held her in his arms. She looked up at him and moved her lips closer. He kissed her open lips and closed his eyes. She tasted of summer wine.

"Remove your mustache, and your turban," she said.

Elijah stepped back, slowly peeled off his mustache, laid it on a table along with his turban, walked back to Sonia and engulfed her in his arms again.

He moved his hands down to her small waist and felt her smooth bare skin. As he kissed her again, her arms went around him, pulling herself closer against him.

He did things with his tongue that she wasn't familiar with. She broke off giggling, saying, "What are you doing?"

He just smiled and went back to kissing her. He gently pulled at her sari along her waist, until it all lay at her feet. He stepped back and looked at her. "God, you're beautiful."

She had on her *choli* -- which was a blouse that exposed her midriff -- and her skirt. He nuzzled her neck and fumbled with the buttons of the *choli*. She put her hand behind her and undid the buttons and let her *choli* drop. He drew in his breath, looking at her beautiful breasts. She put one hand on his face and ran the other through his hair. He knelt down and pulled her to him, kissing her flat belly. "Take off your shirt," she whispered.

She knelt down too and helped him take it off. They embraced again, still kneeling. Her nipples and breasts pressed against his bare chest.

She moved her hands down his back, while they kissed. They were breathing hard. They rose as though with mutual consent. He bent down and put his arms under her legs and lifted her off her feet and slowly carried her to the bedroom and laid her on the bed. He kissed her breasts and moved down, kissing every inch of her. It was like a symphony that built up gradually to a tremendous crescendo, when they finally collapsed in each other's arms. She held him tight in her arms as though she wanted the moment to last forever. After a while she relaxed and caught her breath.

"You are so beautiful," whispered Elijah, also gasping for breath.

They woke up several times in the night and made love. She gazed at him and gently touched his face. He smiled and moved his fingers to her lower lip. Elijah felt he had fallen in love.

He woke up at dawn, and lay staring at her beautiful face. She opened her big brown eyes and smiled at him. "Today is Saturday," he said. "We don't have to go to work."

She looked at him, "I feel so happy."

He smiled and put his hand on the curve of her naked hip and pulled her to him.

She buried her face against his chest and sighed. They lay like that for a long time, enjoying the warmth and comfort of each other. She finally stirred, sat up and gracefully swung her legs off the bed and stood. He watched her, taking in her beautiful body, her breasts, and the flatness of her stomach, and the curve of her hips.

She reached for her robe and pulled it around her saying, "You are going to Simla today, remember?"

He propped himself up against the pillows and said, "I couldn't possibly go anywhere without you."

After they both had showered and dressed, they went into the living room. There sat the meal neither of them had touched. She put things away and made breakfast for both of them. She glanced at him over her cup of tea. "I could come with you to Simla, this being Saturday. But I must return on Sunday. I must get back to work."

"That would be wonderful," he said, throwing his arms upwards and smiling. He watched her chew on a piece of toast. She was a delight to watch.

"Stop staring at me."

He laughed. "You're such an exotic creature that I find it hard to keep my eyes off of you."

She smiled. "Sounds like a song." Then after a while she said, "We could take my car to get there and I'll come back in it, while you stay over and take a taxi after your vacation."

"That's fine. Remember that box that Derek sent. You still have it here don't you?"

"Yes, you explained some things before we left on our trip."

"I'd like to go over some more details."

She brought the box to the living room. He opened it and took out a small wafer thin electronic device and showed it to her.

"This is an electronic transmitter. See this little switch? If I turn it on, it starts sending out radio signals."

He pulled out a larger square box. When he powered it up, a network of grid lines appeared on its screen. "This," he said, "is the GPS Receiver Module. It's called a Global Positioning System and when I turn on the transmitter, this receiver will give the co-ordinates of where the signals are coming from. See I'll show you."

He took the transmitter and moved the switch to "On." Immediately the GPS receiver showed a latitude and a longitude on its screen, and a light blinked indicating the transmitter had been turned on.

Sonia stood transfixed, and gazed at the screen intently. "Is that where we are right now?"

"Yes, those are the co-ordinates of this very room."

"What do you intend to do with them? What's the purpose of these devices?"

"It's just a precaution. If I should get captured again, I would like someone to know where I am."

"Wouldn't it be better to avoid being captured?"

"Yes, I've tarried here long enough. Just two more days and I'll be on my way and out of your hair."

"Is that all you think of me?"

"No, I didn't mean it that way. Of course I've grown to care for you. I could come back or you can come to where I live."

Sonia cast her eyes back to the equipment on the table. "You really think this little device is going to save you? If the CIA gets it they'll use the signal for an incoming missile to destroy the evidence and say, 'Oops, we made a mistake. Destroyed by friendly fire.'"

Sonia's face was clouded in a frown. Her whole face reflected unhappiness. He had never seen this side of her before. He walked over and stood in front of her. She put her arms around him. "You're the first person I've ever started caring about and now there's all these obstacles. Go away to your country and leave me alone."

She untangled herself and walked into her bedroom.

Elijah slowly put the electronic devices back in the box. What obstacles? thought Elijah. She knew all along that the Fundamentalist Muslims were after me. The only alternative I have is to take her with me. He looked around the room, deep in thought and said, "Well, I'll have to marry her first."

*　　　　*　　　　*

In half an hour they were off in the Ambassador on their way to Simla. The terrain soon turned to desolate roads, gradually moving away from the city. The car strained on the incline of the road and she had to change gears. Elijah felt his ears pop as they reached higher elevations. Soon they saw snow on the sides of the roads, where small pine trees grew in abundance. Huge rocks had been pushed aside in the construction of the road. In the distance range upon range of mountains shone in different shades of blue and purple. These were the Himalayas with their Yetis and the home of the Dalai Lama.

Sonia drove in silence with a composed face. Elijah kept shooting side-glances at her, hoping to see her smile again.

"Can you ski?" he asked, hoping to break the tension.

"No, and I don't want to learn now either. Do you?"

"I never learned either, but I would like to see you in a pair of jeans."

"I have jeans," she said smiling. Ah! There it was, the ice was thawing.

She drove into the parking lot of a large structure, the tires crunching on the sanded drive.

Hotel Daulath, constructed from stone and mortar, had mammoth proportions, built in the Victorian style by the British ages ago. He registered, adding her name as Mrs. Davenport. When they were settled in their cabin, he said with the ease of renewed familiarity, "Let's go for a walk in the snow."

"I'm going to change into my boots."

She unpacked, went in and returned shortly wearing jeans and boots. "You look lovely," he said. He got his camera and when they were outside, started taking pictures of her. She clowned for him, and soon they were in a snowball fight. There were lots of other tourists, dressed like them for the outdoors.

Elijah had changed into his jeans and shirt and boots. He had taken off the turban. Now that a week had gone by without sighting Fundamentalist Muslims, he had relaxed and his paranoia of getting caught had faded.

He had forgotten to replace his mustache, when he had removed it the previous night.

"You don't think you need your disguise anymore?" asked Sonia.

"They are probably in the city looking for me."

"I wouldn't bet on it."

"Why, did you see someone here?" asked Elijah in a panic.

"No," she laughed, "but you seem to have lowered your guard."

"I feel uncomfortable, especially those sandals. But I promise to put it all back on when I come back to Jullundur. I may even wear it to the airport."

Towards evening, they went back to the main building and had dinner in a crowded dining area. Sonia was still concerned about the Fundamentalist Muslims group, who had kidnapped him. "What do these Fundamentalist Muslims people want?"

"They wanted me because I'm an American and planned to send me to ISIS."

"ISIS kills foreigners," said Sonia. "Now I do worry."

After dinner they went back to their cabin, the fireplace had been lit. Elijah opened a bottle of wine and poured two glasses. They sat on the carpet with their backs against the sofa in front of the fireplace. She leaned her head against his shoulder. He put his arm around her, looking at the flames as they danced and flickered. Life is so tranquil and beautiful with her by my side, he thought. Soon they decided to turn in.

Next morning broke bright and clear. After breakfast, they said their good-byes. They kissed a long and lingering kiss.

"I'll see you in a couple of days," she said.

Why was he staying back, he wondered, when he'd rather spend time with her? But once they were back at the office, their closeness would be restricted anyway. He decided he would do some exploring. He would never get the chance again of standing at the foot of the mighty Himalayas.

He stood and watched the Ambassador became but a dot in the road leading down.

Elijah went back in the cabin and put on his boots, for a trek on the slopes. There sounded a knock on the door. He wondered if she had changed her mind and come back. He opened the door and three men forced their way in, and before he knew it, two of them pinned his arms behind him. Both wore beards, the shorter one with a scar on his left cheek. The other loomed over him, a giant of a man.

The third man was Abdul Rehman. He had his hands behind him as he strode in front of Elijah. "We meet again. We hadn't seen you for a while. I am glad I did not tell my men to stop looking for you. ISIS still wants you. There are fanatics in our group who would just as easily cut your throat. I have other plans for you. I think you can be of use to a group of villagers. They are my countrymen and I would like to help them. If I'm over-ruled by someone above my rank, then your head is still at stake. Consider this as a reprieve. As long as you work for me, you stay alive."

Turning towards his men, he said in Pushtu, "Bind his hands and feet and put him in the back of the Jeep. Gag him too. We will transfer him to the truck at our camp."

Two men gripped him and he got the powerful scent of Attar. One or both of them had dabbed it on quite liberally. Strong smells always gave Elijah a headache.

One of them coughed in his face as they ushered him out. This was going to be an uncomfortable ride.

He soon found himself trussed and bound like the chickens he had seen in the market place in Jullundur. Their hostility towards him was quite evident. The rope cut into his wrists and hurt whenever he moved them. As they lifted and placed in the back of the Jeep, he looked around to see if he could attract someone's attention, but the place was deserted. It was too early for anyone to go hiking. One of the men pulled down the translucent plastic and leather sidewalls of the Jeep converting it into an enclosed vehicle.

Elijah once again tried hard to hide his frustration and his fear. These men were ruthless. All they had against him was the fact that he was an American. They were fanatics and he would have to bide his time. No point in provoking them. He wondered what kind of work Rehman had in mind. A glow of hope seeped into his mind as he remembered the transmitter attached to his boot. With that thought, his attitude changed from one of anxiety to confidence. Always be on the offensive was the motto.

The Jeep wound its way through mountain roads for several hours. He gave a sigh of relief when they finally stopped. They lifted him out of the vehicle and removed the bindings. When he stood, he almost collapsed, because his legs were cramped. The men held him up. After hobbling around he bent down and rubbed his legs, straightened up and massaged his painful wrists to get the circulation going. They were at a campsite in the hills. Several tents were pitched around a central fire, surrounded by a ring of stones. As he watched, a man threw a log on the fire sending up a shower of sparks. These hills could be either in India or in Pakistan, he thought. Simla isn't far from the Pakistani border.

His anorak kept him warm. They gave him an additional coat, and assigned him a bedroll near the fire.

Abdul Rehman walked over and looking directly at Elijah, said, "I have taken off your shackles, but do not try to escape. They will shoot you if you try." He nodded toward the guards. "What is your name?" he asked.

"Elijah Davenport."

"I will call you Elijah. Do you speak Urdu or Pushtu?"

"*Kooch, kooch* (a little)," Elijah said, in Urdu.

"*Acha.* From now on I will speak Urdu to you. You rest for the night. We have a long journey tomorrow."

The electronic transmitter he had shown Sonia a day earlier was attached to his boot with Velcro. Despite Sonia's outburst he had gone ahead with his plans. Belatedly he wished he had stayed in disguise. He had grown sloppy in his precautions. With the guard's permission, he walked off to relieve himself. In the dark, behind a tree, he bent down and turned on the little switch of the electronic transmitter. He hoped the nickel cadmium batteries would last long enough.

He looked back at the camp from his vantage point in the darkness. The smoke from the fire moved lazily up into the trees. Smells of cooking drifted down, but he wasn't hungry. He trudged back and noticed the guard's rifle trained on him.

Damn, he thought, with suppressed vehemence, one more day and I would have been out of here.

Chapter Seven

Sonia returned to work on Monday. She expected to see Elijah by mid-morning. When noon came around and he still hadn't arrived, she started to worry. She called Hotel Daulath and asked the front desk about Elijah's whereabouts. The clerk, a highly excitable fellow, told her in a high-pitched voice, "No, he hasn't checked out, but he's not in his room either. The cleaning maid said that, there were signs of a struggle and his bed hadn't been slept in. We have notified the police."

Sonia had a moment of panic and a tight knot developed in her stomach. She took a deep breath and said, "He has a small carry-on bag. Could you find it? I'll send someone to pick it up."

"Yes, we have it here in the office."

She composed herself again and said, "Thank you. My name is Sonia. Please give me a call if you find out anything further." She gave him her phone number and hung up. She knew that Elijah's personal effects including his passport were probably in that bag.

She went quickly to her car and opened the trunk and took out the GPS module Elijah had shown her. She switched in on, standing out there in the parking lot. Yes the transmitter of the GPS had been turned on. Her screen blinked, indicating his position. She pressed the button which showed the co-ordinates in longitude and latitude. "Oh, my poor Elijah," she whispered, "what have they done to you?" She turned it off, put it back in the box, closed the trunk of her car and walked back, pre-occupied as to her course of action. Her instructions had been to call Derek. But it was 1:30 PM here in Jullundur, it must be 1:30 AM in Oregon. She called Derek anyway and got his answering machine. She left a message, detailing what had happened and Elijah's instructions. She gave him her home phone number. After she hung up, she began to fret. She bit her knuckles, got up and walked around. No point in telling anyone else as yet, she thought.

She made a list of things to do right away. With everyone in the office around me, I hope my face doesn't betray the turmoil within me, she thought. Mister D'Souza came over to her office and asked her, "Wasn't Mister Davenport supposed to be back today?"

"Yes," she answered, evenly without a tremor, "but he may have decided to stay another day."

"If he calls, let me know, I need to talk to him."

She said she would.

*   *   *

Back at the campsite, Monday morning broke cold and clear. Elijah and his captors had packed up all their gear onto two trucks and started rolling out.

"Where are we going?" asked Elijah in Pushtu. No one answered.

They traveled most of the morning on a fairly good road. They did not pass any traffic going either way. From the location of the sun, Elijah could tell they were going west towards Afghanistan. Towards noon they drove through a large city. He felt sure it was Peshawar. The smells in the air of the town hit him with a surge of longing. He smelled wood-smoke and aromas of cooking. The trucks slowed down in the crowded streets. A Jeep moved slowly ahead of them beeping his horn. The foot-traffic overflowed from the sidewalks onto the road. He noticed people of almost a dozen nationalities. He could make out Chinese by their features and Kaftans from the mountains, Persians with their lighter skins, Indians and Pakistanis from their clothing, a few Englishmen, looking for adventure and a bargain in precious stones or the pleasures of opium. He saw many old men sitting in doorways smoking their water hookahs, stoned no doubt, out of their minds.

A few miles further, they entered the Khyber Pass. It had three parallel roadways. He saw motorized traffic rolling through one while the second had a rail system curving around the bends and the third was filled with pedestrians and a camel caravan. They had entered Afghanistan.

To the north the Hindu Kush Mountains loomed in the distance, eternally snow capped. Nearer, the rolling hills blended in varying shades of green. Elijah noticed the dark green oaks that skirted the lower elevations, while higher up were slender silver birches.

At mid-day they stopped in a shaded clearing. One of the men built a fire and cooked a meal of *kebabs* and *roti*. The smell of roasting meat made Elijah hungry. They sat around the camp on rocks or just squatted on the ground with plates in their hands and ate their meal and sipped tea before starting off again. The skies were pale blue with a few cumulus clouds. He estimated that the convoy had done about three hundred and fifty miles since leaving the campsite.

In the distance he could see buildings shimmering in the heat. "What city is that?" he asked to no one in particular.

"Kabul," said someone.

As they drove through the streets of Kabul in the hot mid-day sun, Elijah was stunned by the many buildings that had been demolished. There were certain areas where re-construction crews worked. The sound of heavy equipment filled the air and the smell of dust floated towards them.

But most of all he was appalled by the sight of Afghan women, destitute and begging to passersby. Most men ignored them as though they were second-class citizens. Where had he seen this before? These were a handsome race now driven to such abject misery. He couldn't believe it. He remembered, Mumtaz Mahal, Shah Jahan's wife, had been an Afghan maiden and considered a beauty in her time.

"Why are they treated like this?" Elijah asked the man sitting next to him.

"They have lost their husbands in the war. With no husband, they lose everything."

"Isn't there an organization to take care of such people?"

"If there was, they wouldn't be here, would they?"

They had been talking in a mixture of English and Urdu. Elijah lapsed into silence. This is awful, he thought. I thought I had problems, but this is beyond belief.

They left the city and towards evening the trucks drove into a small village. A bell rang out and children came pouring out of a brick building, screaming at the top of their lungs.

Rehman came and asked Elijah to join him, while the others started taking out the camping equipment once again. A group of about eight children ran around, curious and shouting to each other. A few women, wearing *burkhas* that covered their faces, with a mesh like aperture for them to see through, stood in a curious group and stared at the stranger.

"What are we doing here?" asked Elijah, "I thought you were going to send me to ISIS. That's why you kidnapped me for, didn't you?"

"Yes," said Rehman, "that was the original intention. As I stated earlier I felt you could be of help to these villagers. You are still at risk. If my commander objects to my decision to put you to work, he can order you sent to ISIS. Do you still wish to argue?"

"No," said Elijah.

"Come let's meet the mullah of this village."

*   *   *

Abdul Rehman had crossed the Rubicon when he decided to put Elijah to work. His main goal now was to help the villagers become self-sufficient. He wanted them to be able to grow crops. Irrigation played a large part in that endeavor. He needed Elijah's help to install the pumps and the diesel-generators to run those pumps.

How this decision affected his standing with the Fundamentalist Muslims was yet to be seen. The organization was large. His superiors could still change things.

He took Elijah to the mullah. Mullah Mansur was in his sixties. He had deep brown eyes and an aquiline nose. His brown beard and mustache looked like they had been dyed to take the white out. His black turban covered most of his hair. He was about five foot ten.

"Salaam Aleikoum," said Abdul Rehman to the chieftain and then introduced Elijah, "This is American engineer. He will help you with the equipment you have lying idle these many years. You will be able to grow some crops this year, if he will help us."

Elijah understood most of what they spoke in Pushtu.

The mullah escorted them both to where two diesel powered generators stood on the open ground. Elijah bent down and wiped the dust off the name plate and read they were one hundred horsepower machines. The starter batteries had long since corroded into grotesque shapes. He could still smell the diesel fuel. He looked at Rehman, "You brought me here to hook up these generators?" he asked. "You could hire people in Pakistan to do this for you, or ask the UN."

Rehman sighed. "No one wants to come here. There is a civil war going on in this country. Everyone including the UN has been waiting for it to end, for ten years. All the people with any professional knowledge have left the country. In the meantime these men, women and children have no food nor any work to do." Rehman had a deep knowledge of the situation facing his countrymen. He wanted to help them. He felt Elijah was a godsend.

Seeing the plight of these poor villagers, Elijah was moved. The women, when they sometimes took off their purdahs, looked so resigned to their impoverished way of life. He pitied the children too. They must have a school of some sort. He had seen them come running out of that building. He had never been asked to do pro-bono work before, but under these circumstances it would be a pleasure to do so.

"I would gladly have come here to help," said Elijah, "you didn't have to kidnap me to accomplish this."

"Mister Elijah, I'm a full-fledged member of Fundamentalist Muslims. I do not like Americans. We did indeed want to kill you at the onset and one more casualty means nothing to us. How many suicide bombers have you read about in the Middle East? But after you escaped I had to get you back or lose face with my superiors. While my men were searching for you in Jullundur, I spent a day in this village on my way back to my own. I saw the apathy and the mullah asked me for help. That was when I decided that you with your training could be of help here. My attitude towards Americans may not have changed, but it has changed towards you, if you will help these people." He paused to catch his breath. This had been the longest he had talked to Elijah. "But my men," he continued, "are militants. That's their way of life. My own feelings are merely a temporary suspension of hostilities as far as you are concerned."

"Once I finish this project will you let me go? Will you take me back to Jullundur?"

Rehman needed Elijah's co-operation. He restrained his anger and said, "There is one more village that needs similar help. After that I will take you back."

"But the guards, I don't like being hemmed in. I don't think anyone does. Can you take them with you while I work here?"

"No they stay," he said with finality.

"So I am a prisoner here. Nothing has changed," said Elijah, his face clouding in disappointment. It is the duty of all prisoners to try to escape, thought Elijah. One way or another I must get out of here.

Elijah stared at the bleak landscape that was going to be home for a while. A day ago I was in Paradise with Sonia, now this. "Where is the stream they get their water from?" he asked, pointing to two women carrying buckets of water.

"Someone will show you."

"Where are all the men?"

"They have been conscripted into the army of the Taliban," said Rehman getting restive again, answering all these questions.

"Are you part of the Taliban?" asked Elijah.

"No. We are a different group with aims of our own. That's all. No more questions."

Elijah looked around making a mental note of items the project would require. "I will need some supplies and tools and a few men to help me," he said to Rehman.

Rehman nodded, "Yes, yes, you write down all you need and I will get them. I have a supply store I do business with in Pakistan. It's a long journey but I can get most anything in building materials. Give me your list and I'll send my men in the morning."

It was light still and Elijah made a survey of the village compound, making notes in a pad Rehman had given him.

The smell of smoke from a small fire around which the women worked floated towards him. He walked around them selecting a site for the power house where the generators would be kept safe from the elements. With no measuring tape, he took a three-foot stride and counted his steps from the stream to approximate locations to get an estimate of distance where the various items like pumps, water taps and the power house would be located.

The children followed him everywhere. He spoke to them in Pushtu, asking their names. Some of the boys answered shyly before running away. The young girls giggled as they watched him counting his large exaggerated strides. The younger girls didn't wear burkhas. He thought they were cute and pretty as they smiled at him.

The guards stayed out of his way, selecting higher ground from where they could observe him.

He continued making sketches in his notepad until it got dark and he was forced to quit.

Rehman came and talked to him. "Let's have a meal with our host, the mullah Mohammed Mansur."

He sat with Rehman and the mullah and the rest of the villagers in a circle on the ground. The women served them lamb curry, roti and tea. The curry smelled heavenly. The crisp roti crackled as he broke it into smaller pieces. The lamb was delicious and he wondered what kind of spices the women had used. Maybe it was something they grew right here. He noticed that the women had pushed their burkhas over their heads while they cooked the roti on their pans over the fire. They had finer features than the men he had seen. Many were blue-eyed and light skinned. The children ate their food quietly though they kept staring at him. When they were done Elijah thanked the mullah and bowed to the women and complimented them on their cooking. He spoke in Pushtu. They smiled uneasily. No men ever thanked them for their cooking. Elijah went back to his notepad making his list of all he required. Insulated wire of different gages and lots of it, now that he had an idea of the estimated distance between equipment and lighting. He needed transformers to step down the two hundred and twenty volt output from the generators to a hundred and ten volts for lights and equipment. Starter batteries. He added concrete mix and rebar for a foundation for the two generators. Next came lumber and plywood for an enclosure. Three wheelbarrows and shovels, a Skill saw, a handsaw and a few other items.

He gave his list to Rehman as they turned in for the night. Elijah had his own tent and as he lay in his sleeping bag the isolation abruptly had him thinking of Sonia and wondering when he would see her again. Surely she knows by now where I am. That blinking light should tell her. What would she do? They had not got so far as to discuss what course of action she was to follow other than to inform Derrick. What could Derrick do thousands of miles away?

With the guards all around, his only chance of escape would be in the night. If he could hike to the next village and get a ride on one of those trucks he had seen on the roads. While he worked at this place his life would be spared. While there was life there was hope. On those thoughts he fell asleep.

Early the next morning two men took one of the trucks and his list to fetch supplies. Rehman took off in one of the Jeeps.

With stakes made from the branches of a tree, Elijah began laying out the perimeter of his power house. Lacking tools, he drove the stakes in at estimated locations using a rock for a hammer. He soon ran out of things to do and sat on a rock and watched the boys kick a soccer ball around. When the ball rolled towards him, he got up and tried dribbling it towards the boys. They joined in trying to maneuver the ball away from him. There were shouts of joy when they got away. Now they had a regular game going with Elijah on one of the teams.

The women were back at their chores and they paused to look at this unusual match being played amid the dust the game was raising.

At noon Rehman drove in with three men in his Jeep. They were young not much older than sixteen or seventeen. With energetic steps they climbed out and followed Rehman to where Elijah sat, their sandals clicking on the dry earth.

"With a lack of manpower here," said Rehman, "I have been able to find these very able men who are just under the age for conscription, from another village." Two of them had shovels with them.

"Good," said Elijah, rising. "Let's put them to work. Come with me." He pointed to the young man with a shovel. "*Aap ki nam*? (Your name)?"

"Ishmael Khan," said the man.

"Ishmael, you dig post holes here," said Elijah, indicating the stakes he had planted and continuing to talk in Urdu and Pushtu and English.

"*Ha jee.* (Yes Sir)," said Ishmael and started digging.

Elijah checked himself. He stopped and shook his head. "I'm jumping the gun," he said to himself. "I need the measuring tape to confirm my dimensions. All this work will be wasted." He called out, "Ishmael."

Ishmael stopped digging, his shovel poised and looked at Elijah.

"Just dig the one hole," he said in Pushtu. "We will determine the position of the other holes when the men come back with the measuring tape."

"*Ha Jee*," said Ishmael and continued digging.

Elijah moved to the next man. "*Aur aap ka nam*? (and you name)?"

"Majid," said the young man about the same age as Ishmael.

"Come with me and bring your shovel." He took Majid to the creek below. "You dig me an area here for a foundation for the pumps." Elijah stuck four sticks in the ground and Majid set to work.

"*Aur aap ka nam*? (and your name)?" He asked the third man

"Saleem."

"Pick up all these stones in this area where the shed goes and collect them in a pile outside."

"*Jee*."

Elijah went back to his sketches and every time he walked to the outskirts of the village, a guard appeared to follow him. He ignored them and went about his work. While the villagers seemed friendly, the Fundamentalist Muslims members were not. He heard a guard say to his comrade, "Americans are arrogant devils."

Elijah clenched his fists and gritted his teeth and turned to face the man, who lowered his rifle. Not a wise move, Elijah told himself, relaxing and turning away. Have to bide my time and keep my cool.

Chapter Eight

The truck came back after a day. They unloaded all the material he had sent for. This must have cost a bundle of money, thought Elijah. He knew the villagers couldn't afford this expense. He was sure Rehman was using Fundamentalist Muslims funds. He picked up the measuring tapes and smiled. One a robust fifty footer and the other a versatile twenty-five footer. "Now I can get started," he mused.

"The first thing we need is a work center," he said to all three men. They smiled, nodding. He showed them how to make a sawhorse with some of the lumber and plywood. The lumber and the plywood gave off a welcome smell of pine pitch. They all took deep breaths and laughed.

He wished he could use the skill saw, but not without electrical power. They used the hacksaw for now. Clamping a rebar to the sawhorse, he cut it to the length he wanted. Next he let them do it. The rasping sound of the saw on the steel caused the women to stop their work and look at them. The children were in the school.

Then using some bare galvanized wire he tied the joints together, to form a box shape. He had Majid nail some pieces of 1x6 lumber to the posts driven around the excavation for the generator foundation. "This will do as makeshift forms for our foundation, keeping it about six inches above the ground," he said to Ishmael. They had already dug the cavity eighteen inches deep. They lowered the reinforcement into the cavity of the foundation.

After measuring the footprint of the mounting holes of the generators, he took a piece of plywood, laid out the hole pattern.

"Ishmael," he said, "use this drill bit to put holes in the places I have marked in the plywood," as he gave Ishmael the tools to do it with. "Make two of them, exactly alike." When Ishmael was done, he came back to Elijah who was working on something else. He stopped and handed Ishmael some large bolts.

"Put these foundation bolts in the holes you just made, with nuts on both sides. Keep the threaded end about three inches above the plywood."

He smiled to himself, thinking about Ishmael always looking for more work. He found the young man very receptive and could rely on him doing exactly what Elijah had intended. Ishmael always asked questions in their quieter moments together. He has an intelligent inquisitive mind, thought Elijah.

"We'll need a lot of concrete," said Elijah. He had done the math. Each foundation measured two feet deep by four feet wide by five feet long, would take sixty of the 90 lb. sacks of concrete mix. "Bring two wheelbarrows. Two of you mix three sacks at a time and empty it into the foundation pit. Do this ten times. Ishmael and Majid, you two do the same with the second wheelbarrow. When we fill one, we move on to the second foundation."

He spoke to Ishmael. "Have the women bring water in these buckets and in all the pots they have available."

Soon they had a train of women handing buckets of water from the creek to the work site.

"Let's start," said Elijah.

They poured water into a wheelbarrow with dry concrete mix. Without electricity and a large concrete mixer, it was a laborious process. Two of the guards were pressed into service too. They worked continuously until one hundred and twenty empty concrete-mix sacks lay in a heap. The men sank down in tired groups. The women walked back to their homes, just as tired, some of them bent over from the heavy lifting.

They were not done yet. Elijah picked up the plywood sheet with the foundation bolts and told Ishmael, "Hold onto the other end and bring it over here." They slowly lowered the sheet, the bolts sinking into the still liquid concrete. One completed, they moved onto the next. It would take a couple of days to cure. None of his helpers had done these things before. Elijah was pleased however and said to his workers, "*Bahouth acha*, you did a good job. We'll start early again tomorrow."

"*Ha, jee* (Yes sir)," they said, happy at their own handiwork.

That night they sat down to eat lamb curry and roti again. They didn't have much to choose from. The children still stared at him from time to time. They had pitched a tent for him on the outskirts of the little village. He had been given a sleeping bag and blankets. They made do with the few kerosene lamps available but Elijah wasn't given one. The six guards rested in their tents at various locations. He made himself comfortable and wished he was back in Sonia's apartment. How do I get out of here with all these guards around? he thought. I'm sure Sonia knows by now where I am. If only I could talk to her. This was Tuesday, his second day of captivity.

*   *   *

Sonia called the American Embassy in New Delhi, and informed them that an American citizen had been kidnapped, and gave them all the relevant details. The aide who took the call asked, "Do you have his passport number?"

"Not right now," she said, "but I can call you back when I find it."

"Very well ma'am, we'll do what we can. I shall pass on the information."

Next she went through a stack of newspapers to get the name of the President of Afghanistan. She finally found it, Hamid Karzai in Kabul. She put in a call to Kabul. Someone at the other end kept passing her to different departments. She finally spoke to a man named Abdul Aziz. She told him about Elijah being kidnapped and detained against his will, and that he was an American citizen. She added, "I do believe he's at these co-ordinates, Latitude N26.23, Longitude E.65.35."

Mister Aziz asked her, "How do you know that?"

"I just do," she answered, "please send someone to look for him."

"Who are you to him?" asked Aziz.

"I'm his wife, Sonia Davenport," she lied. She could hear herself breathing hard, like she had run a race.

"But you have an accent."

"So do you," she said, and wished immediately she hadn't said that. She didn't want to antagonize him.

"We will do what we can," said Aziz.

Sonia wouldn't be put off. She hung on and said, "I read in the papers, that the U.S. Special Forces are at the Shindand Air Base. Is there any way to get in touch with them?"

All Aziz said was, "We will try." He hung up.

"You bastard!" shouted Sonia into the dead telephone line. As the frustration wore off, she realized she was in her office. This isn't good for everyone else to know about my efforts, she thought. She made up her mind and went over to Mister D'Souza's office and knocked.

"Come in," he said.

She walked in and said, "I have some vacation coming, and if you don't mind, I'd like to take three weeks off. There is nothing pending on my file right now."

D'Souza looked at her and smiled, "Yes, of course." Then he frowned and added. "Has this anything to do with Mister Davenport's disappearance? Is there something you know that the rest of us don't?"

"No," she said, "I just need some time by myself."

Although it might be advantageous for more people to know of Elijah's plight, she didn't want her involvement to be common knowledge. Besides, what could they do? What could Mister D'Souza do?

"It's not like Mister Elijah to keep us uninformed of a change in schedule. You take it easy, Sonia."

She walked out, got her things together and left the office. As she got in the car, she remembered the pictures of the journalists, who had been captured in Pakistan and Syria. Their pictures showed that they had been beaten up before being killed. She hoped they hadn't harmed Elijah. Tears welled up as these thoughts raced through her mind. When she arrived at her apartment she wiped her eyes dry.

She opened the trunk and took the box in with her. Besides the GPS module, she found a night vision binoculars, water purification tablets. Packets of dehydrated food, a compass and a couple of flares and three cans of tear-gas. All this against the Taliban, she thought. And what in the world do you do with the tear-gas? She sat at the table, then lowered her head onto her arms on the table and sobbed until she fell asleep.

*　　　　　*　　　　　*

D'Souza stood in his office, looking out his large window. He had things on his mind, when he saw Sonia walking to her car wiping tears from her eyes. He turned away so that she may not see him observing her.

For heaven's sake, he thought, why is she crying? Is someone in her family ill? Does Elijah's absence have anything to do with it? I wish she had confided in me, whatever is bothering her.

He stepped out of his office. The sounds of machinery running in the shop reassured him that all was well. He walked over to the receptionist and asked, "Did Sonia say where she was going?"

"No, but I heard her shouting at somebody on the phone."

"Did she get any calls from any of her relatives?"

"No, I didn't take any calls."

"Let me know if she or if Mister Davenport calls."

"Yes, sir."

He walked back to his office wondering if he could have helped Sonia.

*   *   *

Sonia called Derek again later in the evening. He had got her message. "He has initiated the GPS," she said, " and from the co-ordinates I have I'd say he's in Afghanistan."

Derek was unprepared for this. "It will take me some time to get to Jullundur," he said. "I have to get a passport, and apply for a visa. This might take about three weeks or more. I also have to run the business, Elijah has entrusted me with."

"Well, let me know what your plans are. I'll try to get help here from whomever I can." She hung up. She sat pondering, what can I do?

*   *   *

Elijah was up at the break of dawn. He had been thinking all night. With all the guards around, his mind raced over plan after plan of escape. With no definite strategy his thoughts shifted to the work at hand. He needed to use the skill saw and the electric drill. The cordless drill and the cordless saber saw lasted for a few days then ran out of power and needed to be recharged. The generators were a source of 110 volts. Why not use one of them? A temporary system would allow him to use that power.

Elijah talked in a mixture of Urdu, Pushtu and English, trying to get across his ideas of what he wanted done. He called his main helper, Ishmael, "Take these 2 x 4s, cut them in half along the angle I have marked, so that they form a point." He marked one of the 2 x 4s with his pencil.

He had another man, Saleem, replace the old starter battery on the generator with a new one he had bought.

He mounted a disconnect and a transformer on a piece of plywood, laying it near the generator and using the wire he had ordered, made temporary connections, while Ishmael watched intently.

With breakers and fuses in the disconnect, he was ready to start the unused generator that had sat idle for so long. "Ishmael fill the tank with diesel fuel," Elijah said pointing, "from the barrels over there. Use the hand pump in the barrel and lead the hose to the engine fuel tank." As they worked, the smell of diesel fuel filled the air. Majid had a fit of coughing when the fumes hit him in the face.

Elijah gave Saleem a grease gun and said, "See these fittings? Give them a shot of grease. About six strokes to each fitting, OK?"

"*Ha Jee*," said Abdul, positioning himself, holding the gun with both hands.

Once the fuel was topped off, they put the cover back on the tank. "Wipe off all those spills. It should be clean and dry," said Elijah. He looked around. Everything seemed to be in place.

"Everyone stand clear," he said. He pressed the start button and the engine cranked. He held the button down for half a minute, before the engine coughed and came to life with a roar. Dust flew everywhere. The crew moved back further, wide eyed. Elijah waited for the dust to settle, then went over and felt the generator with his hands to check for excessive vibration. It seemed normal. He flipped the disconnect switch on and checked the voltage with his multimeter. It read 110V. "Good," he said. He plugged the skill saw into the receptacle and tried it. It worked. He could now work at a faster pace. Not that he was going anywhere.

The roar of the engine had attracted the attention of the villagers. The women and children ran to see what was happening. They gathered around the workmen, curious, straining their necks, jostling each other to see the better. They wandered away when nothing new happened and the machine continued running.

By the end of the day they had the four walls of the enclosure up. He had not ordered any trusses for the roof as he had no idea how big the enclosure would be without a drawing and a measuring tape. Now he knew. He made another list. He would give this to Rehman, who was out most of the time, only coming back in a SUV at the end of the day.

"Ishmael bring those two-by-sixes over here," said Elijah, pointing to the lumber. "You may call it something else in this country, but that's what I call it." That was good enough for Ishmael.

"We call it *lakadi* (firewood)," said Ishmael, picking up the lumber.

"Let's bolt these horizontally to the posts on the inside of the enclosure, right here."

Elijah had them mount the two disconnects, the breakers and the transformers on a sheet of plywood screwed to the wall.

The generators still sat on the ground. Ishmael poured water on the foundations to speed up the curing process. He pressed the surface with his fingers and said, "It is hard."

Majid unscrewed the nuts and took off the plywood, leaving the four anchor bolts exposed, ready for the big machines.

It was tedious work showing Ishmael, Majid and Abdul how to run plastic conduit from the panel to the location where the pumps were located near the creek. Then pulling wires to the electrical box for the pumps.

It was mid-day when they had finished this work. The temperature was still mild and light cirrus clouds hung around the hills. He considered it ideal weather for outdoor work. He wondered if the weather would change. His thoughts on escape were ever present. Rain or snow could add to his problems.

Elijah looked at the water inlet to the pump. If he attached a filter to the inlet pipe in the creek, it would plug up in no time with silt and debris.

"Ishmael and Majid, dig an opening along these stakes I have put in. It's about four feet square and make it three feet deep just below the creek water level, and about two feet away from the edge of the creek."

While the two of them dug with their shovels he shouted, "Saleem, bring those pieces of lumber and plywood over here. We will make forms with them for a concrete wall on three sides. This side facing the creek will stay open."

They made rebar reinforcement bent on a simple fixture made of bolts on the sawhorse. The rebar tied with wire went into the cavities, and the concrete poured. They moved on to other jobs while the walls set for a day. Once the sides had set, the forms were removed and they poured a six-inch thick floor slab, also reinforced with rebar. They waited another day for the concrete to set.

"Dig a shallow trough from the creek that will allow the water to flow into the concrete three-walled tub. The water will also help the curing process." When the walled in area filled with water he said, "This is where the pump inlet hoses will be placed. I will put in a stainless steel, half-inch wire mesh to keep the debris out over here. He made a note to add that item on his list for Rehman.

"The water is very cool," said Abdul, smiling. They were quite comfortable working together.

"Let's build a small dam across the creek with boulders to raise the water level slightly and still continue to flow over the dam, downstream," said Elijah, indicating where he wanted the boulders placed

They searched far and near for rocks and soon had a primitive dam that promptly raised the level of water in the inlet trough by about two feet. The stream continued flowing over the dam, gurgling among the stones and pebbles, on its merry way as it always did. They hadn't disturbed the ecosystem.

Elijah had been in this place now for five days. The days were filled with creative work, but the nights were closing in on him. He wanted his freedom and longed to spend time with Sonia. His constant thoughts about ways of getting out of this village always stumbled with the sight of the guards. An idea had crept into his mind. He needed some means of communicating with Sonia. He would put it to work tomorrow. The guards still hovered in the background. He would need a vehicle, one of the Jeeps Rehman used. Rehman had promised to set him free after helping the next village. He no longer had the heart to tarry here any longer. He just wanted out, now.

Chapter Nine

In her apartment Sonia sat down at her dining room table and considered her options. Just a few short days ago she had sat in this very spot across from Elijah. She had grown to like him, and felt comfortable with him. She felt an ineffable yearning in her. Tears welled up. He's a friend, she thought and he needs my help.

I have to do something now. I could follow his trail with the GPS module. But he's in Afghanistan, and from what I've read, it's no place for a foreign woman, and there's a war going on. I will have to disguise myself as a man. They all have beards and mustaches. If this were Mumbai I could probably buy such a disguise. But how am I going to find one here? Maybe I can make my own. I know what I'll do. I'll ask Leela to help me.

She called Leela and told her the plan. Leela was shocked and thrilled. "Oh, my God," she said. "What are you trying to do? Get yourself killed? What will I do if I lose my friend? No, no think of something else, Sonia."

Sonia was adamant. "I'll be there in half an hour," she said. I helped Elijah with his disguise and it had worked very well for more than a week. It was hard to tell what went on the day he was captured. She wondered if he had stopped wearing the disguise. That would do it.

She stopped at a store and bought a bottle of rubberized glue, a plastic bottle of superglue, a pair of scissors, a roll of Velcro tape, and a roll of cotton tape eight centimeters wide and a roll two centimeters wide. She parked her car at Leela's home. Leela let her in with a worried look on her face and gave Sonia a hug. Roy was still at work. Sonia set all her stuff on the living room table. They both sat down looked at each other and burst out laughing. Leela felt the whole project was preposterous and unbelievable. The laughter helped ease the tension for her.

Sonia turned serious and spread out a newspaper on the table. Next, she took the scissors and cut a lock of her straight brown hair and put it on the paper. "That's for a mustache," she said.

Leela looking on at Sonia's efforts started to laugh again. Sonia cut a piece of the narrow cotton tape, and spread some of the rubberized glue on. "This is going to be messy." She got some small towels she had brought with her in a bag. She took some of the hair and began to simulate a mustache, as she visualized one. She stopped, moved her head back and appraised it. Added a few more touches, looked at Leela and said, "Well?"

Leela had nothing to say. She just laughed nervously. Her laughter sounding like bells rung at intervals in a religious ceremony.

Sonia picked up the fake mustache and stuck it under her nose, and again said, "Well?"

"You look like a very handsome young man," said Leela.

"A beard can improve on that," said Sonia, "let's start on the beard."

The beard had to be done in layers, the first starting back under her chin. She cut some more of her brown locks of hair, from the left and the right. She couldn't spare much more. She looked at Leela and said, "Maybe you can give me some of your hair."

"But it's not the same as yours."

"That's all right," said Sonia, "it's brown like mine, and I can use it as filler at the back."

Leela cut long strands from her hair, and laid it on the table. She looked hurt, like a child losing a toy.

"What is Roy going to say?" she wondered out loud.

"He won't notice, if you work on it," said Sonia.

Soon they had made four rows of beard on the wide tape. Sonia put the rubberized glue on the bare side and waited for it to dry. Ten minutes later, she carefully pressed it onto her chin. The front layer was long while the layers behind were a little shorter. Leela helped to trim it, to make it more realistic. They made pieces to add to her eyebrows to make them bushy like a man's. Everything in place, Sonia took out a turban she had brought and wrapped it around her head. She already had on pantaloons. A loose fitting shirt hid her feminine attributes and a waist jacket and a shawl completed the disguise.

Sonia stood and walked to and fro trying to imitate a man's gait.

"I have to 'turn two mincing steps into a manly stride,'" said Sonia, remembering her Shakespeare.

"Keep practicing," said Leela, "you're getting there."

Roy opened the front door with his key and walked in and they both turned towards him. "I noticed Sonia's car in the driveway," said Roy. Seeing Leela and a young man standing in the living room, he said, "Who is this?"

Leela started laughing. "It's Sonia," she said, bending over with more laughter. He walked forward, and peered at the man and said, "Sonia?" He walked all around the man again and said, "Really?" his mouth half open in surprise.

Sonia was serious. She did not smile. She stared back at Roy. If I can fool him, the disguise must work, she thought.

Finally, Roy stopped in front of her, still staring at her, he said, "If that's you Sonia, why are you dressed like a man?"

Sonia remained very serious of countenance. "*Mera nam, Abdul Aziz hi* (my name is Abdul Aziz)," she said, in as low a contralto as she could command. The smell of the rubberized glue almost choked her. Roy couldn't keep it together any longer. He burst out laughing as he walked around. But he sobered up quickly. He had noticed that Sonia still stayed serious.

Roy looked at Leela, "What's this all about?"

They all at the table and Leela said, "Tell him Sonia."

Sonia started narrating her plans, and her intention of going into Afghanistan, in search of Elijah. Leela started clearing off all the material left over from their costume make-up.

"But why?" asked Roy.

"You will do crazy things when you're in love," said Leela, staring at Roy.

"You're in love with this man?" asked Roy, "someone you've only known for two weeks?" His voice was rising to almost a shout.

"I don't know," said Sonia, almost in a whisper. "But I do know that I must help him. I owe him that much."

"One night in paradise doesn't mean you owe him anything," snapped Roy.

"Roy!" exclaimed Leela, "shut up."

"My mind is made up," said Sonia, "I will be leaving in the morning."

Roy looked at Sonia or Abdul Aziz and said, "Afghanistan is no place for a woman."

"I'm supposed to be a man," said Sonia.

"What if they found you out?" said Roy

"Not if I can help it," said Sonia quickly.

"Do you have any weapons?"

"No. Can you get me one?" asked Sonia.

"No," said Roy, "how are you going to get there? You can't take your car."

"Yes. I know," said Sonia, "I'll rent a SUV, a four wheel drive. I'm also going to get a cell phone, and I'll give you the number. If you hear anything, I want you to call me. I can call my home phone and activate my answering machine to read any messages."

"So how long do you expect to be gone? What about food? Once you cross into Afghanistan, there are no hotels between Peshawar and Jalalabad. And it's also desolate between Jalalabad and Kabul," said Roy.

"Yes, I do know that, but there are truck stops. I am taking some dehydrated food and a flask for water. I will do a major refill at the Pakistan border. As to how long I'll be gone? I don't know. I'll follow Elijah's trail to the co-ordinates, where I think he is and if I can get him out, we should be back in a week."

"What if they won't let him go? Remember he was taken by force," said Leela.

"Then I'll stay with him until we can figure out what to do. He's probably in a village. It all depends on how they treat strangers."

"You're one courageous person Sonia, or *bilkul pagal* (completely mad)," said Roy

"As long as that light is blinking and moving around in the GPS module, it means that he is alive. Someone has to make an attempt to help him. I have not heard from his friend Derek either."She stroked her beard with her hand. I think that's how men do it, she thought

"What if you do end up in this village where you think he is," said Roy. "Tell me, what are you going to do? Walk up and say, 'Hey, I want my brother back.'"

"I will say I'm just passing through to Kabul and get to know the situation. Once I know how he is, I may continue on to Kabul and seek help from the Americans there. My presence there will be more convincing than a phone call. Yes it may not be that easy. They may kill him if they saw American soldiers. But what else can I do?" She broke down and started sobbing.

Leela ran to her and put her arms around her shoulders. With a stern look at Roy, she said, "Stop badgering her. This isn't easy for her."

She gave Sonia a napkin to wipe her face with.

Roy walked away and sat down, deep in thought. After a while he stood and said, "If you find the village, Abdul Aziz can't just drive in there. They may have as many as six to eight guards with rifles. They will stop you and ask a lot of questions."

"I thought about that. Since I have the night vision binoculars, I could park the SUV away from the village and observe them from a safe distance, right into the night and find out their routine and where his tent is."

"That's a good idea. However, getting to his tent will be a risky business. If you observe where he works during the day, that area will not be guarded at night. You could possibly leave a message in that place for him and he'll find it the next day. But without weapons what can you do to protect yourself?"

She didn't tell them, but she knew if she were willing to take the risk as Abdul Aziz, he could find and buy weapons and explosives on the streets of Pakistan. While she had no intention of killing anyone, an explosive could be used effectively to disable any of the militant's vehicles. Where was she getting these ideas from she wondered.

Well, they started it, she thought. They took my friend. I haven't the slightest idea what explosives to buy. Abdul Aziz would have to ask the sellers what to buy and how to use it.

"What are you thinking about," asked Roy, after a long silence in their discussion.

"I was thinking I could ask Elijah to leave me a note in reply as to what he would want me to do."

"Yes, but remember," said Roy as though he had read her thoughts, "if you use a weapon, it can be used against you also.

This is dangerous work for a woman. I wish I were going with you."

"No, you have Leela to take care of." Sonia now more composed wiped her face with the napkin. She slowly peeled off her disguise and put it in a bag and she was now once again the "beautiful Sonia" minus some hair. She told them to keep an eye on her place, while she was away.

Sonia drove to a car rental. A salesman walked towards her. "I would like to rent an SUV," she said.

"We have quite a selection," said the salesman. "What color would you like?"

"It has to be black or dark green," said Sonia, thinking it would have to be camouflaged in her travel.

He led her to where a dozen SUVs were parked. Some were black SUVs.

"Would you like to try one of them?"

"Yes," said Sonia.

He opened the door of the nearest black SUV and she stepped in and started it. He walked around to the passenger side and climbed in. She eased it out of its parking slot and drove around the lot.

"I'll take it," she said, bringing it back to the rental office. She signed the papers and paid for it with her credit card. They agreed to keep her car parked on their lot for the duration of the rental. The engine purred smoothly as she drove it away. The smell of petrol fumes hung in the air, but it didn't bother her. It had automatic transmission and she felt comfortable. She drove back to Leela's place, and stayed the night with them. She had all her belongings in two knapsacks. In the morning, she woke up at seven a.m. With Leela's help, and the aid of a hand mirror, she became Abdul Aziz, once again.

As she sat in the SUV a whole gamut of emotions ran through her. Feelings of fear and doubt shook the little confidence she had mustered together to make this trip. But the one question that had brought her so far was, who would help Elijah? "I will," she said through her tears.

Chapter Ten

Abdul Aziz stopped at a large grocery store. As he walked in, the air was thick with smells of a dozen different spices and grains. It must have been the choking smell of dried chilies that made him cough. He stopped and walked to a more neutral corner and told the clerk what he wanted. He bought two sacks of potatoes, two bags of wheat flour, two bags of sugar, two bags of salt, twenty cans of soup, two sacks of rice, and loaded them in the back of the SUV, in plain sight. He paid in rupees. He was still in India. He started the SUV and drove off with only a few curious stares.

At the India-Pakistan border, the armed guards asked Aziz where he was going. Sonia replied in her practiced contralto, in Hindi, "I'm taking provisions to our village in Pakistan."

"Very good," replied the guard, "you should spend more money in India. *Salaam Aleikoum* (Peace be with you)."

"*Salaam Aleikoum*," said Abdul Aziz. The guard let him pass. Abdul Aziz smiled. This was so much pulse pounding excitement. Keeping a calm exterior was the hardest part. I think I'll become a double agent she mused. I'm a natural. As long as I don't have to sing and dance as they do in our movies. The SUV moved on.

It was a sunny day, with not a cloud in the sky. She encountered no traffic on these roads. An occasional man or woman with a burden on their heads was all Sonia saw, for about two hours of driving. A lone SUV passed her going the other way in a roar and the sound slowly faded away, leaving her alone with her thoughts. She now had a new problem. She had on a man's get up and she had to go to the bathroom. She pulled off the road, near a dense growth of trees, shut off the engine and checked both directions, then made a dash into the woods. She had all the privacy she needed. Soon she was back on the road and in another hour went through Peshawar and arrived at the Pakistan, Afghan border, at the entrance to the Khyber Pass.

Abdul Aziz spoke to the Pakistani guard, "*Salaam Aleikoum*."

"*Salaam Aleikoum*," said the guard, in Urdu, "where are you from and where are you going?"

"I'm going back to my village in Afghanistan, after buying some supplies," said Abdul also in Urdu.

"I thought you people speak Pushtu," said the guard.

"Yes," said Abdul Aziz in Pushtu, "but I spend so much time in Pakistan, I am getting used to speaking your language."

"*Bahouth acha*, carry on, *Salaam Aleikoum*. Be careful of the snipers," said the guard.

"*Salaam Aleikoum*," said Abdul. What snipers? she wondered. She slowly inched the SUV forward. She hadn't gone five hundred meters when a shot rang out and the bullet ricocheted of the sign post on the roadside. She gave a start and gasped, "What in the world?" When she heard a second shot. She floored the accelerator and roared off. Soon she was out of range of the sniper. Now the guard's words came back to her.

"Oh, those bandits," she murmured, "why can't they do some honest work for a living?"

Soon the terrain changed to dry sand with parched shrubs and mostly the appearance of a desert. The road had potholes and she had to slow down. The shimmering heat sent rising waves of air so that it appeared as though water puddles lay on the road's surface up ahead. She wiped the sweat from her forehead with her sleeve.

When she had gone about fifty kilometers, she noticed from far away, on the side of the road, a Jeep on its side. She pulled off the road and stopped, got out and walked to the damaged Jeep. It had been completely demolished. The occupants had been long gone and had abandoned it. Nearby, she noticed one of those Russian automatic rifles. She picked it up and immediately dropped it when she felt how hot it was to the touch. It had been lying in the sun. She took out the scarf from around her neck and used it as a glove to handle the rifle and examined it carefully wondering why it had been left behind.

She turned the weapon over and noticed it had a dent on one side. Perhaps this is my lucky day, she thought. Maybe God is on my side. I have to find bullets for this rifle.

She put the gun in the back of the SUV and drove on. There were signs indicating she was approaching a truck stop. Maybe she could get some food and drink there. She took the exit and stopped near a *Chai shop*. The menu was spelled out on a blackboard. The smell of meat cooking on a hot grill filled the air. She decided she'd try the *kheema* and *roti* and a cup of tea. She sat at a table and relaxed. She could see through the window that they had a store. The men in the restaurant hardly gave her a second look. She had to remind herself that she was Abdul Aziz. The food tasted delicious. However as she ate, the mustache kept getting in the way. She wiped her lips with a large red handkerchief. This is ridiculous, she thought. She kept at it till she felt she had got the knack and the last morsel of *kheema* had disappeared.

She drove over to the store, grabbed the rifle and walked in. A clerk came to her assistance. Abdul Aziz showed him the rifle. "Do you have a cartridge pack for this rifle?"

He picked it up and stared at it. "Where did you get this AK-47?" he asked, rubbing his hand along the barrel and slowly turning it. "What you need is a magazine and ammo for it."

"I found it," said Abdul Aziz, looking as honest as her statement was.

"I'll be right back," said the man. He came back with a magazine and a box of ammo. He took the rifle and tried to snap the magazine into place. But it refused to latch on. He turned the rifle around and scrutinized it carefully.

"Oh! Oh," he said

"What?" asked Abdul Aziz, with growing apprehension.

"This is damaged. You cannot use this. You could get hurt. Here let me get a new one."

He returned with another rifle and pushed a magazine with the palm of his hand into the new one. It latched in with a smooth click.

"This is the way it should look." He turned it over to Abdul Aziz.

"How much is the rifle?" asked Abdul.

"Three thousand rupees."

"And the magazine and ammo?"

"Fifty rupees each."

"Would you take twenty seven hundred rupees for the three items?"

"Let's even it out to twenty eight hundred."

"All right," said Abdul Aziz, opening her knap-sack and counting out the money.

"Where did a young man like you learn to bargain like that?" asked the storeowner.

"From my mother," smiled Abdul Aziz.

After the transaction, Abdul asked, "Can you show me how to take the magazine out and put it back on?"

"First I'll show you how to load the magazine with rounds," said the man. "Then I'll show you how to attach the magazine to the rifle."

After the first lesson the man took the rifle and showed Aziz how to snap on the magazine.

"Now let me try," said Abdul Aziz, taking the rifle from him. She struggled with it and the man showed her again, until she could snap it off and back on again like a pro, sort of.

"With delicate hands like those, I think you should wear a pair of gloves if you're going to use that rifle," said the man looking directly into Abdul Aziz's eyes.

Aziz's eyes flickered for a second in panic, but only for a moment.

"Yes, I'll take one of those."

The man went away and came back with a pair of cotton gloves.

"Ten rupees," he said.

Sonia counted out the money.

Sonia climbed back into the SUV and drove off. He probably suspects that I am a woman, she thought. It doesn't matter; I'll never see him again. Now, I have to try out this rifle. When she saw a grove of trees she pulled off, parked, and looked around. She saw no traffic. She pulled on the gloves and getting out the rifle with the cartridge pack attached, slung the rifle onto her shoulder and pointed the barrel at the hillside, and pulled the trigger.

The recoil of the rifle pushed her backward and she fell. As she lost her balance her finger on the trigger fired two more shots into the air.

Lying on the ground in shock, she pushed her way into a sitting position. "God," she said, gasping for breath. "I have a lot to learn."

The loud report caused her ears to ring for a while. She hadn't been prepared for both these reactions. She pulled out her red kerchief and took one corner and gently pushed it into her right ear. She kept at it until it felt plugged up. She then took the opposite corner and worked on her left ear. The kerchief looped around her chin. "I wonder what I look like?" she said.

Once again facing the hill she braced both feet spread apart and holding the rifle firmly against her shoulder pressed the trigger again. This time, she held her ground, and the muffled report was easy on her ears. She had seen where the bullet hit the hill. The lingering smell of gunpowder and oil made her hold the gun away from her.

I hope I don't have to use it she thought putting the rifle in the rear of the SUV. She covered it with a tarpaulin with the potato and onion sacks above it.

Chapter Eleven

Elijah counted the days in his mind. This was the sixth day of his captivity, which was Sunday, if he remembered right. He looked around him. The early morning light crept through the valley. Smoke from the cooking fires curled up lazily and the smell of spices and onions floated around. He went to talk to Rehman who sat talking to the Mullah.

Elijah said, "Excuse me, Mister Rehman, I need some more supplies. Here is a new list."

Rehman stood. "Good morning, Mister Elijah, I can see much progress. Soon we'll have running water here in the compound, and the fields will be getting irrigated." He smiled like a proud father. "And all thanks to you." He rubbed his hands together; it was a happy moment for him. He took the paper from Elijah.

He folded it, and put it in his pocket. Elijah relaxed; Rehman hadn't read Elijah's hand written series of items. One of the items had been for a cell phone, with a note, "Package well to protect during transit." He hoped no one but the supplier would read this note. Rehman looked at Elijah and said, "I will send my man this evening, he should be back tomorrow by noon. Once this is done we move to the next village."

Elijah looked at him. "Why don't you let me go back and we can arrange to send a proper crew to do this work?"

"Mister Elijah, may I remind you that you are still a hostage of Fundamentalist Muslims. They intend to kill you. I have taken it upon myself to bring you here. They may still overrule me and order you killed. The guards you see around this camp do not like Americans. They will shoot you at the slightest provocation. To answer your question, no one wants to come here." He stormed off leaving Elijah standing alone and quite disconcerted. He looked around. The guards were watching him. He strode back to his group of helpers.

Early Monday morning they were back at work. The weather was pleasant. No rain and soon it would be hot. He showed Ishmael, Saleem and Majid how to add Teflon tape to the brass fittings and assemble the shut-off valves to the pumps. He said, "This pump will supply water to the compound water tap, while the second pump will feed the irrigation canals. They both have their own switches to turn them on and off. Here assemble this." He helped them lay the PVC pipe in an eighteen-inch deep trench that led to where the water tap would be located.

"Glue an elbow, right there. We're taking the pipe up to the tap. Now here we change the fittings to copper. Anything exposed should be copper. The PVC will break easily."

He grabbed a length of three-quarter inch copper pipe. "Cut a three foot piece, Majid. Ishmael, hold this copper pipe with your leather gloves. I'll show you how to solder copper pipes."

Using the propane torch he showed them the basics of soldering copper pipe joints.

The smell of the hot flux and the heated copper made Ishmael, who was closest, wrinkle his nose and cough. "Is it poisonous?" he asked, his face anxious.

"Well, don't breathe it in," said Elijah, slapping him on the shoulder.

Elijah looked at the pipe work. It came up above the ground three feet; a ninety-degree elbow brought it horizontal about twelve inches into a water tap. "Now build forms for concrete to enclose those pipes. You're getting good at this."

The pipes might freeze in winter, so he added a drain valve at the lowest point with a box and a cover. Forms were also added for a platform to set pots and buckets on, under the tap. They added rebar and poured concrete.

Elijah studied his system and wasn't pleased with it. It meant that the pump would be running all the time, even when there was no demand for water. They had several empty fifty-five gallon plastic drums lying around.

"Build an eight foot high platform with the steel tubing left over, and set four barrels on top." While they were building the platform, Elijah cut holes for three-inch PVC fittings about six inches from the top of each barrel. He inserted the plastic bulkhead fittings with nuts and rubber gaskets and tightened them to interconnect the four barrels.

The children came running out of their classroom. They saw Elijah and shouted out to him. "Elijah Jee. Let's have a game of football."

Elijah looked up and waved to them. "Later," he yelled back. He turned to Ishmael and explained, "The output from the pump will go into the first barrel. When the water level rises to the height where they are interconnected, the water will flow into the second barrel and so on until the fourth barrel is filled. In this fourth barrel I have installed a float switch about six inches from the top. As the water level rises the float will move up with it and actuate an electric switch to shut off the pump. When the water level drops, through use, it will start up the pump again." He moved down and pointed to valves at the bottom of the barrels. "These valves are for safety or if one of the barrels has to be cleaned out. Do you understand?"

"Ha jee," they said.

"Now you also don't want the generator running all the time, if they're not using the pumps. But this time we'll use a timer, to shut off the generator. If the pumps are not used for say ten minutes, then the timer will shutoff the generator. That will save diesel fuel. To start the whole system again, someone will have to manually push a button to start the generator. We will give that duty to one of you. The mullah can tell us who. Maybe you, Ishmael."

When the platform had been completed, he said, "Are you ready? Let's move the four barrels on top of the platform."

He shook the structure to check for stability. "Now connect that output line to the main pipe to the compound with this coupling." They added railings up to a height about midway of the barrels, to keep them from falling off in a great wind or an earthquake. For safety he added another float switch in the first barrel and wired the switch in series with the switch in the fourth barrel. This would stop the pump in case the first barrel over filled for some reason, like slower flow between barrels.

They were now ready to try out the pumping system, though the concrete was still damp around the water tap. "Majid," said Elijah, "place some blocks and a two-by-six to span the concrete forms and place a bucket under the tap."

Elijah looked at Ishmael and said, "Go over to the generators and start the one that is connected to these two pumps. The other generator is for the lights. *Summja*?"

"Jee," said Ishmael.

Ishmael walked away and they waited. After a few minutes, they heard the generator come on. The children heard it too and stopped playing soccer and ran towards Elijah and his men, shouting, "*Bijlee ah gayee.*" They stopped short and watched when they saw nothing new.

Elijah waited until he saw Ishmael walking back. He didn't want Ishmael to miss the fun after all the work he had done. When he reached the group, Elijah flipped on the switch for the pump. A gurgling sound came from the inlet trough in the creek below. In seconds a gush of water sprayed into the first barrel. Both Saleem and Majid cheered. This was a fruition of their labors too.

The children echoed their cheers joining in the celebration, not knowing exactly what it was.

Ishmael was silent. He expected this. The water rose slowly, and started flowing into the second barrel. Elijah waited patiently. After several minutes, when all four barrels were full the pump turned off automatically. The float switch worked.

Elijah and his men walked over to the tap in the compound. The atmosphere was tense. There was electricity in the air. A crowd had gathered there. All the women folk, the old men and the mullah joined the children who were hopping unable to stay still. They had come to witness the inauguration of their community water tap. The women pushed their burkhas over their heads the better to see.

They all cast their eyes on Elijah. A lull fell over the compound. The children had grown silent too. The women put their hands nervously to their lips. Everyone held their combined breath as Elijah opened the water tap.

It gurgled, snorted and splashed air and water into the bucket. Everyone let out a cheer, even Ishmael. When the water in the bucket rose to the brim, Elijah shut off the tap.

The children danced around screaming in delight. The women shouted, "*Aray pani aagaya* (there's water in the compound). No more carrying those heavy buckets from the creek." The older men hugged each other. The mullah beamed and raised his hands to the sky and said, "May Allah be praised. We will have crops this year. Allah bless this man and give him many children and may they all grow up to be just like him."

Many of the villagers ran to the fields to see the water running through the once parched troughs, moving ever onwards to the many fields. This was a happy day for the village. Even the hostile guards lay their rifles down and joined in the applause.

Elijah's job was done.

*   *   *

The truck arrived at the warehouse in Pakistan. The sign read, "Sulliaman Hardware." The driver parked his vehicle and walked into the store.

"Salaam Aleykoum," said the owner to the now familiar truck driver. "You are one of Rehman's men, am I right?"

"Aleykoum Salaam," said the man, pulling out Elijah's list from his pocket. "Ha Jee, I have another order for you." He handed over the paper. The owner, Talib, looked at the note and read it through.

"This will take a while. You can check with me tomorrow evening."

"Acha Jee. I will see you then."

He left and Talib walked into the inner office and called his assistant.

"Look at these items. The trusses and plywood we can handle. But this cell phone? Doesn't Rehman know we are a hardware store?"

The man he had called over looked at the sheet of paper, then said, "Well most of the items lately have been of a special nature and one more won't make a difference. He pays all his bills. We could possibly get this phone from the store down the street, who carries them. We can just buy it and add it to Rehman's bill as a favor."

"Yes, I guess we can do that. Send someone and get all the information on how to use it and all the fees to be paid. We don't want Rehman getting sore at us. Those trusses and sheets of plywood should be worth a few rupees."

The next day when the truck was fully loaded, Talib took the carefully wrapped phone package and gave it to the truck driver.

"Give this to Rehman, personally," he said. "It is very delicate to be put with the other items."

"Ha, Jee," said the driver taking the package and setting it on the seat beside him.

*   *   *

At about noon, two days later, Elijah heard the truck squealing in second gear up the sloping road to the village. "At last it's here," he said. and waited patiently.

He greeted the driver and went to supervise its unloading. He saw the trusses and the plywood and other items, but the package he was looking for wasn't there. He called to the truck driver.

"There's one item missing on this bill of lading," he pointed out.

"Ha, Jee," said the man, remembering Talib's instructions. He walked to the cab and pulled out the small package and handed it to Elijah.

"Mister Talib said to give it to Mister Rehman personally because it is very fragile."

"I can do that," said Elijah, "it was I who ordered it. Besides Rehman is not here today and we'll need to use it soon." He held out his hand. The man gave him the package. Elijah took it to the shed and placed it on one of the generators and walked back to see the unloading of the trusses.

He picked up a three-foot square, stainless steel, half-inch wire mesh that he had ordered. It was one-eighth inch thick, a heavy enough gage to prevent bending while keeping out debris in the pump inlet in the creek. He went back to where the package was and slipped it into his pocket and walked unhurriedly towards the creek. It seemed a natural thing to do. Nothing suspicious. When he felt he was alone, away from prying eyes. He was just about to open the package, when he heard footsteps approaching. He threw the package into the bushes and looked up. A guard strode into view with his rifle on his shoulder. He looked at Elijah then looked all around. He walked past Elijah to the bush where the package lay. He paused with his hand on the bush. Elijah bent down, picked up the mesh screen and walked to the water's edge, like a grouse hen would try to lead predators away from her chicks. The man turned around and walked back to the compound.

Elijah's heart raced. That was a close call. He dared not open the package now. He pretended to work with the wire mesh screen once more.

He walked back to the pumps and water barrels. Glancing at the retreating back of the guard, he stopped at the bush and picked up the package, opened it and lifted out the cell phone. He carefully read the instructions. Noting down the phone number he made a call to initiate the calling codes and open his account with the cell phone service. This done, he clicked off and wrapped the small phone in three layers of clean wipe rags he had brought with him. Hopefully it would muffle the vibrations of the phone when and if he received a call. He placed it in his pocket.

He went back to the truck trembling with fear and anticipation. They had unloaded the trusses and more plywood and roofing material and taken them to the site of the enclosure.

He directed Ishmael and Saleem, "Put ladders on both sides of the enclosure near the end."

He watched as they moved the ladders into position.

"Now each of you pick up your end of a truss and carefully climb your ladder with it. It isn't heavy."

They followed his instructions and slowly ascended the ladders with the truss.

"Good. Now set it on the end joist."

Elijah added a third ladder at the front end of the enclosure. "Let's start with the end truss." He climbed up and measured the overhang on each side, having them move it slightly, until the overhang measured equal on both sides. While they held the truss in place he nailed it to the joist at one end, and Majid nailed it on the other side. They took a truss to the other end and did the same. The other three trusses went in equidistant from each other. While Ishmael, Majid and Saleem gazed in awe at their own handiwork, Elijah said, "Now let's raise the ridge pole and lay it in the slot provided in the peak along the length of the roof.

He waited as they lifted the ridge pole in place.

"Good," he said. "Now have it aligned at the other end."

"Yes, Saab," shouted Ishmael.

"Now nail it to the trusses."

The sound of hammering filled the air. There were at least three hammers being wielded at the same time with Elijah adding his at certain points. Plywood sheets fell into place and then *Bang! Bang! Bang!*

"Amazing," said Elijah, "none of you have hit your thumb with a hammer as yet."

"Ouch!" Cried Majid just then.

"Maybe I spoke too soon," said Elijah, looking up. Majid smiled down at him. He had faked it; he slapped the roof and laughed.

By the time they got through nailing the rafters and the plywood sheathing the light had faded to dusk. They had a support structure now, from which the generators could be hoisted up. They still had enough light to work by.

First Elijah disconnected the wiring from the generator to the temporary control panel he had used for the skill saw. The two generators were now ready to be moved.

"Ishmael, bring the lifting chain and tie it to the joists above the generator and attach the hook to the manually operated hoist," he said. When Ishmael had it hooked up, he said, "OK, Ishmael, you operate the hoist. Majid and Saleem bring those eight-inch square blocks, all four of them and set them nearby. Ready? Start lifting Ishmael." The generator rose slowly from the ground where it had rested these many years with a rasping sound as the chain rubbed against the lifting eye. When it had risen twenty inches in the air Elijah said, "Hold it. Majid and Saleem, bring those square blocks and set them on the floor. The generator will sit on them. Are they in position? Let's see, Ishmael lower the generator onto the blocks."

The generator swung and turned lazily around. The three of them helped guide it down. When it sat on the wooden blocks, Elijah checked if it was stable by trying to rock it. It seemed to be firm.

"Now disengage the chain from the joist and move it a foot in the direction of where the foundation is. We'll walk it over one foot at a time." Ishmael followed his directions. "Now lift it again slowly. It's going to swing as it leaves the blocks."

He was right. As the generator moved up, it also slid towards Ishmael, who moved back out of its way, at the same time lifting it some more. Elijah and the others provided the resistance by pushing against the machine until it swung clear once again. Three more times they repeated the maneuver to bring it directly over the foundation. The men were huffing and puffing loudly. "This is hard work," said Majid.

"Majid and Saleem, remove the blocks." They hurried to move them. "Ishmael, slowly lower it. Majid, you and Saleem hold the machine and guide it so that the holes in the machine are in line with the foundation bolts. I'll guide this end." The generator swung slowly and they pushed, pulled and lined up the holes in the machine over the bolts, ever so slowly. When all four bolts registered in the holes, Elijah gave a sigh of relief and said, "Slowly Ishmael, lower, lower."

The generator sailed down smoothly and sat down with a thud on the foundation, all four bolts centered in their holes. "Good," said Elijah, "take off the hoist and the chains. Saleem, bring those nuts and washers and a wrench and tighten them onto the bolts."

Another hour and the second generator sat on its foundation and had been bolted down. Elijah gave them all a high five and called it a day. "Everyone gets extra tea today," he said.

"Yes," said Saleem, raising a clenched fist to the sky.

Elijah had been holding back the excitement building within. He wanted an opportunity to call Sonia's home number. All day as he worked with the men, his mind kept drifting back to the call he wished to make. It felt like a needle prodding at the back of his brain. With an effort he had kept focused on what he was doing.

"You seem to be excited, Saab," said Ishmael. Was it so obvious? he wondered.

"Well, it's the end of the project, Ishmael. Maybe they'll let me go home now," said Elijah.

When they had dispersed to their various tents, he walked around inspecting this and that as he usually did.

Finding a place where he could place the call without being seen or heard was a problem. He went into the enclosure they had just worked in. The end wall where the doors would go in stood wide open. The other end had been closed with plywood. It wasn't safe. Children and women still moved around.

He walked back to the pumping station passing a guard on his way. The man turned and stared at Elijah's receding back. They were all just waiting for an excuse to shoot him.

At the platform with the barrels, he casually held the posts and shook them to test their rigidity, then climbed down to the creek. It was quiet and he saw no one nearby. Off in the distance a bird called in plaintive tones. His position hid him from anyone at the camp. Furtively he pulled out the phone, when he felt someone's eyes on him. He looked up and there several yards away staring at him was a young boy of seven or eight. His round eyes got bigger as Elijah looked at him. Elijah was caught off guard. Was the boy spying on him? He waved to the boy, who waved back and then took off. In seconds he was gone. Was he going to call his parents or whoever had sent him? Elijah had no time to waste. He unwrapped the phone and punched in Sonia's number. He could hear it ring. Her recording machine asked him to leave a message. He whispered, "Sonia, this is Elijah..."

Chapter Twelve

Elijah turned it off and rewrapped the phone up again and placed it back in his pocket. It had taken three minutes. Half expecting the boy to be back with the guards his hands trembled as he climbed up to the pumping station and walked to his tent. The villagers had all gathered for the evening meal. He washed up and joined them.

Today they had cooked chicken and rice – chicken was a luxury here. It must be a special occasion, he thought. Maybe the inauguration of the water tap called for a celebration. The adrenaline was still flowing and his hands had a tremor as he took his plate. In an hour or so hopefully Sonia would be calling. A glance at his watch showed it was seven p.m.

He wished he had a bottle of wine to pass around among the guards. But they were Muslims and did not drink.

The mullah sitting next to him smiled. "You and your men worked real hard today," he said. "Almost like there's no tomorrow."

"We got caught up in the excitement," said Elijah, smiling. "Everything just fell into place." He nodded indicating his plate. "The food tastes very good."

"Yes, the women are trying to show their appreciation."

Elijah glanced around and found Ishmael's eyes on him. He smiled at Ishmael and got up. "Excuse me," he said to the mullah with a bow, and he walked over to Ishmael.

"You've learned a lot in these few days, Ishmael," he said. "You have a natural aptitude for doing things with your hands, and you also have a quick mind."

Ishmael smiled. "Thank you saab. You are a good teacher. No one has shown me how to do these things before." He laid his plate down and put his hands together, "*Shukriya, saab*(Thank you, sir)."

Elijah nodded. I would hire him on the spot, if he were back home, he thought. He also noted that during his trip, most everyone said, "saab," instead of the original "sahib." Many words had changed into something easier to say.

They finally retired for the night. It was close to eight p.m. Elijah went to his tent. He was about to curl up, when the phone in his pocket started vibrating. Jumping up he pressed his hand against the phone and counted the number of rings. After six it quit. He quickly took it out, unwrapped it and held it ready to flip it open should it ring again. The minutes ticked by. He looked through the opening. All the guards had entered their tents. In exactly ten minutes, he felt the phone buzz in his hands. He flipped it open and whispered, "Sonia? Is it you?"

*   *   *

Sonia had driven for three hours after she left the truck stop. The dry heat got to her. The disguise made it even worse. She itched all over and she sweated under the heavy clothing. Her watch showed five p.m.. She pulled off the road again and examined the GPS module. It was definitely closer now to where Elijah's tracer flashed. She flipped open her cell phone and called her home number and actuated her voice mail.

It came on. "Sonia, this is Elijah. My number is 0118384911. I am in a village in Afghanistan. There are guards. If you can, call around eight p.m. when everyone is in bed. Let it ring six times then hang up and call again in ten minutes." The machine signed off.

She bubbled over in excitement. She raised her hand above her head and almost shouted, "Yes! I have found him." It was good to hear his voice. She could imagine the excitement of holding him. She smiled to herself as she wrote down the number. She glanced at her watch. Three hours to wait.

Sonia decided to drive further and found a good hiding place for the SUV. At eight p.m. with her pulse running high, she dialed the number. It rang, once, twice, three, four, five, and six. She counted, tense with anxiety, and wondered. What if the guards can hear the phone ringing? Won't they stop Elijah from using it? She shut off the phone. She waited for ten grueling minutes and then rang again. This time on the first ring, she heard Elijah's welcome voice. "Sonia? Is it you?" he whispered.

"Yes, it's me."

"Where are you?"

"I'm quite near where you are. Maybe three or four miles away. I have a SUV and a rifle."

"Stay where you are," whispered Elijah. "No, no, drive about two more miles down towards me and then hide the SUV. Walk down the road, and I'll try and meet you on that road."

"I'm disguised as a man, so don't be alarmed. I'll see you soon, I hope. Elijah, are you all right?"

"I'm fine. I'm looking forward to seeing you," whispered Elijah. He disconnected.

Sonia smiled, absolutely delighted. She clasped her hands together above her head and said, "Yes!" Her quest had come to a successful end. No, not yet, she reminded herself. We're still in the lion's den.

There was still daylight. She put her phone away, made a quick reconnaissance up and down the road, backed out of her hideout, looked at the mileage and moved down the road. When she had gone two kilometers she made a survey for another sheltered area.

She drove slowly and parked within a grove of large bushes. She got out and walked quickly behind the Range Rover, viewing it from the road showed some parts of the vehicle exposed. She took her machete and hacked a few low-lying branches from a tree some distance away and dragged them in place and viewed it again. Satisfied, she took out some dried fruit and chewed on it looking at her watch occasionally. The sun had set on a glorious day and the shadows of night slowly crept in. With the darkness came the sound of crickets and frogs. Birds chirped their last notes before finding perches and nests for the night. Sonia's vigil was only beginning. A wind moved the leaves above, sometimes exposing a patch of cloudless sky and a myriad of stars. She wished she had a better knowledge of the constellations. Where were Orion's Belt and Venus and Mars? Wasn't Polaris the North Star? She pulled out her compass from the knapsack and shone her head lamp she had on an elastic band onto the instrument and followed the indicated north and looked up.

That bright star over there had to be Polaris. She lined up north on the compass with the star. She shut the compass and the light and placed them back in their respective places.

She leaned back in her seat and folded her hands behind her head and closed her eyes. What am I doing here in this wilderness? she asked herself, then dozed off, tired and emotionally spent.

She woke with a start and looked at the illuminated dial of her watch. It was ten p.m. She jumped out of the SUV. What if Elijah has walked past my location while I took a nap? she wondered. In the pitch darkness she could hardly see her way. Her sandaled feet told her she had reached the graveled surface of the road. She turned east and started walking putting the night-vision binoculars to her eyes and searched. It was amazing how clearly everything stood out. No sign of Elijah yet. The pocket on the left side of her pantaloon bumped against her leg with the weight of the head lamp. She looked back with the binoculars at where the SUV was hidden to see if she would recognize the spot on her return. The heat of the engine showed its outline as she scanned the area. How long will it stay hot? she wondered. I better make an indicator that will be easy to spot. My red scarf tied to a branch will do it.

*   *   *

Elijah waited half an hour. No moon shone tonight. In the darkness he slowly crawled out on his stomach. His face was so close to the ground, he could smell the leaves and pine needles lying there. Every few feet he paused and looked around. The guards had not stirred from their tents. The night felt cold. He had on his anorak. Continuing to crawl slowly and softly, he felt rocks and stones against his legs and under his hands. The surface changed telling him he had reached the road. With great stealth he stood up and started walking, ever moving away from the camp and the village. A dog barked somewhere. When he had progressed far enough where his footsteps could not possibly be heard at the camp, he increased his pace. After walking for about an hour, a feeling of anxiety crept over him. Shouldn't she be near?

*   *   *

Sonia continued walking. After half an hour she estimated she had walked about two kilometers. She still measured distances in the Metric system. She stopped and looked again through her binoculars. Yes, she could see someone walking fast towards her. She just as suddenly lost sight of him. Perhaps there's a bend in the road, she thought. She continued walking faster and every so often brought up the lens to scan the darkness. Yes, there he was again. Then her heart froze with horror as she looked; further behind was another figure walking just as fast.

She stayed to the side of the road and touched the trunk of a sapling. They were getting ever closer. When she felt the first figure was within hailing distance, she whistled a warbling note. The figure stopped and listened. She whistled again and he started running now. When he was about fifty feet away, she called, "Elijah."

He had seen her. With out-stretched arms he rushed forward and lifted her off her feet in a powerful embrace. She winced as those strong arms went around her in a grasp that almost took her breath away.

"Oh, Elijah," she said. He held her close and kissed her on her forehead, her cheeks and finally found her lips.

They stayed in a long embrace. He was shocked to feel the beard on her face. He remembered her disguise. He also felt she had something in her hand. She held the night vision binoculars. She whispered, "Someone's following you."

Elijah's world came crashing down. His heartbeat soared as his anxiety grew. He had just begun to feel the thrill of escape. Now what. She passed the binoculars to him. She was right. They revealed someone walking towards them about a hundred yards back. They both moved to the side of the road and waited. When the person strode right next to them, Elijah pounced and had his arm around the man's neck in a vice-like arm lock. The man gasped for breath. Sonia shined the head lamp onto his face. Elijah gazed in utter disbelief. It was Ishmael. He loosened his grip. Ishmael made no attempt to fight back.

He merely rubbed his neck and smiled. "I was going to help you saab," he said.

"It's one of my helpers from back at the camp," said Elijah.

Sonia didn't say anything. She moved the focus of the beam of light away from the man's face.

"Are you coming with us?" asked Elijah.

"Yes, saab."

"We could use your help, Ishmael, if we should be pursued. You know this country."

Sonia led the way. "We should hurry. The SUV is a ways back."

The three of them started running, the sound of their shoes crunching on the gravel road.

In about fifteen minutes, Sonia's beam of light found the red scarf. "There it is," she said, pointing to where the Range Rover had been hidden.

They parted the bushes and climbed in. Elijah taking the driver's seat, started the SUV, turned on the lights and swung the vehicle around so that they were going away from the village. Elijah looked at the gas gauge. The needle hovered at about half. "I have two twenty-liter cans with gas in them," said Sonia.

Elijah nodded in the dark. He looked at the mileage meter. "How many miles is it from the border?" he asked.

"I drove about four hours from the Afghan border, so about two hundred and sixty kilometers."

Elijah figured it out at about a hundred and sixty miles. They had enough fuel to get them across the border into Pakistan and safety. He still counted in miles while Sonia measured distance in metric terms. He drove as fast as he could through the night. He looked at the meter, slowly creeping mile after mile. But it wasn't fast enough for him. He couldn't travel faster than 40 miles per hour. The roads wouldn't allow it.

Night slowly turned to dawn. The sky turned a light pink towards the east. The mountains stood out dark purple in the distance. Soon it would be light and he could imagine the scene at the village he had just escaped from. The guards would be scrambling around looking for him. When they found Ishmael missing, it would add to their consternation. Abdul Rehman had not returned from his trip. They had no leader. They might just decide to get in the trucks and follow the road he had taken. They wouldn't expect him to go further inland. How long would it be before they caught up with him? he wondered. They had perhaps four or five hours head start. Elijah weighed again the danger that still surrounded them. If the Range Rover broke down, they would be at the mercy of their pursuers. He looked back at Ishmael, now visible in the growing light of dawn.

"What do you think, Ishmael? Should we continue on this road or should we try another route?"

"I think we should change our course. I know a village to the north of us. The guards who are after us may expect us to go straight back east. It will buy us some time. I will show you the way."

"They also don't know what type of vehicle we are driving," said Elijah. "You let me know where I should turn off."

"Make a left at the next intersection you see. After a few miles the road gets a bit dangerous. There is a steep drop on one side, with a river below."

Elijah drove on for another thirty miles, before he saw a fork in the road. He asked, "Is this it?"

Ishmael peered ahead through the fog. "Yes, I hope the dust settles down soon. By the time they arrive here we'll be out of sight."

Elijah slowed and drove left on a gravel road, with many bends and turns through hills that soon hid them from the main road. The gradual evanesce of the morning fog made it possible for them to see where they were going. The sun had come up over the mountains and bathed the valley in gold. That's the way it is in mountainous country at dawn, thought Elijah. One moment they had barely enough light to see by and the next the whole valley lit up. The road had been cut into the side of a mountain. The farther they went the steeper the drop on the left side got, until the valley lay nearly three hundred feet below. If another vehicle happened to come from the opposite direction, there would be very little room to spare.

The gravel on the road had turned to larger rocks that made the Range Rover bounce from side to side. Elijah wondered how Sonia was doing and glanced over. For the first time he noticed her beard and mustache and was shocked at the transformation. When he had hugged her in the darkness he had felt her feminine softness against him and also felt parts of her disguise, but actually seeing her brought a smile to his lips.

"Do you have a name to go with that disguise?" he asked.

"Abdul Aziz," said Sonia, turning to smile at him.

"Look out," shouted Ishmael to the distracted Elijah. "There's a truck coming towards us."

Elijah braked and swerved dangerously close to the cliff's edge. He straightened out and gauged how the two vehicles could squeeze by. Then he wondered who are the occupants of the other vehicle? Could it be Rehman's friends?

Chapter Thirteen

At the village where Elijah had spent the last two weeks, everything started out as normal, until one of the guards noticed that Elijah was not up at his usual hour. He made a dash to Elijah's tent and thrust the flaps open and found it empty. He screamed in Pushtu that the prisoner was missing. All six guards rushed to the scene with their rifles on the ready.

After a brief conference, they decided to take the spare Jeep. Abdul Rehman had the other Jeep and had not returned after leaving the previous morning.

"You two stay here and inform Mister Rehman what has happened," said the senior guard. "He is going to kill us if we don't bring the American back."

As the remaining four men climbed into the Jeep, a boy came running up. "Ishmael is also missing," he said, panting.

"Maybe he took Ishmael as a hostage,," said the driver of the Jeep. "But how would he do that without weapons or a vehicle?" They roared off, leaving behind a group of curious women and restive children, in a cloud of dust.

"I hope they don't catch him," said one woman.

"He has done a lot for our village," said another, "Isn't it enough? He has earned his freedom."

"Quiet, here comes the mullah."

The mullah walked into the compound where the group was gathered. One of the guards walked up to him. "The American and Ishmael are missing," he said to the mullah.

"And you have sent the guards with their rifles after them?" asked the mullah incredulously.

"We had orders from Abdul Rehman to keep him here."

"I do not wish any harm to befall the good man. I will talk to Rehman to let him go. His job here is done." He ran his fingers through his beard absentmindedly.

*   *   *

Rehman drove into the village two hours later and immediately sensed something was wrong. The Jeep was missing and only two guards could be seen on duty. He drove up to them. They saluted him and waited.

"Where are the rest of the guards?" asked Rehman.

"The prisoner escaped, sir," said one of the men, "the other guards took the Jeep in pursuit when we found out. He was missing this morning. He is on foot so he couldn't have gone far. Ishmael is also missing."

"Ishmael?" Rehman looked around. Several of the villagers stood nearby. The mullah had seen him arrive and was walking towards him.

"How long ago did they leave in the Jeep?" he asked the men.

"About two hours ago, sir."

"If the American was on foot they should have caught up with him by now. I think he's smarter than that. He had a ride waiting." He took out the phone from his Jeep and dialed.

The guard Iqbal answered from his Jeep, "Hello?"

"This is Rehman, have you found him?"

"No sir, we are almost near the Pakistan border and have not seen them. It's quite possible they got a ride and have taken another road."

"I suggest that you continue on to the border and make inquiries of the patrol there if they have seen an American in any type of vehicle. Call me when you reach the border or if you find them."

"Yes sir," said Iqbal.

Rehman clicked off and turned to greet the mullah. Rehman's mood was not propitious.

"*Salaam Alekhoum*," he said.

"*Salaam Alekhoum*," said the mullah. "I hope you're not thinking of killing the American if you find him, are you?"

"Right now I think I would," said Rehman, vehemently.

"He has done what you asked him to do. The pumps are working, the fields are being irrigated and we have a tap in the compound. The women don't have to walk down to the creek and carry their heavy pots of water anymore."

"Yes, I know." Rehman shook his head, "but I had more work for him. I wanted him to start on another village that is equally bad off as yours used to be. Fundamentalist Muslims officials will question me. They were expecting a statement to the press about another American execution in retaliation for the troops sent here."

"A man's freedom is important. You could only keep him for a short time or he will die trying to escape."

"Actually he was safer here than he thought. Now, out there he is an open target, unless."

"Unless, what?"

"Unless he disguises himself again."

"With all due respect to you, Rehman, I had grown to like him. I pray Allah may preserve him."

"So do I, but I don't like being out-smarted by anyone, least of all by an American. I will get him back. He can go home when I say so. I spared his life didn't I?"

The mullah looked down with troubled eyes. He had tried but it was to no avail. He changed the subject to relieve the tension.

"The men Saleem and Majid know how to operate the pumps and the generators. We can plant vegetables this year. It may be late for wheat or barley or rice. We will try however. We will need seeds for these crops. We will also need a few barrels of diesel fuel."

"I will arrange for the truck to pick up those items before I leave."

"We are very grateful to you, Rehman. We hope to be self-sufficient in a year. *Salaam Aleykhoum*." He gave Rehman the traditional hug.

Rehman turned to the two guards. "One of you take the truck to the place we buy supplies from. Here is a list of items I want you to get. When you're back we'll set out to track the American. There's a chance he's gone north. That's a choice we have to make. We can't go both north and south. If the other Jeep doesn't find any evidence of him at the Pakistan border, then they'll join us on the routes going north and north-east."

The man took the list, saluted and departed. Rehman walked back to the center of the compound and noted that the powerhouse had been completed. All it needed was a coat of paint. Women were filling their pots at the tap. They had gathered there in a group. He was sure the topic they were discussing was the flight of the American and Ishmael. The children remained subdued in a group instead of their usual loud games.

He continued to where the pumps were located and then on further towards the fields. The water flowed through the channels cut into the earth directing the water into long rows for a large area of many acres.

As he neared the pumps on his return, one of the pumps gurgled and shut down.

"What happened?" he asked Majid, who was standing nearby.

"Nothing sir," said Majid, "the pumps to the fields are set on a timer and it shuts off when the timer completes its cycle. We will increase the time the pumps stay on when the seeds of the vegetables sprout and need more water. That saves power and diesel fuel."

"You seem to know your job. Very good Majid."

"Oh, yes, sir, Mister Elijah taught us all we had to know to operate this system."

Elijah seems to be well liked, thought Rehman, he might yet become a folk legend.

"You think you can build a few more houses like the one you constructed for the generators, if I got you the materials?"

Majid hesitated. "Yes, sir. I think so. We may not do as fast. I have been writing down notes on everything he taught us."

I must get him back, thought Rehman, as he walked away. I have one more village that could use his help. He found himself in the presence of the mullah. The mullah seemed to sense Rehman's thoughts.

"Even if you find him and bring him back, he will no longer be motivated. This is creative work. He has to direct people to follow his orders. He may just prefer to be killed than to be taken prisoner again."

"So be it," said Rehman. "We are Fundamentalist Muslims. The money I spend on this village is Fundamentalist Muslims money."

Late that day Rehman got a call. His men had reached the Khyber Pass.

"No one has seen any vehicle with an American or anyone of Ishmael's description in the last twenty-four hours," said his lead man.

"You and your men move north towards Asadabad. There is an Fundamentalist Muslims camp there. We will meet there. It may take us a few days. I will stay in touch."

"Yes, sir. We will move on and meet as directed."

When his man came back the next morning with the supplies, they decided to keep the truck at the village. It was too cumbersome. They took Rehman's Jeep and drove east and took the first road to the north. They didn't know it but they were following in Elijah's tracks. Fate was leading them to a showdown none of them had foreseen.

Chapter Fourteen

Elijah knew if the occupants of the truck coming towards them were enemies then he was in trouble. Sonia had said there was a rifle somewhere on this Range Rover. But his immediate concern was to keep his vehicle under control.

Dust made it difficult to see and he slowed down even more. He hoped the tires would hold. This would be the wrong place to get a flat.

Down below flowed a river and the road ran parallel to it. The truck trundled towards them. Elijah slowed to a stop, hugging the wall as close as he could. The truck moved slowly forward, inch-by-inch, its engine groaning loudly under the load it carried. If he got too close to the edge, the road might crumble and both vehicles could go down. It was a long way to the bottom.

The driver of the truck stopped and shouted to the four passengers in the back. They climbed out carefully and stood on the road. The lorry started moving again. Slowly it made it past the narrowest part of the road and moved towards the center passing the Range Rover.

One of the passengers heaved a sigh of relief and they climbed back in to join the rest of their cargo of goat hides and what looked like spare parts for cars. Elijah was relieved to see the men weren't Rehman's crew.

He inched forward, away from the wall into the center of the road. He said, "I hope they are not stopped and questioned by our guards." Then looking at Ishmael, "Tell me, Ishmael, were you part of the Fundamentalist Muslims gang that kidnapped me?"

"No," said Ishmael, shaking his head, "I was living near the village, where you just left. I was told by the Mullah to help you. So were Majid and Saleem."

The road still felt unpredictable, with rocks and holes that kept the Range Rover bouncing around. It gradually descended and after another two hours of sweaty and dust covered maneuvering, they drove onto level ground, just above the river. They could hear the river gurgling over rocks as it flowed swiftly.

"The village I know is about ten miles further along this river," said Ishmael.

Elijah smiled at Sonia. "How are you doing Abdul Aziz?"

She turned towards him. "All right. That road almost made me seasick. But I'm beginning to feel better. Could we rest a while?"

"Yes, we'll stop and take a break. God, how I wish I could hold you in my arms."

"Not while I'm dressed like this," said Sonia. "If you trust Ishmael, there may not be the necessity to continue my disguise."

"Yes," said Elijah, "I think we can dispense with the disguise for you. But I would feel safer getting back into my disguise. Most of my outfit was left at the lodge in Simla."

"You can use my turban and my mustache."

"I'll also need a robe or *pattu* and a pair of sandals. With my make-up we can say we are husband and wife. But the villagers may wonder what a couple are doing out here. How do we explain that?"

"Perhaps we can say we are with the UN. We are certainly not on our honeymoon," said Sonia smiling.

"I promise you, Sonia, I will get you out of this mess."

Elijah pulled the Range Rover off the road and stopped. The road grew wider here and he parked under the shade of an oak tree with wide branches. Elijah turned to Ishmael and said, "Ishmael, this is my wife Sonia."

Ishmael looked with wonder at Abdul Aziz. Sonia slowly peeled of her mustache, and Ishmael's eyes went wide in disbelief. He jumped out of the Range Rover, shaking his head looking back every few steps. Sonia took off her beard and smiled at Elijah. Ishmael laughed and laughed. He walked back and put his hands together in a salaam and said, "*Salaam Aleikoum, Memsahib.*"

Sonia smiled with her hands together said, "*Salaam Aleikoum, Ishmael.*"

"You have great courage and devotion," he said, adding, "*Ithna bahadur, myne kabhi nahi deka.*(I have never seen such bravery)."

"*Shukriya*, Ishmael," said, Sonia, smiling at him.

Elijah found Sonia's flask of water and poured her a cup. She thanked him. The dry heat had dehydrated all of them.

Elijah took the mustache from Sonia's kit and applied it carefully on his upper lip. He wrapped the turban around his head with an expertise he had learned only a few weeks ago. It did make a dramatic change in his appearance.

"How do I look, Ishmael?"

"*Bahuth acha*. You look like a Pakistani. I will try to get a *pattu* at the village. I'll say it's a spare for myself. The boots can give you away still."

"Try to get a turban also. We can pay for the items. I would like to give this back to Sonia just in case she needs it again."

"I still have the bottle of glue in my kit," said Sonia, "I can make another mustache while we're at the village."

"That's great," said Elijah, "we're beginning to think like terrorists." He paused and turned to Ishmael. "If we tell the people at the village that I was kidnapped, the news may get back to our captors. Let's say we are from the UN, on our way back to Pakistan."

"I think that will satisfy the villagers," said Ishmael, "we can make gifts of some of this food in the Range Rover."

Elijah walked over to Sonia. Without the beard and mustache, he saw the beautiful woman he had grown so fond of, and who had now risked her life to rescue him. She smiled at him. He reached for her hand. Although he longed to hold her in his arms, he restrained himself, because he knew Ishmael was not accustomed to such public display of affection. He could smell her perfume.

"Ishmael," said Elijah, "why don't you check out this rifle that Sonia has and make sure it's not plugged up with dust." Then pointing to the river, "This is a beautiful place. We'll just take a walk, if you don't mind."

"No, no," said Ishmael. "I'll wait here, and check out the rifle. Just don't fall in the river. It's very cold."

Elijah laughed, and took Sonia's hand and they walked down the bank. They had to climb down over the rocks that bordered the road to the sandy edge of the river. Elijah went ahead and helped Sonia over the rocks. They found a path along the gurgling river. It flowed slower here over level ground. Its crystal clear waters glinted in the sunlight as it rushed along on its merry way. The waters looked deep in certain parts. On both banks grew shade trees. Some looked like larch and some like birch and the drooping fronds of some had to be willow. They continued walking, physically aware of each other. The trees now hid them from the road. Elijah put both his hands around Sonia's waist and faced her. She smiled up at him and put her arms around his neck. He put his lips to hers and they kissed a long kiss. Sonia put her head on his chest and sighed, "Oh, I was so worried."

Elijah cradled her head with his hand and held her to him. "I missed you too. I lay every night in my tent thinking of you." He moved his hand forward and touched her face. There were tears flowing down her cheeks and he gently wiped them away. He kissed her forehead then her eyes and then back to her lips. Sonia whispered, "We should be getting back."

"Yes, you're right."

They walked back together, hand in hand. "Isn't this beautiful?" said Sonia. "There are birds of all colors, red, purple and yellow, flying around the water and in those trees. I should write about this place when we get back."

Ishmael had been sitting on a rock. He got up when he saw them. "I cleaned the rifle. It did have a lot of dust; it's in good condition though."

He put the gun away and pointed to the groceries Sonia had brought along. "There's quite a bit of food here. If we had a gas cooker I could serve you some roti and a hot soup."

"Let's wait till we get to the village," said Elijah. "We're going to rest for a while. You should do so too."

While Elijah and Sonia rested with their backs against a tree, Sonia's mind flitted back to the past. It had been in similar settings. She was fourteen and her school had taken a group of them on an excursion. The trip was to the Corbett National Park in Uthar Pradesh, named after the famous hunter and conservationist Jim Corbett. Their group consisted of ten girls and nine boys, all the same age, and two lady teachers. They were dressed for the wilds in shorts and shirts and the excitement ran high. They sang and screamed enjoying the freedom not experienced at school. This was the great Indian adventure into the forests where tigers and elephants and other animals had their domain. The nearest villages were miles away. Only tourists like this bus occasionally disturbed the quiet of the jungle. The chatter of the monkeys forewarned the silent approach of a tiger. They were all familiar with Corbett's tales of man-eating tigers, and had shivered in fright as they read these stories in bed. Now they were actually in those same forests.

The tourists were led to the safety of concrete "*machans*" built and camouflaged around watering holes that tigers and other animals frequented. Sonia and her group were lucky to see a tigress and her two cubs in a concealed location. A pair of binoculars brought them up so close that she was fascinated by the colors and the beauty of the animals.

The park was and still is, made up of thousands of acres of dense forests. They moved on along protected trails until they came to an opening in the jungle disclosing a large river flowing through. A landing with a wooden wharf had a boat tied to one of the posts. The opposite shore looked like an interesting place worth exploring. The waters were slow and boulders showed through at various locations. They decided to row to the other side. The boat would only hold five people including the oarsman. One of the boys rowed them across and Sonia volunteered to row the boat back for the others. When she was mid-stream the boat hit a submerged rock and a large chunk of the weathered hull broke off letting water in until the boat sank. Sonia swam to the nearest shore, which was the one she had just left. As she swam with swift sure strokes she heard one of the girls scream. She looked up out of the water and saw a hysterical friend of hers jumping up and down and pointing down river and continued screaming. Sonia looked in the direction she was pointing and saw the snout of a crocodile gliding upriver towards her while the river pulled her like a magnet closer to the two ugly eyes.

Sonia had a moment of panic. About twenty meters separated her from the reptile and the gap was closing. With her heart pounding she swam like a machine, her arms cutting the water like a waterwheel on a steamboat. Her water soaked shorts and shoes were weighing her down. The water smelled of decaying leaves.

The boys gathered up river rocks as large as their fists and pelted the reptile. The stones just bounced off its amour. Suddenly the crock submerged. Sonia had to see where it was and immediately dived and swam underwater. She could see the monster making straight for her effortlessly. Those big ugly eyes and those big ugly teeth in their big ugly jaws loomed closer. Her hands and feet touched gravel. Pushing herself forward with both arms and legs against a firm surface, she lunged into the waiting arms of the boys brave enough to venture to the water's edge. Together, the boys backing off and Sonia scrambling, her shoes slipping on the rocks made it to dry land and continued running. The crock leaped out of the water the jaws snapping shut on empty air. It lay on the water's edge moving its head from side to side trying to sense if it's prey was near. It then slithered back into the river and disappeared.

Sonia walked around huffing and puffing with her hands on her hips trying desperately to catch her breath. The girls stopped screaming and the teacher collapsed in a near faint.

That was a long time ago. She stirred from her reverie and wondered if she should tell Elijah about the episode.

*   *   *

While Sonia and Elijah rested, Ishmael also took a break and sat on a rock overlooking the river. His mind floated back as far as he could remember. His father had joined the Afghan Army against the Russians. In one of the Russians many bombing raids, his father had been killed. His mother was a teacher in the local school where she taught in Pushtu. Ishmael had been one of her students. He had a younger brother and a sister. They survived on the meager earnings of his mother. Ishmael had one more year of schooling left. But when the offer came of a job helping an American engineer at another village, he took it. He got paid a daily wage, and at the end of each week when Abdul Rehman handed out money to each of the workers helping Elijah, Ishmael walked all the way home and gave the money to his mother, and then came back the same evening.

After working with Elijah, Ishmael felt he wanted to be an engineer. He had developed a great desire to go back to school or college. After all he was only nineteen. Nearly six feet tall with a muscular build blue eyed and light skinned. A white turban covered his brown hair parted in the center and combed backwards. He had broken with tradition when he started shaving revealing his clean-cut features. He still maintained a trimmed mustache. He also carried a scabbard with a curved knife at his waist. A gift from his uncle on his eighteenth birthday.

Now that he had joined Elijah in their escape, he would not see his mother or his siblings for a while. The thought bothered him, but his mother still worked and with him away, it meant one less mouth to feed. He knew this was temporary, and would go back to his family later. Just now Elijah *saab* needed his help.

They had rested for almost an hour. Elijah started up the Range Rover and they were on their way. At the village Elijah parked the vehicle and Ishmael went looking for the headman. Several brick buildings surrounded a compound and women cooked at outdoor fires. Elijah recognized the aroma of kebabs and fried onions. Ishmael came back with an older man. The man smiled at Elijah and Sonia. "They are foreigners," he said to Ishmael.

"Yes," said Ishmael, "he is Pakistani and she is his wife from India. They work for the UN and are on their way back to Pakistan." He pointed to the man and said, "This is Mullah Abad Rashid."

Elijah extended his hand, saying, "*Salaam Aleikoum.*"

But the Mullah put his arms around Elijah and gave him a mighty hug, saying, "*Salaam Aleikoum.*" This was Afghan hospitality. He next looked at Sonia and put his hands together in a salaam and said, "*Salaam Aleikoum.*"

"*Salaam Aleikoum,*" said Sonia, putting her hands together in a similar salaam.

"We have some gifts for you," said Ishmael. They walked to the Range Rover and Ishmael lifted out a sack of rice, looking at Sonia who nodded and smiled.

"Wait," said the mullah, looking around, "let me get some help." He called out loudly and two young boys aged twelve or thirteen came running. They helped carry the sack of rice to one of the brick buildings. Next Ishmael gave them a sack of potatoes, a sack of wheat flour, a sack of sugar, and a sack of salt. They kept the rest in case they had a need for them at some later time.

If he noticed the presence of the rifle, the mullah did not refer to it.

"Why don't you join us for a meal," he said, "come, follow me."

Ishmael covered the rest of the food and the rifle with the tarpaulin. Sonia had come well prepared.

Abad Rashid was in his late fifties, with brown eyes and dark brown beard and mustache. He wore a stripped turban and a black jacket over his loose shirt. He walked with a sprightly gait and had a winning smile. He was nearly six feet tall. He took them to his own home, where his wife moved around preparing the mid-day meal. She did not wear a *burkha*. He introduced his guests to her. She smiled and gave Sonia a hug, and touched her cheek to Sonia's on both sides. She made more kebabs and *roti* and fried potatoes. Elijah breathed in the aroma and said, "Smells delicious."

She smiled when her guests attacked their food with such gusto. They were hungry.

Rashid asked Elijah, "What do you do at the UN?"

Elijah replied honestly, "I am an engineer and I try to fix electrical and other equipment. I noticed you have a good river nearby. Do you need any help?"

"Yes, there is always something that needs fixing. But you look tired. You rest today and we shall talk again tomorrow. We do have a house you and your wife can use. A family is away at another village and will return in a few days. Ishmael can stay with us. We have enough room."

Elijah wondered if this village was off the beaten track and would be safe from Rehman and his crew.

Chapter Fifteen

Rehman and his two men moved along in their Jeep in silence. They travelled east. He grabbed the phone and dialed. Iqbal in the second Jeep answered.

"There's a change in plans," said Rehman, "turn back and find the first cross road going north. I will give you detailed directions when we meet at a truck stop."

"Yes sir, we are on our way."

Rehman told his driver to take the next road left. He conjectured that Elijah and his party were perhaps a day ahead of them. That was not a big lead. We can still catch up.

After several dusty kilometers they came to a truck stop. Rehman indicated with his hand to take the exit. They stopped near a *Chai khanna* that was part of the truck stop. They parked and got out.

The sound of trucks pulling in to fill their tanks kept the place humming with business.

"Make casual inquiries if they have seen three or four people in a SUV or van," said Rehman. "Tell them that one could be a foreigner."

Their rifles were well hidden in the Jeep. They spread out.

One man answered Rehman's questions, "Maybe yes, maybe no. What's in it for me?"

Rehman pulled out a sheaf of Afghani money and took out several and put it in the man's hand.

"Yes, I did see two men and a woman in an SUV. One of the men was perhaps Pakistani."

"Was there anything unusual about the SUV? asked Rehman. "Is it easily recognizable?"

"Yes," said the man. "It was a brand new black Range Rover."

"Thank you," said Rehman, a smile creeping onto his face. He peeled off two more five Afghani notes and handed it to the man. "Which way did they go?"

"They took that road, east," he said, pointing.

"How long ago did you see them?"

"About two days ago."

"Salaam Aleikoum."

"*Aleikoum salaam.*"

He moved away and nodded to his men, who climbed back in the Jeep.

"They took this road," said Rehman. His driver nodded. "They are two days ahead of us."

"At least we're on their track," said Suleman the driver. "Let's ask again at the next truck stop or village."

They drove in silence. So there's a woman involved, thought Rehman. I wonder who she is? Since the other man is Ishmael, it must certainly be she who brought the SUV they are driving. We could use a few women like that ourselves. She must be a regular Jhansi ki Rani.

*   *   *

While Elijah and Sonia relaxed at the village of Abad Rashid, storm clouds were gathering on the horizon for them in the form of Rehman. They didn't know it, but the relentless Fundamentalist Muslims had picked up their scent. Every time they relaxed the gap was closing.

*   *   *

The waning light told Rehman and his men they would soon have to pull off the road and camp for the night when Rehman noticed a car or a SUV in the distance. "Try catching up with that vehicle up ahead, before it gets dark," he said, leaning forward. The Jeep shot forward with a roar. The needle crept slowly from eighty kilometers per hour through ninety-six and steadied at a hundred and twelve kph. They were getting closer. Suleman squeezed the accelerator even further and the light Jeep hurtled at a hundred and thirty kph.

Rehman and the rest hung on to their turbans and *patoos* flying in the breeze. The high pitched whine of the engine sounded like a banshee in pain. One of the men in the back seat looked around nervously. Surely, he's not going to kill us all, he thought. If he hits a pothole we'll all go flying onto the bruising road. Iqbal is a better driver than this maniac.

The Jeep was now only a hundred meters behind. The vehicle ahead of them was indeed another SUV. This could be it, thought Rehman. Soon they could make out a man and a woman in the back seat. Suleman slowed down to hundred kph. The driver of the other SUV kept nervously looking in his rear-view mirror. As they drew closer, Rehman discerned them to be English or American with an Afghani driver. The SUV was definitely not a Range Rover. It was a Ford Explorer. But he couldn't give up hope.

"Could the man be Elijah," wondered Rehman aloud. "Try passing them carefully."

At the speed they were racing along, in minutes they drew up parallel with the other vehicle. The man and woman turned to look at them.

The man wasn't Elijah. The driver was having a hard time staying on the road and looking over at this vehicle that had suddenly appeared out of nowhere.

Rehman and his Jeep passed them with a roar. When they were a hundred meters ahead, Suleman slowed down to his normal eighty kph.

"Find a place to camp," said Rehman in a disappointed voice. He next called Iqbal and gave him directions. "We are camped about two hundred kilometers east from the truck stop with the large sign of a restaurant called, "On the Rocks."

It was late at night when Iqbal and his men found the campsite.

*   *   *

After their sumptuous meal, Elijah and Sonia walked out into the sunshine. "It's good to be free," he said extending his arms skyward, his face breaking into a smile.

"We have a ways to go," said Sonia with raised eyebrows.

"See you in a little while," he said. His smile disappeared as he turned to join Ishmael and the mullah, who was taking them to see his irrigation system.

It was close to one p.m. Sonia walked to the river.

"She likes this place," said Elijah to Rashid. The farmers and young men walked back to their chores, some to the fields after the lunch break.

Sonia heard the birds chirping as she climbed down the bank to the stream. She walked leisurely enjoying the sun dappled shade of the trees, the water sparkling like a myriad of diamonds, until she came to a large boulder partly submerged in the river, the other half stood on dry land. She stepped on smaller stones until she could climb onto the top of the rock.

Once settled comfortably, she looked around her. A kingfisher flew across the water, dipped until it touched the surface.

The river had its own voice. It sounded like a loud murmur, but if she paid attention, she could hear the water break around rocks in a gurgle.

The water flowed swiftly at this point. Fallen leaves sped by in a great hurry, until a rock in their path made them bounce around and she lost sight of them. Near the rock where she sat, the water looked deep and clear. She saw the sandy bottom, where little minnows darted around. She felt I could sit there for ages. Though peace reigns here, miles away in Kabul the thunder of warfare and the cries of the destitute is a contrast and a realty for these people.

It was easier to sit and daydream, and she did just that, when a sudden gust of wind brought the smell of flowers. She lifted her head and breathed in deeply. Surely that was the scent of lavender. There must be a field of them nearby. That smell triggered certain memories of her childhood and her mother's perfume. She thought of her mother and of her father. She would have to tell them about Elijah. They might object, but they loved her and would never stand in the way of her happiness.

Though Kabul was in ruins, these villages were so beautiful, yet she felt fear for Elijah and herself. His captors were not going to sit idly by. They could be on our trail, she thought. We should make a bold dash for the border. I wonder if they'll target me once Elijah goes back to the States. She climbed down from her rock and went looking for that field of lavender. She noticed through a gap in the trees, a field of red in the distance. They were red flowers swaying in the breeze. It looked like a carpet of scarlet. Row upon row and field after field as far as she could see, poppies dominated the landscape.

"Oh my God," she said. "These are opium farmers."

She found Elijah and Rashid in an animated discussion. Elijah looked at her, "Were you able to relax?"

She smiled. "It was good. Did you notice what they grow?"

"Yes," said Elijah. You had to notice it. The red flowers were everywhere.

"I'm searching for some other flowers. I'll let you continue with your work. I think they're further down that way," she said pointing.

She walked down a slope and there in a hollow, stood a host of lavenders in full bloom waving their heads in the wind. She bent and picked a handful of the sweet scented flowers and held them to her breast. She sat on a fallen tree and waited for Elijah. The wind blew a sigh through the fields of poppies.

He found her, staring into the distance, her mind far away. He sat by her waiting for her to break the silence.

"We have a problem here, don't we?" said Sonia.

"Yes," said Elijah, "Rashid says, they get well paid for their efforts and the money buys food and supplies. I offered to help him find alternate crops and funding from the UN. He seemed interested but I don't think it's going to happen. There are many people involved."

"Are you going to stay and help him with his irrigation system?"

"Yes, he has some burned out motors on his pumps and he has various spare parts in his maintenance shed. We'll spend a day or so, if that's all right with you."

"Well, as much as I love these mountains and these lush valleys, I do long for the safety of my home."

They both stood. With Sonia holding her flowers in one hand, Elijah took her other hand and they walked back to the village, both deep in thought. This place had that effect. It felt like ghosts from the past dwelled here. Just as they reached the compound, they heard the village muezzin's call to prayer. Everyone spread prayer towels on the ground and knelt. Elijah and Sonia stopped and Sonia spread her shawl on the ground. They knelt, in deference to the customs of their hosts. Elijah said his own thoughts, as did Sonia.

After the prayers, everyone dispersed to their own homes. Ishmael stood with a group of young men engaged in a loud discussion. When he saw Elijah and Sonia, he came over and said, "Maybe we should move the Range Rover into the compound and park it near the house where you're staying and I think we should also take the rifle in with you for safety."

"Yes," said Elijah, "I agree. It might be prudent to be vigilant, with all this opium lying around. Thanks, Ishmael, I'll ask the mullah if it's all right."

It was turning to dusk, the light fading and the village prepared for the night. Rashid walked over to them with a kerosene lamp and some blankets over his shoulder. He offered the lamp to Sonia and said, "Here are some blankets for the night. It is always cold here." He handed the blankets to Elijah.

Elijah thanked him, and then broached the subject of moving the SUV closer to the building.

"Yes, of course," said Rashid. He noticed the flowers in Sonia's hand. "You like those flowers. We have many different kinds. My wife can show you more of them in the morning."

Sonia thanked him, "*Shukria*," she said, her hands together.

*   *   *

At last they found themselves alone together. Elijah set the lamp on a small table. The room had two small cots. The floor looked clean and dry. Sonia laid the blankets on one of the cots, gave a sigh and sat down.

"Well, it will be warmer than camping outside," said Elijah. He looked at her. "You do brighten up the darkest room, Sonia."

She smiled, not looking up. "You're the nicest person I've ever met."

He walked to her, knelt and put his hand under her chin. "I know this isn't the safest place in the world. We're on the run and have ended up in a place that makes opium. But we'll be out of here tomorrow. I will get you back home safely."

She moved forward, put her arms around his neck and pressed her head to his chest. He could feel the tears roll down. They held each other for a long time. He smelled her perfume again. When she finally let go, she looked up and kissed him on his lips. "Are you all right?" he asked.

"Yes," she answered, standing up.

Elijah took the blankets, folded them and laid them on the floor. "We might fall off those cots," he said.

Sonia laughed. There was something musical about her laughter. She took off her *pattu* and dropped it on the cot. She stood there in her skirt and her *choli*. "I've always wanted to do this," said Elijah moving behind her and undid the buttons of the *choli.* When he took it off, he moved around to look at her round breasts. Gravity has no effect on them, he thought as he put his lips their nipples sticking out. Her hair fell to almost her waist. She moved her hands around him and held him to her. After a few moments he stepped back and she pushed her skirt and panties past her hips and let them drop to the floor.

*   *   *

Sonia had dressed and was combing her hair when Elijah woke up. He kissed her good morning and she showed him a bucket of water in the kitchen area to wash in.

Rashid and Ishmael walked with Elijah to the pumping sump. There were two pumps with burnt out motors. Elijah showed Ishmael how to take the motor and pump assembly apart, and put a new motor on, from the spares that Rashid had. "Make sure the tang shaft registers in the corresponding slot of the pump shaft," said Elijah, showing Ishmael the details.

Sonia went with Rashid's wife, Sohrab to a field with wild flowers. Sonia became so excited at the variety of species and colors of flowers, she decided she would take seeds of as many of them as she could. She found that the flowers had their individual scents. She smelled them and laid them in rows on the ground, cataloging their names and perfumes in her mind. She said, "This small petalled bloom is different. What's the name of this one, Sohrab?"

Sohrab gave her the names of the flowers, as she knew them in Pushtu. Sonia made packets out of the pages of her notebook, putting a name on each with the corresponding seed.

By mid-day Elijah, Sonia and Ishmael gathered together ready to leave. Sonia gave Sohrab a great hug. "Thank you for all your help. You are a dear, dear person. I hope I see you again."

"*Ha, behti,* (yes daughter), you are a very smart girl. God bless you," said Sohrab. They hugged again. There were tears in Sohrab's eyes.

Elijah shook Rashid's hand, saying, "And thank you for your hospitality. You are very kind. I hope we meet again. I will send you help to get you started in new crops." After the handshake, Rashid gave Elijah his Afghan bear hug.

"*Salaam Aleikoum*," said Rashid. "I am happy to have met you. May Allah be with you." Turning to Ishmael, "And you too my son. God bless you." He gave Ishmael his mighty hug. He put his hands together facing Sonia, "*Salaam Aleikoum, behti.*"

"*Aleikoum Salaam*," said Sonia, with her hands together.

Elijah started the Range Rover and soon they were on the dusty road again. They had information about a truck stop just thirty miles away. Elijah wanted to fill up with gas and buy blankets and a gas stove and a *pattu* for himself. He felt getting back into a full disguise may be a good idea. He definitely looked foreign in spite of the mustache and the turban and Rehman's men were sure to make inquiries as they followed.

"I made you a mustache," said Sonia, digging into her purse. "This one's a little larger. Could you try it?"

Elijah pulled off the road and very carefully pulled off the disguise on his upper lip and handed it to Sonia, He looked in the rear-view mirror stuck the new one on. "OK?" he asked looking at Sonia.

She reached out and pressed the edges and said, "Yes, off you go. That looks a lot better."

Ishmael sat quiet for a while. He looked nervous and kept wringing his hands. At last he blurted out, "I was talking to some of the men in the village. They said there was a rumor that there may be a stoning in a village nearby. It's about a hundred kilometers further down. I think we should go there before it's too late and try to prevent this from happening."

"What!" said a startled Elijah. His face flushed and his brow furrowed. Sonia too looked alarmed. She chewed on her lower lip.

"This is terrible," she said, "we have to do something."

"I've seen the terrible way women are left to fend for themselves on the streets of Kabul," said Elijah. "Now this. Let's try saving this woman." He pondered for a moment then added, "Sonia, can you put on your disguise once again?"

"Yes." She looked anxious, as she grabbed her knapsack and started putting on her beard and mustache and finally her turban.

They needed an element of surprise, felt Elijah, and a woman in the group would make the mob bolder than when faced by three men. Besides, should they escape, the village would be looking for three men.

Elijah drove through the truck stop. They would have to come back for supplies. There was a life at stake. Ishmael gave Elijah directions. As they drove, Elijah had time to reflect on this decision they had made on the spur of the moment. Here they were on the run, trying to evade being captured again and now they were going to get involved in more trouble in a country foreign and hostile towards westerners. He was partly disguised which was a plus. But the idea of a medieval sacrifice overcame his fear and doubts. To hell with the consequences, he thought.

In an hour and a half they arrived near the village. Elijah made a turn onto a gravel road. They drove almost a mile from the main road before they saw buildings. A large growth of alder trees loomed ahead. A crowd had gathered in the compound. Their ritual chants stained the air.

Chapter Sixteen

Elijah drove slowly to avoid the attention of the crowd. About a dozen brick buildings stood scattered around the square near a hand-operated water pump. Instead of a group of women gathered to fetch pots of water and gossip, today the women all thronged together at the compound, part of the curious crowd.

The murmur of the crowd grew louder as they got nearer. It obscured the noise of the SUV. Elijah parked behind a grove of trees and they jumped out. He grabbed the rifle and threw the ammunition belt across his shoulder.

The three of them crept along the trees that bordered the open area where men, women and even children had congregated. The villagers had not seen them as yet. From that vantage point, they could see and hear the drama unfolding before them. There, in the middle, in a pit that came up to her chest a woman cowered, dressed in black with a purdah over her face. Her hands were tied in front of her and she was shaking in terror.

In a loud voice, a man began intoning in Pushtu.

Elijah and Sonia both understood Pushtu. The man had read the charges against the woman and decreed, according to Islamic Law, she should die by stoning for infidelity.

Was there a judge and a jury? wondered Elijah. He wished they had more than one rifle. It was too late now to go back to the truck stop. He looked all around and spotted one man with an AK-47 and an ammunition belt. The celerity in its execution would determine the success of the rescue. They could not give the mob time to think and react. He pointed to the man and whispered to Ishmael, "Are there any more with rifles?"

"He's the only one armed that I can see."

"All right, we'll come up behind him and I want you to take his weapon and ammo."

The man with the gun was so intently watching the scene he did not hear them until Elijah prodded the muzzle of his gun in the small of his back. The man turned around swinging his weapon instinctively into position. Elijah had no choice, he clipped him on the jaw with the butt of his rifle and the man went down. Ishmael grabbed the weapon before it hit the ground. The people nearby started to scatter. Ishmael now had the rifle pointed at the crowd. Elijah fired a shot in the air. That got everyone's attention. They parted like a wave before him and Ishmael. The men and women dropped the stones they had in their hands. The man with the decree in his hand, his face contorted in hate and anger, screamed, "Who are you to interfere in our sacred rites?"

Elijah pointed his rifle at the man. "You do not have that right," he shouted in Pushtu and fired a shot just inches from the man's feet. He jumped backwards, into the crowd with a scream, sprayed by the gravel the bullet kicked up.

Ishmael gave his weapon to Sonia –now Abdul Aziz – saying, "Here, take this, I have to help her."

Sonia grabbed the AK-47 and pointed it at the crowd. She knew how to use the gun and fired another shot in front of the man who had dropped the decree. He screamed and jumped further back into the crowd. Someone shouted, "Oh, Allah."

Ishmael ran to the woman in the pit and bending down, shouted, "Raise your arms."

The woman lifted her bound hands towards him. He grabbed both her arms and shouted, "Dig your feet into the wall of the hole and climb."

He pulled with all his might. The woman felt light though the leverage worked against Ishmael. She managed to get a footing on the wall. She moved upwards a small amount. Ishmael pulled again. She kept moving up. For one moment they hung in the air, balancing each other. She could pull Ishmael into the hole with her. He gave a final tug and she came flying out of the pit, falling on top of him. He twisted his body, letting her roll off, and got up quickly, and looked around. The crowd had backed off. The woman pushed herself up and stood, her purdah askew.

"Cut these ropes," she said, panting audibly.

He grabbed the woman's hands still tied together, took out his knife from its scabbard in his waistband and cut her bonds. She pushed her purdah up onto her head so that her view wasn't obstructed. He grabbed her hand and yelled in Pushtu, "Run." Together, they galloped towards Elijah and Sonia. The woman seemed light on her feet. She ran as fast as Ishmael did.

"Give me the rifle," shouted Ishmael when they reached Elijah and Sonia. Sonia gave him the machine gun and turned around and latched onto one of the woman's hands and together they ran towards the Range Rover. She released her hand, so they could run faster. Ishmael joined Elijah to face the mob.

The crowd roared their disapproval. They wanted blood, and now were going to be denied it.

Elijah and Ishmael slowly walked backwards, holding this mass of humanity at bay. The crowd smelled of sweat. Both men and women started following them, though at a distance. They shouted threats and invectives. Someone threw a stone at them. It went wide. They walked under several large alder trees. Elijah raised his rifle, aimed and shot at a six-inch diameter by ten-foot long branch above the crowd. The branch splintered, broke and bent downwards but still clung to strands of bark and strips of wood. The crowd screamed and ran in all directions to get out of its way. Again shouts of, "Oh, Allah," came from various sources.

Elijah aimed again and fired at the remaining strands of the branch which came crashing down forming a barrier in the path of the pursuing crowd.

Sonia and the woman had made it to the SUV. Sonia started the Range Rover and sat tensed, ready to go. Ishmael and Elijah each fired a round over the heads of the crowd and everyone ducked for cover, looking upwards in fear of another branch coming down. The two of them climbed into the SUV and Sonia put it into gear and roared off. The crowd screamed as they ran after the vehicle.

Sonia drove back the way they had come. When she had gone a couple of miles, she stopped, put it in park and moved to the back of the Range Rover. Elijah moved over to the driver's seat and they were off again.

Elijah turned to Ishmael. "Give her a shawl to use as a turban and ask her to remove the purdah. That will attract less attention from passing vehicles and the people at the truck stop."

Ishmael handed the girl a long sash and spoke to her. She did as she was requested.

Glancing backwards, Elijah couldn't help notice that the woman was barely a teenager. She had fine features, light skinned with green eyes and long brown hair. These Afghans, thought Elijah, were a handsome people. But how could a young girl like her be guilty of a crime worthy of a stoning?

The young woman sat by Sonia's side, her eyes cast downward in utter humility. Sonia's heart went out to her, empathizing with the woman's devastated feelings. She is perhaps seventeen or eighteen, thought Sonia.

With the wind blowing and the roar of the SUV, Sonia had to shout to be heard. "I am also a woman, but I am disguised to look like a man."

The woman turned and stared at Sonia, who was carefully peeling off her mustache. She screwed up her face as the glue tugged at her skin. In spite of the turmoil within her, the girl smiled, as though a great burden had been taken off her shoulders.

"I had been wondering, who you people were," said the girl. "What am I getting into, they are all men. Now I thank Allah, one of you is a woman. You can understand why I'm still afraid?"

Sonia reached over and patted her hands and still holding them asked, "What's your name?"

"Aiyasha, Aiyasha Khan."

"My name is Sonia, that is Elijah *Bhai* (brother)," pointing to Elijah, "and Ishmael *Bhai* (brother). We will keep you safe from harm, you poor thing." She hugged Aiyasha, who started crying like the floodgates had been opened. The strain of the past few hours had been too much. Sonia held her until her sobs subsided and she calmed down. Aiyasha sat up and wiped her face with her shawl.

After driving for a while Elijah asked Ishmael, "Does this happen very often?"

"No, not in Afghanistan," said Ishmael, "this has started only a few years ago. Ever since the Taliban took over the country. I hate to tell you this, but America supported the Taliban against the Russians when they were here. Now the Americans are against the Taliban because they allowed Osama Bin Laden to move in here."

They had supplies to get. Elijah drove back to the truck stop. It was late afternoon and they would be camping out tonight. If the villagers followed them on foot, the truck stop would be an easy place to find them. They had to put as much distance from the village as possible. They were fugitives once again.

In an hour they were back at the truck stop they had passed earlier. Elijah gave Ishmael money and told him, "Get two pattus, one for me and one for the girl. I'll try to find a tent and some blankets and a gas stove. Also get some kebabs and *roti* from those food stands."

"Ha jee," said Ishmael as he went off on his errands.

Smoke rose from the coal fire at the portable outdoor cooking stands. The smell of spices and cooked meat filled the air.

Elijah had an attendant fill the Range Rover with gas. "Fill these two carry on containers also with petrol," he said. Sonia and Aiyasha stayed in the SUV.

He went looking for a store where he could get blankets. Choosing the largest shop, however he found they didn't have any tents, but a couple of Kalashnikovs, also known as AK-47s, and ammunition caught his attention. Purchasing two of these along with a few cartridge packs, four blankets and a gas stove. He turned around and there stood Ishmael ready to help him carry all his purchases back to the SUV.

"I don't like back tracking on the road we just came on. Is there another way out of here?" he asked Ishmael.

"No, we are going northeast. Tajikistan is to the north of us. If we go east we should come to the city of Asadabad. I'm not sure how far that's from here, which is close to the Pakistan border.

Elijah started up the Range Rover and followed the road back the way they had come. It was now five p.m. They ate their dinner of kebabs and *roti* on the move. Ishmael had also bought four large plastic bottles of water.

What if the villagers had come down and blocked the road? thought Elijah. He told Ishmael and Sonia, "You both keep your rifles ready, in case we run into trouble."

The evening light faded. Twilight shone on the hills ahead. Elijah kept looking at the mileage meter and adjusted his speed to sixty MPH. The meter had both indicators, MPH and KPH. In a half-hour he had picked up his speed slightly. The needle crept to sixty-five MPH. His body grew tense with anxiety. In another half-hour they reached the road to the village where they had rescued Aiyasha. He saw no roadblocks. Elijah began relaxing and breathing easier, as he drove on.

"All right," said Elijah, "cover yourselves with your blankets. It's going to be cold. I'll turn on the heater and hopefully we'll be warm enough."

As he drove, he looked to the north, the mountains loomed dark and bluish. Pine trees abounded. The contours of the hills below were a rolling dark green. As the light faded further, he turned on his lights. The roads were not in good repair, forcing him to slow down to 40 MPH.

They didn't have a tent; there was no point in camping anywhere. He continued to drive. After three hours, he felt sleepy. He looked for a place to stop for the night. When he found a dense growth of trees, he pulled off the road and slowly guided the vehicle until he reached a spot well away from the road, surrounded by large pine trees. He turned off the lights and engine and covered himself with his blanket and curled up into as comfortable a position as he could. He turned to look at the others. All three had the blankets pulled snugly around them and were fast asleep.

At daylight, Elijah was the last to wake up. He looked around and saw Ishmael had the gas stove running. He smelled the aroma of cooking. Sonia and Aiyasha sat on a fallen tree, sipping on cups of tea. He could hear the sizzle of something frying. He sat up and saw Ishmael had eggs in a skillet.

The trees were alive with the early morning song birds. The air felt chilly. He lay in his hard bed thinking about the last twenty-four hours. We are digging ourselves_deeper and deeper into the bullfighter's arena and taken the bull by the horns. We have to hang on or get gored to death. But it was worth it. We worked as a perfect team and saved an innocent girl from a terrible death. I would do it again. No other country does this to their women. If we get out of here in one piece, we must start a campaign to help the women of the Muslim world. That will go over well, like stirring a hornet's nest. So what do we do?

Nothing? Focus, focus. Just now our immediate goal is to get out of here. He slowly got up and put on his boots.

Sonia sipped her tea and pondered what they had been through recently. I came _to help Elijah and now we're fighting the whole of Islam. And poor Aiyasha. What terrors she must have gone through even if she's guilty. But it's for her to tell us what happened. Look at her, so young and beautiful, on the threshold of her maidenhood, to be murdered like a sacrifice to some heathen god? I've heard of such things but to witness it firsthand makes me as mad as hell. The poor child will bear the scars of what happened in the past few days for the rest of her life. What can one person do against such injustice? There must be a way. If we do get back, I will write letters to people of prominence everywhere. She looked at Aiyasha and put her hand on her shoulder reassuringly.

Aiyasha turned and smiled at her. "Thank you," she said, "for saving my life." She got up and putting her hands together, bowed to Elijah and Ishmael. "*Shukria*," she said. They both nodded to her.

"Where are we going?" she asked of both of them.

Sonia answered, "We are trying to get back to Jullundur in India. It hasn't been easy. Some people kidnapped Elijah *Bai* and we managed to escape from them. You can come with us unless you wish to do otherwise. Tell us if you have a place you would like us to take you."

Aiyasha looked bewildered. "I do have relatives, but I have never been outside my village. I have my parents and a brother, back there," pointing in the direction they had come from. "The mullah, tried to molest me. I escaped and ran home. He made up a story and accused me of all kinds of things. He even had some men support his accusations. My poor parents couldn't do anything against the powerful mullah." She started to cry. Sonia put her arms around the girl. Aiyasha sobbed on her shoulder.

"You can come with us," said Elijah, when she had calmed down. "We'll help you as best we can. I have written down the location of your village with the help of my GPS locator. Someday you can contact your family again. Were you going to school at your village?"

"Yes," said Aiyasha, "I was. I want to be a doctor, but after my high school, I would never have had the chance to further my education, not in Afghanistan."

"When we get to India," said Sonia, "we will try and see if we can help you with your education."

Aiyasha smiled and gave Sonia a warm embrace.

They all sat quietly, while Ishmael was washing up after making breakfast. He didn't have very much water for cleaning up. He tried to preserve most of it for tea. He swirled a little water in the pan and pitched it, then used a clean rag to wipe it dry.

While doing these chores his mind was also miles away. What is happening to my life? What's happening to my country? My mother is barely able to survive with my brother and sister. This girl Aiyasha could easily have been my sister. I wouldn't have let that happen to my sister. Oh, yes, that mullah was lucky I wasn't in his village. He put the last of the utensils neatly stacked in the rear of the Range Rover.

As they all sat quietly each with their own thoughts, Elijah turned to Sonia and asked, "What do you think about the rescue?"

"I think we have interfered in one of Islam's major laws," said Sonia. "Not that I regret having done it. They are not likely to forget it and soon we may have a price on our heads."

"From what Aiyasha has said, she was not guilty," said Ishmael, who was standing nearby.

"But," said Elijah, "we didn't know that at the time. It just didn't seem right to us, whether she was guilty or not. The penalty seems far too great to fit the crime."

"I don't understand it either," said Ishmael, shaking his head.

"I like the way the people scrambled when they saw that branch come crashing down on them," laughed Sonia. "They were so blood thirsty. Weird."

"That's what happens in a mob," said Elijah, "people lose their reason."

"We have two enemies now," said Ishmael, "the Taliban and the Fundamentalist Muslims. I think we should get rid of the Range Rover. Everyone will be looking for it."

"Yes," said Elijah, "at the earliest opportunity we should look for another vehicle."

Sonia put her arm around Aiyasha's shoulders. "It will take some time for you to forget about the terror you've been through. But remember, we are here for you."

"I wish that mullah were dead," said Aiyasha, her anger welling up.

Elijah stood and said, "Okay, let's pack up and put some distance between this place. We're going in the wrong direction, but that can't be helped, with all these people after us."

An Asian koel called out plaintively as though in answer to Elijah.

The skies were pale blue with a few white clouds over the mountains in the distance. The road gradually gained altitude. Pine trees grew in abundant clusters on both sides of the road. I'm sure Genghis Khan didn't take this road, thought Elijah. It didn't lead to India. They were going north instead of east. After two hours of driving, Ishmael staring at the landmarks said, "There is a village nearby and a town further down with a UN office."

"I would guess it'll be safer at the village," said Elijah.

"I think so too, but we can probably buy a tent at the town."

*   *   *

Rehman and his six men reached the village where Abad Rashid was the mullah. It had been two days since the departure of Elijah and his party. He sought out the mullah.

"We are looking for two or three people." He gave Elijah's and Ishmael's descriptions. He added, "We are not sure of the third person with them."

"Why are you after these people?" Abad asked. "Have they done something wrong?"

"So they did pass this way?" asked Rehman, getting a bit annoyed.

"I didn't say that. We give shelter to many people passing through. What is your interest with these people?" persisted Abad.

"I noticed you have an opium production here. It will be to your advantage to cooperate with us. We are members of Fundamentalist Muslims."

Abad showed signs of surprise. "This is not a clandestine operation. Many villages produce opium. It's our only source of income. Anyway, we didn't see the people you are looking for. You're welcome to stay for a meal."

In the distance a group of youngsters played soccer amid a lot of shouting. One of them yelled out, "Goooall."

One of Rehman's men came up and whispered to him. "I have been asking the children in the village. Three strangers did stop here in a Range Rover. Two men and one woman. One of the men was dressed as a Pakistani."

Rehman turned back to Abad, "That won't be necessary. We do thank you. We must be on our way. *Salaam Aleikoum.*"

As they walked back to their Jeep, Rehman murmured, "Did they say how long ago?"

"Yes, two days ago."

"We're on their trail now. We should stop at every village and truck stop and make inquiries."

There was a smugness about his features and his facial muscles tensed as he clenched his teeth. "We'll have you in our sights soon, Mr. Elijah," he said.

Chapter Seventeen

Aiyasha had grown up with her younger brother, a mother who loved them both dearly and her father, a farmer who tried his best to eke out a living from working in the fields. In her teen years she began blossoming into a beauty. She was blessed with fine features and light skin like her mother, green eyes and long straight brown hair. Her budding breasts were noticeable through her loose garments. In a small village all the young men and some of the not so young stared at her whenever she walked by.

Her mother, Fatima, made her sit in front of her, while she combed her hair. "My little girl has grown into the prettiest girl in the village," she would say.

"Oh mother, you embarrass me. Don't talk so loud."

Her mother laughed and hugged her. "I love you, my dearest daughter. You bring joy to my heart. Come here, sit down," she said pointing to a low stool. She took a mixture of henna and sandalwood ground to a paste and decorated her daughter's hands. Intricate designs she had learned from her own mother. The smell of sandalwood followed Aiyasha wherever she walked, waiting for the henna to dry. Fatima taught Aiyasha how to cook simple dishes. When her father and brother returned from the fields, her father said, "Something smells good. I'm very hungry."

"Your daughter cooked today," said Fatima.

"Ma," said her son Abdur, "you should teach me also. I like to cook."

"Tomorrow I teach you."

The brother and sister attended the little village school. They learned to read and write Urdu and Pushtu. Besides the usual subjects, they also studied the Koran daily.

Aiyasha loved school. Everything they taught her, she absorbed and came up with questions of her own. Some queries that the teacher had no answer for. She liked everything especially physiology. The working of the human body intrigued her. The muscles, the heart, the stomach were all fascinating subjects. English was taught as a foreign language. Most schools had restrictions on girls attending once they reached puberty.

But the mullah at this village allowed the older girls to be part of the system and he himself taught the Koran.

Aiyasha was now seventeen and her brother Abdur thirteen. At the village compound they sometimes showed movies or television shows that depicted doctors doing operations. She wanted to be just like them, a doctor with a stethoscope hanging around her neck. Her mother sat before a fire cooking. "Mother," said Aiyasha, "I would like to become a doctor. Then I can look after you and father when you get old or sick."

Her mother looked troubled. "I wish we knew how we can make your dream come true, my dear. You are very clever and if we can send you to a school where they teach doctors, I'm sure you will become one. We shall talk to the mullah if he can help us."

She was a healthy girl, strong in wind and limb, and often persuaded her brother Abdur to race against her on the playing fields at school. Just when she knew she would be surging past him, she would ease off, so that they arrived at the finish line together. She loved her brother. But Abdur screamed, "I almost beat you."

"Soon you will," said Aiyasha, panting.

She realized that it wouldn't be long before she would have to wear the burkha when she turned eighteen. She despised the woven head cover women had to wear, with the rows of holes for them to see through. "Why do women have to wear this thing?" she asked her mother. "It always smells of sweat."

"Wearing it is part of our custom, and our religion," said her mother.

"But it doesn't make sense. We have seen movies of the rest of the world, where women don't have to wear them. So why hide our faces?"

"We live here and those are our ways, our traditions," said Fatima.

"What will happen if I refuse to wear one, when I am older?" asked Aiyasha.

"The people of the village will not like it. The mullah will not like it, and they will make it difficult for your father and me to live in this village."

"But isn't that a kind of discrimination against women? I don't see men wearing a burkha. Are they above this law? Some of them should hide their faces."

"Now Aiyasha, be sensible, my dear."

"Someday I will go to another country, like India. They won't mind if I did not wear a burkha or a purdah."

"You are watching too many Indian movies. Allah knows they make a lot of them," said Fatima.

Her brother walked in. "Say Aiyasha, show me how to do this math problem."

"Yes, my brother dear, come sit here," said Aiyasha, "Let's see." She worked with him and soon he understood the method of attacking the problem.

"You are very good, Aiyasha," said Abdur, "you should become a teacher."

"No, I want to become a doctor," said Aiyasha. "What do you want to do, when you grow up, little brother?"

"I don't know," said Abdur, "but I don't want to be a farmer like father. Perhaps a soccer player."

Aiyasha laughed, "That is a sport, I'm talking about a career."

"Have you heard of Pele or Beckham?"

"Who is Pele? I'm talking about engineers, doctors or scientists."

"But I have never seen an engineer or a doctor in these villages," said Abdur.

"But there is life outside these villages. If you go to Kabul, you will meet these people," said Aiyasha.

"Kabul has been bombed and destroyed and the people have left the country. You should know that."

Aiyasha was hard pressed not to agree with her brother. She sighed, "That is true, my brother, but if the war does not stop, we have to get our learning outside, where it is safer. We can always come back."

"And how are you going to do that?" said the young man who didn't like the way this discussion was going. "When will there be peace?" he asked.

"I don't know, Abdur."

*   *   *

Aiyasha's mother, Fatima Khan, had her own set of goals for her daughter. Aiyasha would be coming of age soon. Her husband, Mohammed Khan, and she would have to find a suitable match for their daughter. Once she is married, she will leave this home to live with her husband. It may even be in another village. There were tears in her eyes at the thought. "I will surely miss her," she said to herself.

As she did her cooking, she mused at the early years, when Aiyasha was a bouncy baby. She was so strong. When she liked something, she would lift it up in her baby arms and carry it around with her. They had a small globe of the world. Aiyasha carried this from one room to another, wherever she decided to sit down and play. Another time her uncle, Fatima's brother Adnan, brought her a large stuffed ladybug. It measured as big as she was tall. She dragged this around everywhere she went, until other things caught her interest.

"Now she wants to become a doctor. How is this possible in a country torn by strife? I am proud of her, but what can one do?" She said it out loud.

One day when Aiyasha was alone with her, she said, "Aiyasha, you are now reaching the age when you turn into a woman. Your father and I should be looking for a suitable young man for you to marry."

"Oh no, Mother. If I marry, then that will be the end. I will never become a doctor. Men are so controlling." Aiyasha was adamant. She stamped her feet -- she always stamped her feet to make a point -- and said, "You can't do this to me now. Maybe after I become a doctor, you can do your searching. But remember, he should be good looking." She laughed and gave her mother an affectionate embrace.

That was the last time they had talked about it, before the trouble with the mullah erupted.

*   *   *

After Rehman and his six men left Abad Rashid's village they came to a fork in the road. One led north to the mountains of Afghanistan. The other led east to Pakistan and India. They stopped their vehicles and got out to confer.

"It seems logical that Elijah and the Indian woman would go east towards India," said Rehman.

"Yes," said one of the men. "But are we sure?"

"What are you saying? That we should split up?" asked Rehman.

"I don't know," said Suleman.

"But that would waste time," said Rehman. "We are only two days behind them. If we split up, one of us will be wrong and when we get together again we will have given them a larger lead."

"Then you tell us. What do you want to do?" said Suleman. The rest of them remained silent.

"What do you think, Iqbal?" asked Rehman.

"Going east makes sense," said Iqbal.

They travelled for a day. They passed no farms or villages. The land bordering the road showed rocks and stones, the remains of a glacial period in their distant past. Pine trees struggled to take a hold onto every patch of soft soil. In some areas they thrived in groves before fading out to more rocks and boulders. The convoy drove through.

Suleman drove one of the Jeeps with Rehman in the passenger seat. Rehman's thoughts were on whether he should kill Elijah or take him to ISIS. It didn't make much difference to him anymore.

A blast of warm air through the trees brought the scent of pine needles. He became aware that they were running low on gas. He took out his cell phone and called the others to stop for a conference.

"Maybe we should camp tonight and one of you take a Jeep and find a gas station," said Rehman. He turned to Iqbal. "You go, Iqbal. We'll look for a camping site soon. It's getting late." As the others returned to their Jeeps he continued talking to Iqbal. "Check at the gas station if Elijah and party went through there. If they didn't then we've given them a three day lead."

Chapter Eighteen

Meanwhile Elijah drove north for perhaps an hour, when they came into a valley. The day grew sultry with not a cloud in the sky. The mountains in the distance still had snow on the higher elevations. It was late May. The hills were covered in pines and at the lower levels deciduous trees spotted the landscape. They looked like alder or maple. A stream ran through the valley. Goats and sheep grazed along the banks. Elijah noticed an absence of cows.

The beauty of the place struck Sonia. It hadn't been touched by the war that they had seen all around them in their flight through Afghanistan. Green meadows covered the village far below with mulberry and apricot groves spread lushly as far into the distance. They drove further down and parked the SUV in a secluded grove of trees. The four of them got out and stretched their arms and legs.

"This is what Shangri-La looks like," said Elijah.

"It is beautiful and peaceful," said Sonia, sweeping her gaze at the panoramic view before her. Aiyasha hardly saw anything. She was still too depressed.

Ishmael was in good humor too. It felt good to walk around. The sense of urgency had faded. They hid the rifles under the tarpaulin in the Range Rover.

"Aiyasha, could you put on Sonia's disguise?" asked Elijah.

Aiyasha looked surprised. "Why?"

"News about your escape could travel fast," said Elijah, "we would like to delay your being recognized."

"Oh! What about my hair?"

"I'll help you," said Sonia, getting her bag and taking out the various pieces that made up the disguise. "Sit right here."

Aiyasha took a deep breath. Everything in the bag smelled of Sonia's perfume. She eased herself onto a stump, her eyes roving from left to right as Sonia moved around her, applying the beard and the mustache. "Stop doing that," laughed Sonia, "you're making me nervous."

"Do I get to see myself?"

"You can use the mirror on the SUV," said Sonia finishing off the eyebrows. She gave Aiyasha the jacket and draped the pattu over it to cover her feminine attributes. She then started on the turban. "Hold this end," she told Aiyasha as she wrapped the rest of the fine cloth around Aiyasha's head covering her hair and finally taking the other end from Aiyasha's hold and tucking it in neatly.

"Now go look at yourself," said Sonia, tapping Aiyasha on the shoulder. "Your name is Abdul Aziz."

Aiyasha walked to the mirror on the side of the Range Rover and looked at herself. She raised her eyebrows and started to laugh. She walked to where Ishmael was sitting and posed beside him with her hands on her hips.

"Ishmael I am now your older brother."

Ishmael stood and put his arm around her shoulders, "*Kaisa hi bai* (How are you brother)?"

Elijah looked on with amusement. A goat bleated in the distance. A pheasant took up a cry that was answered by its mate. They all paused to listen to its plaintive notes. Elijah put on the *pattu* that they had bought. It didn't change his identity; he still looked like a foreigner. The excellent disguise that Sonia had helped make for him had been left back in Simla when he had been captured. A mustache and a turban had changed his looks quite dramatically. "Let's go find this village that grows apricots and other fruits," said Elijah.

Ishmael and Abdul Aziz led the way with Elijah and Sonia following. As they walked side by side, Elijah moved his right hand until it touched Sonia's hand. Instinctively her fingers curled around his. He squeezed her hand gently. She turned her head towards him and smiled as they walked towards the village.

Elijah noticed several houses built of brick with tiled roofs huddled together. A woman cooked by an outdoor fire with a flat wok like pan supported on stones. It looked like Nan or chapatties. She did not have on a burkha. An older man sat nearby with a baby in his lap. They both looked up and Ishmael and Abdul Aziz raised their hands and said, "*Salaam Aleikoum*."

The man smiled and said; "*Salaam Aleikoum*." The woman did the same and continued with her cooking.

"We need some water to drink and to fill our flasks," said Ishmael, "we can pay for some food if you have any to spare."

"*Ha jee*," said the woman, "please sit down and make yourself comfortable." She looked up across the fields that sloped down to the creek. A man up there worked with a hoe and two young boys helped him break up the clods of soil. Still others worked on fields to the west.

Elijah had disengaged his hand from Sonia's as they approached the woman. While Ishmael and Abdul Aziz sat down, the two of them walked down the slope to the creek. As they got closer they could hear the familiar sounds of a rushing stream. The gurgle and splashing sound of water lulled their sense of urgency. After what they had been through, the peace and quiet away from people was like a healing salve on a painful wound.

Sonia sat on a rock and the movement of the water seemed to mesmerize her. "This is such a beautiful place," she said, "it belies the danger we have been through. Why won't people let these Afghans live their lives in peace? They are such a friendly people when there are no Taliban around. Oh, my heart aches for them."

Elijah looked at her and shrugged.

What will we do if they catch up with us, he wondered. We can't fight them. The best means of escape would be to disappear into thin air. A disguise for myself and Sonia would do it, now that Aiyasha also had assumed a new character taking the only outfit we have. Wish we had a helicopter. Maybe we can steal one. But who knew how to pilot one? That thought gave him an idea. What if I called Mister D'Souza at the factory and asked him to find a helicopter and send it to a location whose co-ordinates I can give him? We could be lifted out of here to safety. He turned to Sonia, "Could you dial the factory and get Tom D'Souza on the line? Maybe he can get some help."

Sonia was taken by surprise. "What kind of help?" she asked as she took out the phone from her deep pocket in her skirt. She dialed the number and when it started ringing, passed it on to Elijah.

"Jullundur Machines," said the receptionist.

"This is Elijah Davenport. Can I talk to Mister D'Souza, please?"

"Yes, sir, just a moment please."

After a minute, D'Souza's voice came loud and clear. "Mister Davenport! Where are you? Are you all right?"

"Yes, I'm OK. But we could use some help. Sonia is here with me and we are in Afghanistan. Could you charter a helicopter to lift us out of here? I could give you the co-ordinates of exactly where we are. There are no landing strips for small planes."

"I can try. Give me an hour and I'll call you back. Let me have your number." Elijah gave him the number and they clicked off.

Sonia looked at him inquiringly. "Mister D'Souza is going to try to get a helicopter to lift us out of here. I should get the GPS and get our position to give him when he calls back. I'll be right back." He walked swiftly back to the Range Rover and wrote down the location on a piece of paper and slipped it into his pocket, and walked back to where Sonia waited.

Elijah noted that this village looked different from those that they had been to before. About twelve families lived here. The farmers raised corn, wheat and barley and fruits and vegetables. They had walnut and almond trees in groves and further down were the groves of mulberry and apricots they had seen. On the hillside the sound of lambs making the familiar "Baa," reached them.

While Elijah made these observations, Ishmael walked over to him. "Let's have a feast," he said. "I can cook. Why don't you come with me, Sahib and help me buy some raisins, pistachios, flour and rice. This seems like a nice place to rest for a few days. The women could use some rest and peace of mind."

"That's an excellent idea," said Elijah. "I didn't know you had all these talents. You can cook too. Very good Ishmael."

By mid-day all the farmers started streaming back from the fields. Elijah's phone rang and he quickly flipped it on.

"Mister Davenport," said D'Souza. "There are no helicopters in this part of Jullundur or Ludhianna. The Indian army has them but won't make them available to private concerns. I have put in calls to New Delhi and am awaiting their response. Don't be discouraged, we may find something yet."

"All right, keep trying and let me know as soon as you find a positive answer. But let me give you the GPS co-ordinates of where we are. Thank you, Mister D'Souza." He read off the numbers and clicked off.

He looked at Sonia and shook his head. "No luck yet," he said, giving her the phone back.

Elijah and Ishmael went to meet the farmers. The farmers were curious about Elijah and could tell that he was not Afghani. They smiled at him. Elijah introduced himself and Sonia as his wife. The headman's name was Sayed Hassan. He invited them to partake in their meal of *rhoti* and kebabs and tea. During the meal Sayed said to Elijah, "Where are you from? What brings you here?"

"I am an American," said Elijah, "disguised as you can see as a Pakistani. I came on business to India. The Al-Qadia kidnapped me and brought me here to a village further west. I escaped with the help of my wife Sonia. We are trying to make it back to India."

Sayed looked at Sonia, with raised eyebrows. "You helped him escape from the Fundamentalist Muslims? That is remarkable. They are not Afghans. They are made up of Saudis and other groups." Then looking at Aiyasha, he said, "*Apka nam kya hi* (what's your name)?"

Aiyasha looked up, her hand taking a piece of Nan to her mouth and hesitated. "Ji, Abdul Aziz."

Sayed nodded. He was in his late sixties and his benign features spoke volumes of his natural hospitality to strangers. He had blue eyes and a light brown beard and mustache with streaks of white. He squinted slightly making his face take on a thoughtful look. A little of his hair peeped through from the bottom of his white turban. A loose fitting shirt was draped over with his pattu that hung from his shoulders. He looked a little over six feet in his leather sandals.

Elijah explained to Sayed what Ishmael had in mind. He wanted to cook a feast for everyone. "That's a wonderful idea," Sayed said. "We have not had a feast in a long time. We will help you as best we can." Then looking at Elijah he said, "You can spend the night with us. We will find you room."

"First, we will go into town to buy some of the things that Ishmael needs."

After the meal the men returned to the fields and the women to their chores. Elijah and his party got in the Range Rover and in half an hour were in a small town just as Ishmael had predicted. The first they did was to fill the SUV with gas. Elijah told Ishmael, "Let's find out if there is a Red Cross Medical Center." They soon found one. Now Elijah wished he didn't have the *pattu* on. He knocked on the door and introduced himself to the man who answered. The man was tall with a kindly face, brown eyes and light brown hair. He had bushy eyebrows and was clean-shaven. He wore a gray shirt and Khaki slacks.

"Hi," said Elijah, "I'm Elijah Davenport."

"How do you do," said the Red Cross man, "I'm Michael Pierson." He had an English accent.

"Where is this town?" asked Elijah. "Does it have a name?"

"It's a county of the larger town up north known as Taloqan," said Pierson.

"I was wondering if you can help us," said Elijah. "We are trying to get back to India. I was kidnapped by the Fundamentalist Muslims. It's a long story. Right now we are running short of money. I do have my credit card and my checkbook. Is there a bank in this town?"

"Why yes," said Pierson, "there's one here and I'm sure they can help you. But if you should have problems, come back and we'll see how we can help you. In fact why don't I come with you? I'll take you there." He closed the door behind him.

While the rest of the group waited in the Range Rover, Elijah and Pierson walked down the road to a small brick building. With an introduction from Mr. Pierson the manager was eager to help and Elijah soon had enough dollars and Afghanis in his pocket.

They walked back to the SUV, where Sonia, Ishmael and Aiyasha were standing around stretching their legs. Elijah said, "Sonia, this is Mr. Pierson." Then turning to Pierson, "my wife Sonia."

The Hunt for the Rajput Princess

Pierson extended his hand. "Mrs. Davenport, what a pleasure meeting such a beautiful lady." He took Sonia's hand. "I wish I had known, you could have waited in my office."

"Nice to meet you," said Sonia, smiling. She was dressed as an Afghan lady, without a *pardah.*

Elijah completed the introductions with, "This is Ishmael Khan and Abdul Aziz." Ishmael smiled, looking dashing in his Afghan attire with his knife in its scabbard at his waist. He stepped forward to give Pierson a hug, as was his custom, when Pierson proffered his hand. So he shook it saying, "*Salaam Aleikoum.*"

Then he shook Abdul Aziz's hand saying, "*Salaam Aleikoum.*"

"*Salaam Aleikoum,*" said Aiyasha.

Elijah thought, thank goodness he didn't give Aiyasha a hug.

"Why don't you all come in for a cup of tea," said Pierson, with a formal gesture towards his office.

Elijah looked at his watch and said, "It's getting late and we do have to make some purchases. But we will come and see you again before we leave." Elijah thanked him again and shook his hand with great fervor.

They drove to a store that looked promising and Ishmael bought two large cooking pans and two gas stoves. They moved on and stopped at a butcher's shop. Various cuts of lamb hung on hooks. The smell of raw meat permeated the air. Flies buzzed around.

"Take your choice, Ishmael," said Elijah, swatting at a fly.

Ishmael pointed to a large leg of lamb. "This one," he said to the butcher, who hefted it off the hook and set it on his cutting block. With his cleaver and a band saw he cut it to smaller sections the way Ishmael directed him to. He wrapped it up in newspaper and gave it to Ishmael. They moved to another store and Ishmael bought a sack of rice and a sack of potatoes. Still further down Ishmael stopped and pointed. "Live chickens."

"What are we going to do with chickens?" asked Elijah.

"They will make a good gift to the villagers," said Ishmael. "How much?" he asked the poultry merchant. After some haggling they settled on a price. He bought a cage with a rooster and six hens. When he carried it to the SUV, Aiyasha looked at them and the chickens clucked at her. She was so taken aback that she started laughing. Sonia, seeing Aiyasha so happy, joined in the laughter.

Elijah looked at Ishmael; "Can we go back now?"

"Yes," said Ishmael, "we have all we need. Wait, we need some boots for Abdul Aziz. Remember she has chappals."

"Oh, yes," said Elijah, "I forgot."

Ishmael asked one of the hawkers where he could find boots and shoes. The man pointed to a store farther down the street.

Now they had a problem. Aiyasha had henna dyed designs on her feet, and she was dressed as a man. Ishmael wasn't fazed. He took one of Aiyasha's flip-flops and used it to size the boot he needed. Elijah paid for it and took it back to Aiyasha who tried it on. It fit. Soon they were on the road again, with Aiyasha smiling at her new socks and boots. Aiyasha stretched her legs and said, "I can wiggle my toes, but the socks feel so warm."

"You'll get used to them," said Sonia with a smile.

At the village, they carried all the things that Ishmael had so carefully selected. It was three p.m. and the men were still working in the fields. Ishmael called one of the young boys who were playing in the creek. The boy accompanied him while he carried the cage of chickens to the open ground away from the dwellings and set it down. The chickens kept clucking softly.

Ishmael said to the boy, "What's your name?"

"Jahan."

"Jahan," said Ishmael, "these chickens are for the whole village, but you will have the fun of feeding them every day. Do you think you can do that?"

"Ji ha (yes)," the boy said, nodding.

"And when the chickens start laying eggs, the first six eggs will be yours. Do you like that?"

Jahan nodded again, smiling, *"Ji."*

"I will talk to your dad this evening when he comes in and ask him if that's all right."

Ishmael got out the two gas stoves and set it up. He brought water and the pans and soon had rice cooking. He called Abdul Aziz and said, "Can you watch the rice? I'm going to make pilaf."

"Yes, I know how," said Aiyasha.

Next he laid out the cut pieces of lamb on a board he found and started sorting out the various spices. Sonia walked over and asked him, "Can I help too?"

Ishmael gave her the job of shelling a large amount of pistachios and a bag of almonds. "They both have to be sliced, and the onions to be peeled and sliced also."

The women of the village seeing the activity going on came to watch and help. Sonia spoke to them and they brought her knives to do the chopping. Ishmael had some of them build a fire like they usually did and soon had them frying somosas that smelled delicious. The odor of food floated in the air and drew more children to the area.

Sonia told them to sit down. "Here, you children, peel these onions." Some of them soon had tears in their eyes. Elijah sat and watched.

After about three hours of continuous activity the meal was ready. Ishmael was pleased. He ran back and forth checking everything one last time. Tasting a dish here and hurrying off to the next. The men trickled in from the fields, washed up and spread their prayer cloths on the ground and the headman Sayed lead them in prayers. Ishmael and Abdul Aziz joined in the prayers, moving away from the fire and the cooking, kneeling on their own prayer cloths. Elijah and Sonia also knelt down, each quiet in his and her own prayers. When they were done, Ishmael went over to the headman and invited him to start the meal.

They brought plates of their own and partook of the feast that Ishmael and company had prepared. The pilaf had chunks of lamb buried in mounds of yellow rice, cooked with raisins, almonds and pistachios and topped with a layer of onions fried to a crisp. There was mutton soup, kebabs and *samosas*, and yogurt and *raitha* sauce.

The women served the children who gathered together as a group. When all had their plates filled and had settled down cross-legged on the ground, Ishmael and Aiyasha filled their plates and moved back to the spot where Elijah and Sonia and Sayed were seated. Sayed addressed Ishmael; "You have honored us with your exquisite cooking. We will remember this day for a long time." Turning to Elijah he said, "Thank you for the chickens."

Before they retired for the night Elijah and Sonia sat on the veranda of Sayed's house along with Sayed and his wife and talked for a while.

Elijah wondered where Rehman and gang were. Sayed had told him that the Taliban was known to have a stronghold in Taloqan. Perhaps they should turn east towards Pakistan.

*   *   *

Iqbal travelled about six kilometers before finding a village with a gas station. After filling up with gas he called Rehman. "I found a gas station," he said. He gave his location and paused to look around. No one nearby. "I checked with the owner and no Range Rover with the type of passengers we're looking for have come this way."

"I guess we should turn north then," said Rehman, sounding disappointed. "However, we'll join you to fill up before we backtrack. We've lost a day. But we'll find him." He clicked off and swore in Arabic.

Chapter Nineteen

Elijah had broached the subject on Islamic Law and Sayed was hard pressed to answer some of the questions. "Well," said Elijah, "take the extreme case of the stoning of women. How can one man or a group of only men, be the jury and the judge against a woman? Doesn't she have the right to express her side of what may have happened? And even if the woman is guilty, isn't the punishment too severe? How many men have committed the sin of infidelity and have never been censured?"

Sayed was visibly getting uneasy in his bearing. His hands opened and closed as if he wished he didn't have to look at that side of the picture. He seemed a patient man as he looked down contemplating the question Elijah had put so bluntly. Finally he took a deep breath before he spoke. "These are important points you bring up. But no system is infallible. In your own country you have smart lawyers who can twist the interpretation of the law. I believe a jury found O.J. Simpson not guilty, when everyone believed he was? We read the news too. How many innocent men have you sent to the gallows?" Sayed was getting excited. His usual calmness had been rattled. An owl hooted in the stillness of the night air.

Elijah had no intention of putting Sayed on the defensive. He tried to bring the discussion down to a lower key.

"Yes," Elijah said softly, "justice may not have been served in the cases you mention. But they all had legal representation. Mistakes may have been made. But I am talking about basic rights. Why do women have to hide their faces and their heads? The Taliban has made up a list of rules for women that is unthinkable anywhere else in the world. A woman doctor may not be alone with a male patient? Women may not wear cosmetics? These are just a few that I have read about."

"Yes, the Taliban have made a list of rules that have no bearing on Islamic law. But you must admit, some of these things you refer to are traditions, like the wearing of the burkha. Many women like to do so."

"Yes," said Elijah, "but they should be given the choice. They should never be compelled to wear them. Therein lies the difference."

"You are a very wise man," said Sayed, "why don't you stay here a while. We can have many discussions."

Sonia sat near Elijah though she didn't voice an opinion. Ishmael was resting under a tree after all the work he had put in preparing the feast for the village. Aiyasha also was resting with the young girls of the village. They seemed to gravitate towards her. What they had in common was their youth and the school studies they wanted to share with her.

Elijah and Sayed talked on. Sonia was on the verge of falling asleep when she became aware of a sweet scent that pervaded the night air.

"What is that sweet scent?" asked Sonia.

"That is *Rath ki Rani*," said Sayed. "Also known as Queen of the Night." He paused to take a deep breath. "It could have come from India. The history of Afghanistan is varied. He moved to a more comfortable position. "Did you know," he continued, "that Alexander the Great, the king of Macedonia, when he marched through Afghanistan to invade India became wary of his retreat back to his country being blocked. He spent three months in a ruthless campaign against the Afghans. So cruel were his methods that his name has not been forgotten, even after twenty-three hundred years. Each generation has passed on these stories to the next. To this day, Afghan mothers use his name to hush their babies. Many Afghans are light skinned and have blue eyes, because many of his men settled in Afghanistan."

"I didn't know that," said Elijah, "it's fascinating history."

"Well," said Sonia. "I'm ready to hit the sack. It's been an exciting day and now I must bid you, Sayed and Mrs. Sayed a very good night."

"Good night, Mrs. Elijah," said Sayed's wife in Pushtu.

*   *   *

Early the next morning, they loaded up the SUV once more. Ishmael left one of the gas stoves with Sayed. Elijah noted that they needed a vehicle with a little more space and perhaps a larger gas tank. He addressed Ishmael, and Sonia, "If we get a bigger vehicle, like a passenger van, we could all probably sleep in it too. We won't need a tent. What do you think?"

"I think that will work," said Ishmael

"But what will we do with the Range Rover?" asked Sonia.

"Perhaps Mister Pierson can help us in that regard," said Elijah.

"I only rented it. I don't own it, we can't just trade it in."

"Yes, I know. But we could negotiate something and perhaps the dealer you rented it from could pick it up from here. We'll give them a call once we find a suitable alternative. We'll find out when we're back in town."

The men were back in the fields. The noise of the children was absent. Probably in school, thought Sonia. Sayed Hassan gave Elijah a bear hug and Ishmael was next. He put his hands together in an Indian Namaste to Sonia. She did the same, raising her hands to Sayed, *"Bahuth shukria* (thank you very much),*"* she said smiling

Aiyasha had retired to the SUV. Elijah said to Sayed, "Abdul Aziz is slightly under the weather. He said to thank you." He knew Aiyasha didn't want to be hugged by Sayed for obvious reasons. Those were some of the pitfalls of being in disguise, thought Elijah.

"Allah be with you all," said Sayed.

*   *   *

Back in town, Elijah once again sought out the Red Cross Center. Pierson came out to meet them. "We need your help again," said Elijah, "we need a larger vehicle. Is there a place we can find something like a passenger van, something bigger than our SUV?"

Pierson considered the question for a minute and said, "Yes, there is a dealer of sorts. He may have something you like. What about the Range Rover?"

"That's the other problem," said Elijah, "this is a rental from Jullundur in India. We need to get it back to them."

"Let's go over to this dealer I know and find out if he has any suggestions," said Pierson.

The people on the sides of the road plied their trade as usual. The aroma of cooked meat filled the air. The butcher's shop where they had stopped at yesterday was open for business. Sonia and Aiyasha waited in the SUV while Elijah, Ishmael and Pierson went to see the car dealer. As they waited, an Afghani woman walked up to Sonia.

"You want to buy precious stones?" she asked in Pushtu. Aiyasha looked at Sonia. "Did you understand?"

"Yes," said Sonia. She turned to the woman and said, "Can I see them?" She stepped out of the SUV. Aiyasha joined her.

The woman took out a package from a band around her waist and carefully opened a rolled up scarf and there in her palm were some of the most beautiful uncut precious stones Sonia had ever seen. For a moment Sonia felt she had been swept back in time to the fabled land of Ali Baba. She pointed to four stones as big as marbles.

"What are these?" asked Sonia, picking one up and running her fingers around it. "It has sharp edges."

"Those are uncut diamonds," said the Afghani woman.

"Are these Pigeon's Blood Rubies?" asked Sonia pointing to yet another group of six stones.

"Yes," said the woman, "from Burma."

"And these?"

"Those are Aquamarines from Ceylon, and these are Pearls from the Persian Gulf."

Sonia was open-mouthed with wonder.

"How much do you want for them?" asked Sonia.

"Ten thousand Pakistani rupees," said the Afghan woman.

Sonia figured it out. At forty rupees to the dollar that was almost two hundred and fifty dollars. That was a bargain by any standards, if the stones were genuine. That's a chance she would have to take. She looked in her purse. She had about ten thousand Indian rupees, which were about the same in exchange rates as the Pakistani rupees.

Sonia studied the woman. "Why are you selling these stones?"

"These belonged to my husband. He just died in an accident and I have no money. I have two small children and I would like to take them with me to my father's house in another village far to the north. My husband would never have sold them, but I need money for food and travel."

"I'm sorry to hear about your husband," said Sonia continuing to talk in Pushtu. "May Allah protect you and your children. I'll give you all that I have. It's nearly twelve thousand rupees." She took all the money in notes and handed them carefully to the woman.

The Afghani counted them, then rolled them back into a bundle and wrapped it again in a scarf and tied to her waist. She gave Sonia the scarf with the precious stones.

"How did you pick me?" said Sonia. "You could have gone to a store."

"You look different," said the woman smiling. "I intuitively believed I could trust you. I'm afraid of the big stores. They will always rob you." She raised her hands in a salaam and walked away down the road. Their eyes followed her for a while until the crowd blocked their view.

"Those are very beautiful stones," said Aiyasha, as excited as Sonia.

"Yes," said Sonia, "I hope I have enough money to have them cut and polished."

"My mother gave me a diamond," said Aiyasha, "I still have it with me."

"Really? Didn't the men search you before they imprisoned you?"

"They did but I had it on a chain around my waist where it still is."

"But why would you wear it there?"

"I moved it from my neck to my waist when all the trouble started."

"You poor girl," said Sonia and pressed her shoulder with her free hand. She took out her own silk kerchief from her purse and moved the stones to their new home. She wrapped and tied it put them in the depths of her bag and zippered it shut. She threw the old scarf away and watched it go flying in the wind to land on the side of the road.

"I hope there's some way to verify if these stones are genuine," she said to Aiyasha.

"You just bought a prince's ransom in jewels," said Aiyasha.

"Where did you learn to talk like that?" asked Sonia.

"Oh, I read as much as I can."

Elijah, Ishmael and Pierson came back. They had found a car dealer. Sonia and Aiyasha got in and Elijah drove to the parking lot filled with a variety of pick-ups and trucks. What had caught Elijah's eye was a '97 GMC Savana passenger van. It had plenty of room and a large enough fuel tank to give them a lot of mileage, about four hundred miles, between fill-ups. They negotiated a price and Elijah's credit card was capable of taking the burden of the transaction. Using his satellite phone he let Sonia talk to the dealer in Jullundur into leaving the Range Rover at the location where they were. She let the dealers talk to each other until they came to an agreement.

Ishmael was highly appreciative of the new vehicle. Together they moved all their equipment to the new land cruiser, including the rifles. Elijah got a map from the dealer. Ishmael, Sonia and Aiyasha climbed into the back, while Pierson got into the passenger seat and Elijah drove him back to the Red Cross Center.

Pierson stepped out and beckoned to Elijah to follow him. When they were alone he said, "Since you're being followed by the Taliban and Fundamentalist Muslims I think I can give some ammunition in case you're forced into a trap."

"What kind of ammunition?" asked Elijah. "We have three rifles and enough cartridge packs."

"This is a little more sophisticated," said Pierson. "I salvaged it from the US army when I was working with them. They let me keep it. Would you like to see what I have?"

"Yes," said Elijah, intrigued by the word "sophisticated."

Pierson took him into a garage and opened a safe. He took out a package and laid it on a work table and opened it. He separated the items carefully. He picked up something that looked like putty and handed it to Elijah. "This is semtex, a plastic explosive that can be easily shaped around a detonator." He opened another package and gave Elijah a small device. "These are the detonators which have a timer that can be preset."

He turned a dial which had seconds and minutes calibrated and turned it back to zero. "It gives an electric pulse after it counts down." He put it back in its box. There were five of them. He next took out a gadget that looked like a TV remote. "And this is the remote that triggers the detonator."

"Oh, my God," said Elijah. "I can't think of a scenario where I could use this."

"It's up to you," said Pierson. "It's yours if you want it. Store them in their packets separately."

"I'll take it," said Elijah. Pierson helped carry it out to the van where Elijah placed the large box in the rear of the van. He looked at Ishmael who was watching him. "Remind me to explain what this is," he said.

"Yes, *saab,*" said Ishmael.

Sonia walked up to Pierson and said, "Excuse me. Is there a jeweler in this little town?"

"Yes," said Pierson, "just a hundred yards in the opposite direction."

"Thank you," said Sonia, then to Elijah, "Could we try and find this store? I just invested all my savings in some uncut precious stones."

"Really?" said Elijah, surprise on his face. They said goodbye to Pierson and he started the van and pointed it in the direction Pierson had indicated. They found the "Afghan Jewelers" store. Sonia took her purse and went in, with the others following.

The owner of the store came to help Sonia. She took out the scarf with the stones and spread it on the glass counter and asked, "Could you tell me how much these stones are worth?"

The jeweler bent down and looked at them. He then placed his loop to his eye and looked at each stone in detail. "These are very good stones," he said. "Normally the Afghan men and women never sell their stones. They hang onto them for generations. These are worth about three or four thousand US dollars. If you want me to authenticate them I will have to charge you a fee."

"Let's do that," said Sonia. "I hope it won't take too long."

"No," said the jeweler. "About half an hour."

"We can wait."

The man sat at his work table with a loop on his eye and began the process of scraping and cleaning and putting the stones under a microscope.

Elijah moved around looking at all the jewels on display. He finally stopped in front of a display case with diamond studded rings. He stopped in his tracks and stared. He had been telling everyone that Sonia was his wife but there was no evidence of a ring on her hand and nor on his.

The jeweler finished his assessment of the stones and gave Sonia a detailed certificate as to the quality of each item. "It's as I said," said the man. "They are all authentic and of fine quality. You are very lucky."

"Thank you," said Sonia, paying the fee.

As they trooped out to the van, Elijah hesitated. "Why don't you wait for me," he said and walked back into the store.

He talked to the jeweler again, pointing to various diamond studded rings. Finally satisfied, he paid for his purchase and put the package in his pocket.

*   *   *

Rehman and his group waited at the cross-road in their Jeeps. It was three hours later that the call came through from Iqbal.

"What did you find?" asked Rehman anxiously.

"Not very much," said Iqbal. "I found a gas station but they have not seen anyone of the description I gave them."

"That means they went north," said Rehman in disgust. "Stay there," he continued. "We'll join you and fill up our tanks before we retrace our steps." He clicked off and gave the other men the news.

They reached the gas station with its one store and filled up their tanks.

"There's a change in plans," said Rehman. "There's no point in in four of us following Elijah. Why don't Suleman and I go north while the other two Jeeps go east to Jullundur. They must eventually end up in that city. You stay out of sight and make enquiries and keep vigilant."

"Seems like a plan," said Iqbal and the other two men.

The two Jeeps continued east and Suleman and Rehman went west until they reached the crossroad and turned north. The wrath in Rehman's mind against Elijah made him curse again in Arabic.

Chapter Twenty

It was six in the morning and they were ready to leave Sayed Hassan's village. Elijah pointed to the route on his map. "We'll go south along here," he said, "and once we hit the main road, we turn east and make a beeline for Peshawar, and then Jullundur."

Aiyasha had been quiet as usual. "May I say something?" she said quite abruptly.

"Yes," said Elijah, looking up at her.

"You have saved my life and I'm grateful. But I'm still distressed about how they will treat my parents." She related the whole sequence of events that had led to her being accused and condemned to be stoned.

This was the story that unfolded before them. They could well imagine Aiyasha with her good looks had begun filling out as she blossomed into a young woman and drew the attention of all the young men including some older fogies, one of whom was the mullah Hammid. He taught the Koran at the local school, and started taking a special interest in Aiyasha at this stage. He was about fifty-five years old. It started with him bending over her from behind, looking at her work. It moved to touching her on the shoulder, as he corrected her exercise or making a point of something important. Aiyasha liked the special attention. She was an eager learner and naïve enough not to comprehend what was going on.

One day he asked her to stay after class to instruct her further. When all the students had trickled away to their homes, the mullah, the man of God sat down next to her and continued the exercise of the day from the Koran. Before she knew it, she found his hand under her skirt on her thigh. She was alarmed, and wondered, what do I do now. His hand moved further up her thigh. She jumped up with a cry. The man tried to restrain her. The table prevented her from fully standing up with the man's arm around her; they fell backwards onto the floor. Aiyasha felt dazed and so was the mullah, in a semi-conscious state. She jumped up, grabbed her books and ran out of the building and did not pause until she reached home, her breath coming in loud gasps. She found her mother in the kitchen, cooking, and burst into tears, telling her all that had happened.

At first her mother couldn't quite believe her story, "But a mullah won't do such things. Are you sure, my dear?"

Aiyasha nodded and clung to her. Fatima didn't know what to do. "We'll have to tell your father when he comes home."

Her father looked at her in amazement. "He is a mullah. Who will believe you against his word? We have been making plans for your betrothal to the son of one of our friends in another village. Now with your good name at risk, they will surely change their minds."

"You have been making arrangements for my life and you haven't said a word to me," asked Aiyasha incredulously.

Mohammed Shalhoub stared at his daughter and walked away into another room.

"Soon I heard about the mullah's and the Elders' decision that I had been accused of having relations with three men and had declared the ultimate penalty of a stoning in three days," said Aiyasha.

The news of the mullah's and the Elders' decision spread like wildfire. Aiyasha couldn't believe it.

"But, mother, she said, "they are lying and so is the mullah." Her mother was in tears.

"Oh, Allah!" Fatima said in despair, "why did this have to happen to us? I tried talking to the neighbors. I told them this was a bunch of lies. But they wouldn't listen to me. They are afraid of the mullah and the Taliban. What has happened to this country?"

"There is a ray of hope," Mohammed said, "we can try to take you to another village, tonight, when it's dark." Her brother Abdur couldn't understand all that was happening. He was worried and scared.

Aiyasha sat fretting, wringing her hands over and over again. Why am I running away, she thought, when I haven't done anything wrong? Is this how women are treated all over the world?

Her mother packed a few of her clothes in a knapsack and amid tears, hugged her and bid her farewell. Abdur was asleep in his room. Aiyasha left with her father into the dark night.

But the mullah had planted guards at various points for just such an eventuality. A throng of villagers with lighted torches escorted Mohammed and Aiyasha back to their home.

Aiyasha stayed home, like she was under house arrest. Her thoughts were dark and hopeless. Is there no one I can appeal to for help?

On the third day, the mullah and his men came for her. They bound her hands in front of her and lead her away. Her mother, unable to bear her feelings of despair, fell into a deep faint.

The whole village had gathered in the compound. They had dug a hole into which she was lowered. Her shoulders and head stuck above ground. The obvious target when the stoning started was the head of the victim. The compound buzzed with the chatter of the crowd. Not one of her friends and neighbors showed any pity on their faces. Someone lowered the burkha over her face.

It was into this melee that Elijah and his party had so abruptly intervened and saved the girl's life, leaving a very disappointed, angry and dangerous mullah, who could still make life miserable for Aiyasha's parents and her brother.

*   *   *

All three of them, Elijah, Sonia and Ishmael sat silently as though turned to stone while listening to Aiyasha. It had taken an hour for Aiyasha to recount this painful chapter of her life.

When she had finished her story, she looked at all their faces. "I would like you to take me back to my village and I will confront this mullah and tell the villagers the truth. I'd rather die than have them believe this of me."

Ishmael was the first to speak up, "We have to go back and challenge this man and give Aiyasha a chance to be acquitted, and let the people see him for what he is."

Elijah agreed, but he wasn't sure of a plan of action. "This is your country," he said turning to Ishmael, "do you think a woman can speak out against a man, much less a mullah?"

"There are mullahs and mullahs," said Ishmael. "Most are good but some are worthless. We will add our voices if we get a chance."

Elijah shook his head, frowned deeply and walked to and fro. "It doesn't look good," he said swinging a fist into the palm of his other hand in frustration. "It's dangerous to go back. I'm an engineer for Christ's sake, not a soldier," he said to no one in particular. He stopped in his tracks. "Maybe Sayed Hassan can help us. I could ask him to accompany us." He turned to Aiyasha. "We have to be honest with him and tell him your story. The first thing to do is take off your disguise." He turned to Sonia. "What do you think?"

"It's worth a try," said Sonia. "You don't want this hanging over her head for the rest of her life when she's innocent."

Aiyasha slowly took off her disguise and Sonia put the various pieces in her knapsack.

We're going back to the lion's den, thought Elijah, and the delay will give Fundamentalist Muslims a chance to catch-up with us. Why hasn't D'Souza called back about the helicopter? He took out the phone and made the call. When he had D'Souza on the line he asked without preamble, "What have you found out?"

"Still no positive answers from all sources, Mister Davenport. I have sent one of my men to Delhi to find a private firm who will rent a helicopter with a pilot to go to Afghanistan. So far he hasn't had any luck. One company has the equipment but they refused. They think they'll be shot down by terrorists or by American artillery. It doesn't look good, Mister Davenport."

"All right, but keep trying. Thank you Mister D'Souza, I'll call again." He told Sonia about the call, shaking his head in disappointment.

Elijah got them together in the van and drove back to the village they had left earlier that day. It was now about eight in the morning. When Sayed saw who they were he walked towards them. This time he saw Aiyasha dressed, as she was, an Afghani maiden. Elijah, Sonia and Ishmael told him her story and asked him if he would talk to the people at Aiyasha's village. Sayed shook his head sadly. "Sometimes these things happen. I will come with you. We will try and convince them of her innocence."

"Now here's the plan," said Elijah. "We have not endeared ourselves to the people of that village the last time we were there. Their reaction when they see us will be to kill us all if they can. Ishmael, Sonia and myself will carry our guns and stand by while Aiyasha and Sayed make their appeal. But if things go wrong and they rush us, the three of us will shoot to kill until all of us are back in our vehicle and we make a run for it once again. We can only hope they don't have weapons of their own. This is a very risky operation and Sayed is putting his life on the line too for us. I shall put it to a vote to all of you. Do you still want to go through with this?"

Ishmael nodded and so did Sonia. Sayed who had been listening said, "Yes." Aiyasha was silent knowing the great sacrifice each of them was making on her behalf. Sayed turned to Elijah and said, "Let me get some men to help us. We can pick them up from a place nearby."

They all got in the van and drove a few miles north and stopped at a chai shop with a few ramshackle buildings. Sayed went alone into the teashop and after a while came back with three men who carried their own rifles. Elijah got out and opened the sliding door. Sayed introduced the men who nodded and climbed into the van. Ishmael and the two women made room for them. They now had six rifles. Elijah hoped this show of force would get them through the next few hours.

It took four hours to drive back to Aiyasha's village. During the long drive, Sonia, kept thinking about what Elijah had said. "We will have to shoot to kill." God, I don't want to kill anybody. I don't even think I can hit something I aim at. What if I kill a poor innocent child? It's too late now for target practice. I think I'll shoot at their feet.

It was close to noon when they drove in cautiously and parked near the buildings. Elijah, Sonia and Ishmael each took a rifle and stepped out, and the three men joined them. Sayed and Aiyasha walked forward with Elijah behind them. Aiyasha did not have her burkha or purdah on. Sonia, Ishmael and the new recruits waited by the van with their rifles ready. The women and children saw them coming and let out a cry. "Aiyasha's back," yelled many who had recognized her and a crowd soon formed and moved towards the visitors.

Sayed held up his hands and stopped them. "It's 'Sayed the Preacher,'" shouted a young boy.

Sayed spoke in a deep powerful voice. Elijah had never heard him speak like that before. It was as though Sayed was performing on a stage, assuming a new character.

"Where are your elders?" his voice boomed. "Have them step forward." Several men moved towards him. A murmur ran through the crowd as more of them recognized Aiyasha. The mullah was there with the elders. Sayed spoke in his commanding baritone as though his whole being was transformed. He was an actor on a stage, playing a part that all their lives depended on. His six foot three frame towered over the crowd as he raised his arms with his garments falling about him like a modern day Moses parting the Red Sea. His eyes glinted and the passion in the words he spoke held the crowd captive.

"I can't believe it," whispered Elijah. "The last time we were here this crowd wanted our blood. Now Sayed has them under his spell."

"You have accused this woman and not given her a chance to defend herself," said Sayed. "Where are the three men who said they had sex with her? Will you please step forward."

The mullah tried to speak, but Sayed raised his hand again to silence him. Sayed had taken on an aura of authority. Each movement of his arms and tilt of his head held his audience. When he took a step forward the men standing nearest to him retreated a step forcing those behind them to do the same. "Will you step forward," he roared.

Three men reluctantly moved through the crowd and stood in front of him.

"Did this woman have sex with you?" asked Sayed, his eyes holding them in his hypnotic gaze. No preamble for him, thought Elijah. He went straight to the point.

All three of them shook their heads. "No, the mullah asked us to say so and we agreed, because he is a very powerful man."

Sayed now looked at Aiyasha and said, "Tell us exactly what happened." A deadly hush descended over the crowd. Never before had a woman been asked to testify against a man. Now a mullah had to face a common woman. Such was the power of Sayed's presence.

Aiyasha moved forward. "This man," she said, pointing to the mullah. "Under the pretext of teaching me, after everyone had gone home tried to molest me. I fought him and ran away to my mother. That is the truth and I had to come back and testify so that you may know the truth. Yet all of you were willing to believe him." She said pointing again at the mullah. "You wanted to kill me." She emphasized, stamping her foot, with tears in her eyes.

Sayed looked around again and raised his hand for silence. "The laws of Islam are quite clear. We live by the truth of an Allah who is kind and merciful. A mother corrects a child so that he or she may learn that there is a difference between right and wrong. What a child learns at its mother's knee may well determine the greatness of the man or woman that child grows up to be.

"We do not have kings to stand in judgment of our acts. We have elders and mullahs to guide us on this journey we call life. But when that person who has the scepter of power breaks that trust, we have indeed broken Islamic law. Being called a mullah does not give that man the right to bend the very laws he has been entrusted to uphold. This has happened in the past and will happen again, because someone somewhere did not learn those truths at their mother's knee.

"*Andah Vishwas*. Blind belief is dangerous, if that belief is not grounded in truth."

He continued, holding his audience until every adult there had a tear in his or her eye. "You have done a great injustice to this young woman who is innocent," his voice thundered. In an open compound no audio system could have made his words more deafening.

A mighty hush fell over the crowd. Sonia who was close to Aiyasha and near the jury of Elders, trembled in anticipation. She searched each face. Which way will they vote, she wondered. The evidence is clear. It was the mullah who had lied. But would the Elders defy the mullah who had ties to the Taliban?

Chapter Twenty-One

Finally, an elder found his voice. They were speaking in Pushtu, "We have been blind and it will not happen again. The mullah in question is no longer a member of this village. Though I say this, we shall put it to a vote. Please raise your hand, those in favor of letting this mullah go his way." Several hands went up. "It is decided then, you may leave as soon as possible. You are now considered no longer a member of this village from this day onwards."

The mullah is given the uncomplimentary title of Persona Non Grata, thought Sonia.

"You cannot do this," shouted mullah Hammid, finding his voice at last. "I have the support of the Taliban and they will not be happy to hear about you," he said pointing a finger at Sayed.

"You have been proven guilty without a doubt of lying and manipulating evidence by witnesses who have confessed of being bought by you," said Sayed, without having to raise his voice. "You have also molested an innocent girl. How would you explain that to the Taliban? In fact you should be placed under arrest and taken to the Taliban."

Under this onslaught, with all eyes now on him, the mullah slowly slunk into the crowd who let him pass and he disappeared.

The Elder who had spoken last, turned to Aiyasha and opened wide his arms. "Welcome back, my dear child."

Aiyasha's mother ran forward to hug her daughter, followed by her brother and her father. They stood in a group talking while the crowd slowly dispersed.

Sayed addressed Aiyasha's father, "Mister Shalhoub, you are welcome to come and make your home in our village."

"I thank you, for bringing Aiyasha back and for inviting us," said Shalhoub. "But things should be better now that the mullah has left and my daughter is faultless."

Elijah walked down from where he had been standing by the van, observing the drama. He met Sonia and Aiyasha with her parents.

Aiyasha put her hand on her father's shoulder and said, "This is Mr. Elijah and his wife, Sonia. They have been very good to me, Father and I'm going with them."

She has acquitted herself before the village, but she has not forgiven them, thought Sonia.

"But my dear daughter," said Fatima. "Now that you've been proven innocent, we can continue with our preparations for your betrothal. And you will move to your husband's village." She looked pleadingly at Aiyasha.

Aiyasha shook her head. "I don't wish to get married just now, Mother. This lady, Sonia, has promised to help me with my education. There are no opportunities here to do that, you well know, Mother and Father."

"Who are these people?" asked Fatima. "We know nothing about them. It's true they saved your life, but what are their intentions?"

They were talking in Pushtu and Elijah and Sonia could over-hear some of what was being said, but they held their council. Elijah was nervous. Things had gone too well and he was eager to get the hell out of this place and not have anything change the outcome.

"I will come back, Mother. Things have changed drastically here for me. I cannot stay another day with these people who betrayed me. Please understand. I do love you both."

Fatima could not contain her tears. She grabbed Aiyasha in her arms and held her to her bosom. "We lost you once and we are losing you again."

"I will write to you, Mother," said Aiyasha. Then taking out a piece of paper she gave it to her mother, "Will you please write down our address?" She turned to Elijah as though to explain. "I have never had occasion to write to anyone."

Elijah gave her a pen and her mother spent a few minutes writing, using Aiyasha's back as a support.

Aiyasha extended her hand to her brother, "Come here, you." He came towards her with a nervous smile and they hugged. He smelled the attar perfume she used. Aiyasha had tears in her eyes, "Goodbye little brother. I will come back and see you again. You keep studying hard and you'll be a great man one day." She released him and put her arm around her mother and father. Together they walked to the van.

Ishmael was the first to greet them. "We heard everything," he exclaimed excitedly, "we are happy for you Aiyasha."

Sonia embraced Aiyasha again and said, "And Mister Hassan spoke with the wisdom of Solomon."

Aiyasha looked at Ishmael and said, "These are my parents, Mohammed Shalhoub and Fatima Shalhoub."

Ishmael moved forward, swinging the rifle down to the ground and gave Mohammed a hug, then putting his hands together faced Fatima, saying, "*Salaam Aleikoum.*"

Aiyasha continued, "And this is Ishmael Khan." She put her arm around her brother's shoulder and pulled him forward and presented him to Ishmael, "And this is my brother, Abdur Shalhoub." Ishmael gave him a great hug then picked up his rifle and swung the strap back onto his shoulder.

Elijah climbed into the driver's seat with Sayed beside him. The sliding door of the van being open, Sonia and Ishmael got in the back and waited for Aiyasha, who turned back and gave each member of her family a last hug and ran back and stepped into the van. Ishmael pushed the door shut with a bang. Aiyasha was crying.

At Sayed's village, Elijah couldn't fully express his gratitude and the great respect he had developed for Sayed. He did not want to leave. He wished he could stay longer in the company of this unsung hero.

"You were absolutely magnificent, Sayed," said Elijah, "you commanded the respect of those people."

"I only said the truth. People listen when it comes from the heart."

"I know of several places where a man like you could make a difference on the world stage."

"My place is here with my people in this village."

"I am honored to have known you, Sayed. It is with great reluctance that I must take my leave. May God bless you and may we meet again someday."

"May Allah bless your day. *Salaam Aleikoum,*" said, Sayed, smiling as he gave Elijah his Afghan hug.

Aiyasha stepped out of the van and so did Sonia and Ishmael.

"*Shukria bapuji* (thank you)," said Aiyasha giving the kind man a hug.

"*Salaam Aleikoum, beti,*" said Sayed, returning her embrace.

Sonia now stepped forward and raised her hands together, "*Salaam Aleikoum,*" she said.

Ishmael followed and soon the group was back on the road again. They were on their way. This time, hopefully all the way back to Jullundur.

*   *   *

Rehman, and Suleman made discreet inquiries at a truck stop. Yes an SUV with four occupants had stopped there. There was also a story of a woman being rescued from a stoning at a nearby village by three men.

"Interesting," Rehman said, "looks like they're not afraid of their own safety."

They made their way to the village. After making inquiries they found out that the mullah had been sent away. An Elder was willing to talk with them. Rehman got the whole story, including the return of the woman with her rescuers and her acquittal.

"According to you, the woman was innocent?" asked Rehman.

"Yes," said the Elder.

"You were going to kill a woman who had done no wrong?"

"It was the mullah who was responsible for the whole thing."

"In other words the three men did a good deed by saving her?"

"Yes, thank Allah, they came along."

"How long ago did this happen?"

"The last incident happened about two days ago when the woman and Sayed a mullah from another village came with her. He talked like a Moses. For some reason the three men who had accused the woman confessed that they had lied and that put our mullah in trouble. We sent him packing. He's afraid of the

Taliban now." The Elder looked apprehensively at the six men. "Who are you people?"

"We belong to Fundamentalist Muslims." He paused then asked, "What were they driving?"

"A van," said the Elder.

A group of curious villagers had gathered around them, hoping for some new excitement. On the outskirts stood Fatima who had heard the questioning by the strangers. As Rehman and his cohorts elbowed their way back to their vehicles, Fatima whispered, "May you never catch up with them."

*   *   *

The van with Elijah and his group sped down the road to Peshawar. Elijah kept thinking about Rehman and his men. He could use all the help he could find against those men.

He turned to Aiyasha and said, "We will be getting another rifle tomorrow, for you Aiyasha."

She looked up, wide eyed. "Me? I don't know how to use one, and I don't want to kill anyone. Remember, I would like to be a doctor someday."

Elijah nodded. "So you will. But just now, we need all the help we can get. We will show you how to fire a rifle."

"*Ha jee*," said Aiyasha, hesitantly.

"Ishmael," said Elijah. "When I find a good spot I'll pull over and we'll give Aiyasha a lesson on how to use a rifle."

"Very well, *Jee*," said Ishmael.

It wasn't long before Elijah spotted a hill near the road. He pulled over and stopped.

"Good," said Ishmael. "I need to make a target," he said to Sonia.

She tore a page from her notebook and gave it to him. He used her pen to draw wide circles on it and took the rifle and walked over to the small hill. He used a twig pushed into the clay hill to hold the target about five feet off the ground.

They had all followed him and waited about thirty feet behind. He walked back and Aiyasha stood beside him nervously wringing her hands.

"Wait," said Elijah. "The report of the rifle is very loud. Why don't you and Sonia bind your scarves over your heads covering your ears like this." He took a scarf from his pocket and wound it around his head ending up under his chin.

Aiyasha and Sonia turned to watch him. He tied a knot in the scarf and adjusted the cloth so that his ears were covered. He then took the loose ends and pushed them into the ear cavity.

"Try that," he said.

Ishmael joined Sonia and Aiyasha in binding a scarf around their individual heads and soon looked like they were part of a costume party.

"Like this?" asked Aiyasha.

"Yes," said Sonia helping her push the ends into her ear cavity.

"Got it," said Ishmael. He looked at Aiyasha and said, "Are we ready?"

"Yes," said Aiyasha.

He pointed the rifle at the target and showed Aiyasha the stance to take, and how to hold it firmly. "Then you squeeze this trigger, like this. Are you ready?"

Aiyasha and the rest of them said, "Yes."

Ishmael pulled the trigger and the sound was enormous. The rifle bucked in his hand. Aiyasha threw up her hands to cover her ears in spite of the headband.

"Now it's your turn," said Ishmael, handing over the rifle to Aiyasha, who timidly took it, pointing it at the hill. He had her make some adjustments to her stance and her grip on the rifle.

"Go ahead and gently squeeze the trigger." Aiyasha did, and there was another report that shook the valley. Aiyasha looked pleased. She did falter backwards with the kick of the rifle. She frowned and sniffed the air.

"What's that smell?" she asked.

"That's cordite," said Elijah.

"That's the gunpowder in the cartridge," said Ishmael.

"Is it poisonous?" asked Aiyasha.

"No," said Ishmael. "Don't worry about it." He pointed to the target. "Try five more times."

Aiyasha got back into her sharp shooter stance.

When she was done, Ishmael said, "*Bahuth acha* (Very good)."

Elijah patted Aiyasha on her shoulder saying, "*Bahuth acha*, you will be our back-up when we need help."

Sonia had been watching Aiyasha's training and she felt this would be a good time to improve her shooting skills. Here was a target all set up and ready.

"Could I get some practice shooting at the target too?" she asked.

"Yes, of course," said Elijah, handing over the rifle Aiyasha had just used.

Sonia took the stance and sighted and squeezed the trigger. A hole appeared on the far right of the square target. She sighted again, held her breath and aimed for the center and fired. This time the hole appeared closer to the center. She tried again until she had three holes bunched together in the center.

"You're getting good at this," said Elijah as he took the weapon Sonia handed back to him.

"I would like to practice again, tomorrow," said Sonia.   .

"Me too," said Aiyasha, who wanted to imitate Sonia.

"All right," said Elijah, smiling. He had two gun happy women on his hands.

They piled back into the van and continued their journey.

*   *   *

Two days after Elijah's departure, Rehman and Suleman drove into Sayed's village.

"Yes," said Sayed, "we had some visitors. But who are you and what's your interest in them?"

"We are Fundamentalist Muslims," said Rehman, trying to assert his authority. "Our interest is purely political. We would appreciate you giving us any information."

"I see," said Sayed, beginning to realize this was the real thing. These men were ruthless and he had a village to protect. "What do you wish to know?"

"What were they driving and how many in the group. Did they say where they were going?"

"They were driving an SUV. They were all Afghani, two men and two women. They did say they were going to Pakistan."

"Was one of them the woman you helped acquit from a stoning at another village?"

"Yes, the poor woman was completely innocent. I'm glad I was able to help."

"Thank you for your help. *Salaam Aleikoum*," said Rehman, turning on his heel and walking away.

"*Salaam Aleikoum*," said Sayed, watching with relief as the men drove away.

A child cried in the background and a woman called out to Sayed. "Who are those men with guns, Sayed? They're not going to hurt our friends, are they?"

"They are after Elijah and his friends," shouted Sayed. "There's nothing I can do to stop them."

"I pray that Elijah makes it back," said Sayed to himself.

Chapter Twenty-Two

They all curled up in their blankets and Ishmael turned on the propane heaters he had bought. It made the van a lot more comfortable than it had been in the last few days. Elijah cracked open a couple of windows to keep air circulating.

At dawn, Ishmael cooked his breakfast of eggs and roti and they were on their way.

Elijah Looked at his map and traced a route with his finger. Southwards would take them to the main road, then east to the Khyber Pass.

Elijah turned around and asked Aiyasha, "Do you read and write English, Aiyasha?"

Aiyasha had been daydreaming about her family. Elijah's question brought her back to reality.

"We were taught in Pushtu at school, and also some English too. Why?"

"Well," said Sonia joining in the conversation. She turned to look at Aiyasha and then back again to the road, "Since you want to be a doctor, we can help you train to take the entrance exams to a good medical college in India. It's not easy, and they teach in English. You can stay with me in Jullundur. Would you like to do that?"

"You mean that?" asked Aiyasha, her face animated in a smile from ear to ear. "But how will I pay you back?"

"We won't worry about that."

"Maybe I could make a suggestion," said Elijah. "You could work at the factory part time. What do you think Sonia? You're vice president of marketing. Maybe she could become a trainee to type up reports. I don't know. You could think about it, you may come up with something."

"That's a possibility," said Sonia. "We'll have to persuade Mister D'Souza to hire her."

"As the new owner I wouldn't want to be heavy handed. Yes, Aiyasha, there will be a period of training as in everything."

"Allah be praised," said Aiyasha. Then turning to Sonia with a big smile, "You mean after my training I'll be paid? Oh, that would be wonderful. I'll actually be making money."

"I remember my first job," said Sonia chuckling at the memory. "It was so satisfying that someone would pay me for my work. It wasn't much but it was a start."

"What would you like to do, Ishmael?" asked Elijah. "Would you like to go to school to learn more about the things I have been showing you?"

"Yes," said Ishmael, "I know I'm a good mechanic, but it would be nice to know the why of things. How machinery works and the electrical part that goes hand in hand."

"Very good, you know where your heart is. You just need the opportunity. We will find you a school. You're just nineteen. There's plenty of time."

"I'm seventeen," said Aiyasha, eager to be included in the conversation. They all laughed.

So it was settled, Elijah and Sonia had taken on the responsibility of helping them get an education. They would take it one step at a time, when they reached the security and safety of Jullundur.

*   *   *

As Elijah and his group traveled south to meet the main road that would take them east to the Khyber Pass, Rehman and his men were frustrated in their search for the fugitives. They had no evidence that the group had gone through to Peshawar. They drove their two Jeeps westwards retracing their steps, hoping to encounter the elusive Elijah.

They roared past the road, where forty miles to the south, Elijah and Sonia were talking about the futures of Aiyasha and Ishmael. Rehman was in a foul mood. "Where can those infidels have gone?" he asked loudly.

"What about these side roads?" asked Suleman, pointing to the one they had just passed.

"Why would they take a detour when they're so close to the Pass?" wondered Rehman. "Keep going," he commanded.

*   *   *

To give Elijah a break Sonia decided to drive. She made good time driving a larger vehicle than she had been used to. Aiyasha watching her felt a surge of pride in her mentor. "Will you teach me to drive too?" she asked.

Sonia looked back at her and smiled. "Yes, of course, but one thing at a time. When you're ready we'll give you lessons. I'm sure Ishmael would like to drive too?"

"It would be nice to handle a car," said Ishmael. "I will be the envy of all my friends, if they should see me at the wheel of a car."

After driving for about six hours Sonia pulled over to the side of the road and Elijah took the wheel again and Sonia relaxed with Aiyasha beside her.

They traveled through mountainous country now. The road had taken the form of a wide and high bridge with shear drop offs on both sides. Further down it gradually became a valley.

Elijah had read that, millions of years ago, India had been a landmass close to the African continental plate. It had taken those millions of years to slowly drift away from Africa, until it crashed into Asia. The Indian sub-continental plate wedged itself under the Asian continental plate, pushing up what is now known as the Himalayas and the Hindu Kush Mountains, where they were now. At twenty thousand feet elevation they had found seashells, telling of the origins of the area. The Indian plate is still moving further under the Asian plate causing massive earthquakes at unpredictable intervals. The mountains are still growing.

Since the time Edmund Hillary and Tenzing Norgay's conquest of Mount Everest in 1953 the peak has grown by six feet.

They turned a sharp curve in the road and there, not thirty yards away blocking the road, stood about twenty men with rifles and enough ammunition on their belts across their shoulders to stop an army. They had run into a gang of Afghan bandits.

Elijah braked hard. "God damn it," he swore. "Aiyasha," he shouted out, "put on your disguise. Ishmael, we still have some of those packets of the plastic explosive. Give Sonia four of those and four detonators, quickly."

As Ishmael scrambled, Elijah turned to Sonia. "Put them in the glove compartment."

Sonia grabbed the packages from Ishmael stuck them in the glove box and snapped the lid shut.

Ishmael moved things around trying to hide the remaining explosives in their boxes. They worked like a team of well-oiled gears, meshing smoothly.

Aiyasha got her beard and mustache on and was frantically trying to twist the turban around her head. When Ishmael saw her struggling, he paused in his task, took the strand of turban, wound it around expertly and tucked it inside the tight folds for her. "*Shukria*," she gasped. He went back to covering up the explosives.

The van came to a stop, just yards in front of the men standing in the narrow road effectively blocking their path.

Elijah waited. Ishmael and Aiyasha – now Abdul Aziz – had their rifles in their hands. Elijah said, "We are outnumbered. Don't use your rifles. You may hold onto them so they know we are not afraid."

The bandits moved forward surrounding the van. Elijah rolled down his window. The bandits smelled of sweat and Elijah and the rest in the van turned their heads away expressive of distaste. The lead man pointed his rifle at Elijah. "Get out of the van," he said in Pushtu.

"You stink," said Aiyasha.

"Don't provoke them," said Sonia.

Elijah opened his door and stepped out. Ishmael and Abdul Aziz, still with their rifles in their arms stepped out. Two men moved forward and reached for Ishmael and Aziz's weapons. Ishmael raised the butt of his rifle and shouted in Pushtu, "Back off."

Abdul Aziz not only raised the butt of his rifle but actually made contact with the man's chin. He crumpled to the ground. Someone shouted and fired into the air, "Drop your weapons."

Both Ishmael and Abdul Aziz reluctantly threw their rifles down. The nearest man kicked them away.

Sonia opened her door and stepped out. The effect was electrifying, Elijah noticed. Most of the men's faces split into wide grins. A chant recognized as English went up, "Actress, actress, actress...." Apparently a lot of them had seen many an Indian movie, Elijah guessed and they believed they were looking at one of those actresses. Sonia had put on some of her jewelry in that short time. She smiled at them on cue. She was playing a part.

Elijah walked to her side, then looking at the group said in a mixture of Pushtu and Urdu, "Actress from India. We are from the UN. We do not have anything of value and would request you to let us go on our way back to Jullundur."

One man stepped forward; he was tall, bearded with a wide smile. "You are foreigner. You American?" He had a funny gait as though acting a part.

"No, I'm Pakistani," said Elijah, tagging the man as the village clown. "I work for the UN."

"Where is Jullundur? In Pakistan?"

"It's in India. The Pakistan border is close by."

"You still look foreign. You are not Muslim," said the Clown.

"But he respects the ways of Islam," said Ishmael.

"These two are Afghanis, where are they going with you?" said the Clown.

"They are my associates," said Elijah. "We work together for the UN. I am an engineer and they help me."

The leader of the group moved forward and the man who had all these questions stepped aside. "We want your van," said the leader without any preamble.

"I'm afraid that is not possible," said Elijah. "We must be on our way, we have appointments to keep."

The man turned to his gang. "He has appointments." They all roared with laughter, then quieted down when they noticed Sonia frowning. She had a hold on them.

"We have a Jeep," said the chief. "Why don't you follow us to our camp. Some of my men will come with you. We can't stay on this road all day."

Elijah and Sonia got back in the van. Ishmael and Abdul Aziz were joined by four of the bandits in the rear of the van. They followed the Jeep and the rest of the gang to a campsite off the road.

The men had seen all the items in the van. They unloaded everything from the van. Elijah and Sonia sat on a rock and watched helplessly. Ishmael stood nearby, his anger growing within him. "I don't think they know what those packages of explosives are," whispered Elijah.

"I hope they don't," whispered Ishmael. A few expletives escaped him in Pushtu. "After all the trouble I took trying to hide them," he added, looking away to hide his anger.

Still sitting on her rock, Sonia smiled and said, "Oh, Ishmael," trying to soothe his feelings.

One man walked over and said, "No, no, a lady such as you should not sit on a rock. Come, we have a special chair for you."

Sonia stood and glanced at Elijah who nodded to her. She walked beside the man and was led to a chair covered in a bearskin. She sat in it regally and smiled. All the men clapped their hands in approval. She was going to be the Queen of the Bandits. They may not want to let her go, thought Elijah. They may consider her as a lucky talisman.

The day was waning. Soon it would be evening. Ishmael went to the chief and said, "I could cook some of the food on the gas stoves."

"All right," agreed the chief.

Ishmael hurried to where they had stacked all the supplies from the van and got to work. Before long he cooked a meal of rice and kebabs.

The men came and served themselves, including Elijah and Abdul Aziz. Someone took a plate with food to Sonia, still seated on her fancy chair. She smiled at Elijah as though to say, "I'm beginning to enjoy this."

Elijah looked away, hiding a smile. After the meal Elijah approached the chief. "It will be cold in the night. Would it be all right if we slept in our van with our blankets?"

The chief mulled it over. Their Jeep was parked in front of the van, while to the rear was the wall of the cliff that ran up several hundred feet. He said, "Yes, but tomorrow you can take our Jeep and continue on your journey. We keep the van and all that is in it."

Not if I can help it, thought Elijah. He looked around him.

The members of the gang sat gathered round the fire, talking to each other. Out of the dark night a voice rose in a beautiful verse from the poet Mujim E Azam. The voice started out as a rich baritone but slowly rose to clear tenor notes, sustained with delicate nuances. Ishmael and Aiyasha translated the verses into English and Hindi. Elijah was moved at the intensity of feeling it conveyed. Sonia had tears in her eyes. It was a *gazal* that she had heard before.

They all curled up in their blankets and were soon asleep except Elijah. He kept running the possibilities at his disposal. He still had the four boxes of explosives and the detonators. He looked up at the men around the campfire. Two guards were on duty. We will have to play this one by ear, he thought.

The day broke sunny with not a cloud in the sky. Ishmael cooked roti and tea on his gas stove. He had taken over as cook for the whole tribe of bandits. Men sat around cleaning their rifles.

Sonia decided to take a walk around the camp. She found some men playing cards. They looked at her as she approached and smiled at her. One of them asked in Pushtu, "Would you like to join in the game?" She shook her head smiling and continued her walk. She saw Abdul Aziz helping Ishmael wash the cooking utensils. Yet another group was playing a game that she did not comprehend. It involved the throwing of a couple of dice and moving colored pebbles along a framework sketched on a board. Once again they paused in their game to smile at her. One of them called out in Pushtu, "You stay with us, you are the Queen of the Bandits." The whole group roared with laughter.

"*Shukria*," said Sonia, smiling and walking on. She passed a stack of rifles with men nearby keeping guard. She wondered, where are the women? Surely these men are from the villages nearby. Do they go visit their families every so often and then return? Do they have wives, mothers and children of their own? It struck her as unnatural that men should be separated from women for such long periods of time. Without the softness of women, coarseness and savagery could set in. She shuddered at the thought as to how dangerous her position was as the only woman in a camp of wild men. The only restraints were the presence of Elijah and Ishmael, and they could easily be disposed off. It was only a matter of time.

The wheels were already spinning in the minds of the men and Elijah was jolted out of his complacency when the chief walked over and said, "I have changed my mind. We need the Jeep and the van for ourselves. You stay with us for a while. We will travel together and when we come to a junction, we will leave you there. That way someone will find you. You won't die in this wilderness. But the woman stays with us. Our men are lonesome and could use the charms of a woman. You will find another."

Elijah could barely restrain himself from striking the man down there and then. His worst fears had been confirmed. Elijah's face drained of all color. They were kidnapping Sonia? And to what end? He couldn't even imagine what they had in mind.

"What do you mean by that?" demanded Elijah, suddenly throwing caution to the winds. "She works with me and is under my protection. She leaves with us. You can have the van and its contents."

"We will have whatever we want," said the chief, in a snarl. "The men like her, so she stays."

With clenched jaws and his heart thudding violently he sat down on a rock and looked into the distance. His thoughts were in a jumble as to what to do. He wanted so badly to take Sonia back home to Jullundur. Back to the comforts of home. Back where one's neighbors were not a constant threat. His dark mood swiftly changed to anger. He did not ask for this. He wanted to hit back and with a vengeance. He shook his head in his anger and clenched his fists. Sonia had been observing him with alarm. She casually walked over to him so as not to attract any attention. She placed her hand on his arm.

"Calm down Elijah," she said in a soothing voice. "It is a bad situation. But we have been there before." She could feel him shiver with pent-up feelings. With an effort he forced himself to slow down his breathing. He didn't tell her what they had in mind for her. There was no point in upsetting her too. He would have to solve this one by himself.

Chapter Twenty-Three

Ishmael brought two plates with breakfast. Sonia took her plate and Elijah, forcing a smile, took his.

The remote control for the detonators was in the glove compartment of the van and the plastic explosives and the detonators were still in their possession. It would be a risky operation, but it was worth a try. He was determined to put it into motion that night.

At noon at a shout from the chief, the men jumped up grabbed their rifles and fell into a line like regular soldiers. They went through a series of exercises and then set up a large piece of cardboard with circles drawn on it and commenced target practice.

Very impressive, thought Elijah. Which means they will be alert and a formidable force to overcome with just the four of us.

He watched from the sidelines. After six hours of training they trekked back to camp tired and ready for another night around the many campfires.

When everyone had settled down in their sleeping areas, Elijah and his group were back in the van. Elijah reached into the glove box and withdrew one of the boxes of the plastic explosive. He stuck a detonator into its center, pushing the soft plastic to mold around the trigger mechanism. He set the timer for one minute and 30 seconds. He put it back in the box and gave it to Ishmael. "While doing your cooking tomorrow," said Elijah, "try to place this under the Jeep." Ishmael nodded and hid it in the folds of his garment.

Elijah took out a second box and repeated the procedure. He was fast as he worked with his hands, constantly looking around, ever vigilant. He set the timer on this one for exactly one minute. He gave this to Abdul Aziz. "I want you to move very carefully without drawing attention to yourself and place this one among the stack of rifles not being used. Try walking by and gently throw it as close as you can. They will be observing you." Aiyasha's hands trembled as she took the box and put it in her pocket.

After working on the third one, he offered it to Sonia. "I've set the timer on this one at one minute and 15 seconds. Take it and dispose of it near the highest concentration of the group. After the first detonation you will have fifteen seconds to get rid of it. Most of the men will probably rush to find their rifles. When they find them gone, they will turn towards us. Use your judgment and throw it where it will be most effective." Sonia took it and slipped it into a side pocket in her skirt. "I didn't know skirts had pockets," said Elijah.

"Some of them do," said Sonia.

He worked on a fourth unit, set the timer and stowed it in his own pocket. "I will initiate our plan just as Ishmael starts serving the food. Sonia, you're the only one vulnerable, since you will have your bomb still with you. Let's all get some sleep."

Everything is going as planned, thought Elijah. Ishmael made his rounds and started cooking. That told Elijah the explosive had been set under the Jeep. But the timers on the detonators would start when he pressed the remote. Abdul Aziz was walking around somewhere.

Suddenly there was a commotion, a great deal of shouting, and everyone jumped up. Elijah could see Abdul Aziz held in an arm-lock by one of the men. "Hey!" the man shouted, "I think this one's not a man."

"What?" shouted another. "There's one easy way to find out." He moved forward and yanked down Abdul Aziz's pantaloons, which fell at his feet.

"Remove his pattu," shouted another.

Elijah could see Aiyasha struggling and this changed his plans. He moved away from the crowd. Two men had a hold of the hem of Aiyasha's pattu and had raised it slowly. It had reached her knees. With a jerk they raised it to her waist.

Elijah reset the timer to zero and threw the plastic bomb into the crowd behind the man holding Aiyasha, simultaneously pressing the remote.

"It's a woman," said the man. "We can have fun tonighiiiaeee. . ." He and the man holding Aiyasha were bodily lifted in the explosion, Aiyasha with them. She twisted her body as she flew through the air so that she landed on the man. The explosion had thrown bodies in all directions.

The smell of semtex filled the air. Elijah thought it smelled similar to cordite. It would be a minute before another explosion could happen. He ran towards the stack of rifles and grabbed one. The bandits opened fire and Elijah felt bullets spattering all around him. He shot back in the general direction from where the flashes appeared. He saw Sonia to his right, running towards him. When she reached his side, they dived behind a rock.

Men were running to get their rifles. "Don't let them get to their weapons," shouted Elijah.

Sonia pulled out her box, opened it, turned the timer knob to 5 seconds and threw it into the group of men picking up their rifles. It was a good throw, landing smack among the stacked rifles. The explosion sent bodies and rifles flying. The bomb that Aiyasha had dropped among the guns ignited and exploded adding to the noise and destruction, sending missiles in all directions.

Where are Aiyasha and Ishmael wondered Elijah.

Aiyasha felt the wind knocked out of her when she landed heavily on her back. She looked around to get to get her bearings. Her captor's grip loosened. The man had been knocked unconscious. She pulled up her pantaloons and ran blindly looking for Elijah and Sonia. She turned a corner and saw a guard in the cover of a rock, with his back towards her and firing his rifle. She grabbed a large stone and brought it down. "That's for pulling off my pants," she shouted with pent-up fury. The man's turban took most of the impact, but he collapsed unconscious. She grabbed the rifle and peering through the smoke, she looked for Elijah and Sonia. She ran towards where she had last seen Elijah. She found a boulder and dived behind it. Breathing hard, she raised her head and looked around. Crumpled bodies lay everywhere.

When Ishmael heard the first explosion he realized that the plan had been pre-empted. He hadn't placed the box under the Jeep as yet and now had thirty seconds to get rid of it. He took it out and threw it as far as he could but it was nowhere near the Jeep. Another explosion rocked the air.

That must be the Jeep, thought Aiyasha. She pulled off her turban and dropped it. She wanted Elijah and Sonia to recognize her. She stayed hidden, waiting for the smoke to clear.

*   *   *

Elijah and Sonia squinted through the dust and smoke trying to discern whether Ishmael and Aiyasha were safe. Several bodies lay around them. When the smoke lifted, they could see the stack of guns had disappeared and more bodies lay on the ground in grotesque positions. Elijah counted fifteen bandits either disabled or dead.

The minutes ticked by and more of the smoke cleared. Three men stood up with their hands raised.

"Walk forward into the open," shouted Elijah in Pushtu. He stayed hidden with just his rifle and his head visible. The men advanced and stopped. That accounted for all but two of the bandits.

From behind a rock another man rose, holding a knife against Ishmael's throat.

"Drop your weapons," the man shouted in Pushtu. Elijah hesitated. He stood up with his rifle and waited.

"Drop it," shouted the man again, moving forward with his left arm around Ishmael's neck.

"No," screamed Aiyasha, moving out of her cover into the open with her rifle raised.

"Aiyasha don't," shouted Elijah. "You could hit Ishmael." Aiyasha shook her head. She still burned from anger and humiliation at how they had handled her.

"Take it easy, Aiyasha," said Sonia, now standing up.

Aiyasha stared straight ahead, concentrating on her target. "No," she shouted, moving her rifle up to her shoulder as they had taught her.

The man holding Ishmael froze. "I will slit his throat before you can pull that trigger," he yelled.

Aiyasha moved sideways, her left foot moving to the left her right crossing behind to the left, moving to get a better shot at the man's head. The man could read her intention and turned keeping Ishmael in front of him. But his body was now exposed to Elijah and Sonia. Elijah slowly raised his rifle. The man must have sensed the danger of his position. He jumped back pulling Ishmael around to face Elijah. This gave Aiyasha the target she was looking for. But was her aim any good? Could she hit the bull's eye as she had at practice?

The man holding Ishmael had lost his turban. Aiyasha stopped breathing and imagined the man's ear as the 'red dot' and squeezed the trigger as she had done so many times before. A piece of the man's skull flew away followed by a spurt of blood. He collapsed dragging his knife along Ishmael's neck as the blade fell from his lifeless hand. Ishmael put his hand to the wound and jumped to his left away from his captor. He could feel the blood. He grabbed his *patoo* and held it to his neck.

Aiyasha collapsed in a heap overwhelmed by what she had just done. Elijah and Sonia rushed to Ishmael's side. While Elijah held him in his arms, Sonia peeled away the cloth to look at the wound. He was bleeding but the jugular had not been cut.

"You'll be OK," she said, to reassure him. She pushed the cloth back in place and Elijah eased Ishmael to the ground to a sitting position.

"Give me your knife," said Sonia. Elijah searched in his pocket and handed it to her. She made a deft stroke on the hem of her skirt to a depth of three inches, made a cut parallel to its border. She pulled the piece that ripped evenly all around. She rolled the band of cloth into a bandage and once again removed the cloth from Ishmael's neck. With Elijah holding Ishmael by the shoulders, she wound the strip, holding one end in place with her fingers of her left hand and pulling the cloth gently to go around his neck. Soon he looked like a professional nurse had worked on him.

"That should hold it for now, Ishmael, until we can get some medication as an antiseptic," she said, patting him on the shoulder.

They helped Ishmael to his feet and observed Aiyasha standing guard, holding her rifle covering two of the bandits.

With his rifle at the ready, Elijah began his search for survivors. He found two more men, injured and the fight knocked out of them. They raised their hands as he approached. He moved them to where Aiyasha had the other two with their arms still raised. He motioned for the four to sit on the ground. Sonia, who now had a rifle joined him along with Ishmael also armed with a gun.

"Let's put all these rifles in the Jeep, Ishmael," said Elijah. Addressing Sonia, he said, "You and Aiyasha keep these men covered."

It took them the better part of half an hour to round up all the guns and ammunition. They made a heap in the rear of the Jeep.

Elijah drove the van up close to it. "I'll try and siphon out the fuel from the Jeep into our van," said Elijah, looking in the toolbox of the Jeep. Not finding what he wanted, he opened the rear door of the van and looked about. He came back with a piece of rubber tubing. He unscrewed the caps from both gas tanks. Kneeling on the ground he lowered the tubing into the Jeep's tank and started sucking until he got a mouthful of fuel which he spat out immediately. He now bent the hose to clamp it then inserted it carefully into the van's tank and released his manual clamp to let the fuel flow. He raised the tubing to make sure there was flow. He held it in that position for about half an hour when the flow dribbled and finally stopped.

"That should leave enough to move the Jeep where I want it," he said. He took the hose out, wiped it dry with a rag, put the caps back on each vehicle and drove the Jeep further away from the camp out in the open where the nearest tree was some fifty kilometers. He walked back and spoke to Ishmael. "Put a charge among the rifles in the Jeep and bury it deep." Ishmael moved off to get the materials from the van.

Sonia and Aiyasha were still holding the four men at gunpoint. "You both can get back in the van," said Elijah, his voice curt and his nerves still taut. As they walked away, he addressed the bandits in Pushtu, "We didn't ask for this. You give your men a proper burial." He turned and started walking away when one of the men shouted out, "You have appointments to keep?" It was the Clown. Elijah shook his head and continued to the van.

Elijah sat at the wheel and the magnitude of what had just happened hit him. He didn't notice Sonia beside him. He was responsible for almost all the dead men out there. The sudden guilt he felt washed over him and he let out a cry of despair.

Sonia reached out and put her arm around him. As she consoled him with her touch. The scars from this day are going to run deep for all of us, she thought.

Ishmael shouted in Pushtu to the bandits, as he was about to enter the van, "Don't move from your position." Elijah drove about a hundred meters and pressed the remote, sending the Jeep and the rifles up in a fiery mass of metal and debris. After a while he drove on. The fuel gauge showed three-quarters full. "There's enough to take us to Peshawar," he muttered. But as he turned onto the main road going east, storm clouds were gathering in the skies to the south.

Chapter Twenty-Four

Elijah drove the van making their way south. We're getting close to the Khyber Pass, he thought. When he reached the main road he turned east. Off in the distance he looked at the Hindu Kush Mountains. It was June, yet it felt cold.

As the dark clouds moved towards them, Aiyasha got extremely nervous. She had a dread of thunderstorms. It wasn't the lightning that scared her; it was the anticipation of the rolling thunder they presaged that took her breath away.

"I wonder what it would be like crossing this Pass in winter?" said Elijah.

"It may be closed with snow drifts," said Sonia.

He drove on and in fifteen minutes the rain pelted down in a deluge. A heavy fog descended and soon he could hardly see more than five meters ahead. He pulled off onto the shoulder and turned off the engine. "I can't see anything out there," he said. "Let's wait this one out."

"Where did it come from?" asked Sonia in amazement. "We have gone through -- how long has it been? -- over a week of sunshine and now this freak storm."

"It's just a cloud-burst," said Elijah. "I think that's what the weatherman calls it."

"The darkness is depressing," said Aiyasha.

"I think I have something to change your moods," broke in Ishmael, as he rummaged in his supply-bag. He withdrew a small package and opened it, then handed out what looked like dried cakes.

Sonia bit into one and chewed, "What's in it, Ishmael?"

"Dried Mulberries and crushed walnuts."

"It has an interesting taste, sweet and tart. When we get to Jullundur, you should show me how to make them."

"I can show you," Aiyasha said, "my mother used to make them."

"Very well," said Sonia, smiling.

Elijah sat munching on the cakes, his mind still running over the events of the past few hours. I might need the help of a shrink after this, he thought.

They waited and waited. Outside, little rivers formed by the side of the road. Elijah wiped the moisture on the inside of the windshield. Sheets of water blanked out all visibility.

*   *   *

Elijah and his van had changed their course from going south on the main highway when they had been captured by the Bandits. Rehman had passed that location on his rush towards the border.

Once again the guards at the outpost gave them the thumbs down sign of not seeing any of the fugitives. Rehman and his men were becoming familiar faces.

"*Nahi mila* (didn't meet them)?" asked a guard on the Pakistani side.

"*Nahi bai, ek dham bayhosh ho gaya.*(they have quite disappeared)."

Rehman decided to press on to Peshawar where he made inquiries and even paid for information but found nothing with a lead. For some of the men this was the fourth time they had passed through the Khyber Pass in the past week, and the landmarks were becoming easy to find.

They decided to retrace their steps. They hadn't gone far when a thunderstorm hit. Both Jeeps kept moving slowly in the massive downpour, until the lead vehicle couldn't take it anymore without crashing into some unseen vehicle or barrier.

"I can hardly see a few feet in front of me," said the driver. He turned on his blinkers to aid those behind him.

"I think we should wait it out," he said. He signaled he was pulling onto the shoulder. The Jeep behind did likewise. They parked and waited.

The roar of thunder and the noise of the rain drowned out all conversation. After an hour of enduring the storm, Rehman shouted with impatience, "How long is this going to last? I have never seen anything like this."

After another hour the storm slowly let up. Gradually the mist rose giving them more visibility. The men stepped out. They saw a van across the road, which had also pulled over just as they had done.

Rehman pointed to the van and said, "Could it be them?" He tapped Iqbal on the shoulder. "Come with me, bring your weapon," he whispered. The others heard him and turned alert. Rehman pulled his Mauser from his belt and ran across the two-lane road. He yanked open the driver's side door of the van and stuck the muzzle into the surprised driver's neck. "Get out," he shouted, while his men surrounded the vehicle and pulled open the other doors.

The driver trembling in terror stepped out, his hands in the air. Rehman had been mistaken. They were all Afghans.

"What do you want?" stammered the driver, "we are on our way to Peshawar to buy supplies for our village." Rehman slipped the safety back on his gun and returned it to his belt.

"We thought you were someone else," he said and walked across the motorway, without making any apology. His men, equally disappointed, returned with him in a huff. They had hoped for an easy victory.

*   *   *

A mile away to the east on the same road, Elijah wiped his windshield again and Sonia used a handkerchief to clean her part of the glass. It had been two hours since the onslaught had started. It now slowly ebbed and finally stopped. Elijah started up and moved onto the empty road.

Sonia sat in a trance absolutely shaken. She was having a delayed reaction to the events of the past few hours. She stared straight ahead, then put her hands to her face and blurted, "Oh, my God. We just killed sixteen human beings." She broke down in sobs, shaking her head from side to side.

Elijah turned and looked at her with concern on his face. He quickly pulled off the road and parked. He moved closer and put his arms around her. She continued shaking with uncontrolled sobbing. She leaned her head on his shoulder.

"That was the only option we had to protect all of us," said Elijah, the strain of his emotions pulling the corners of his mouth downwards. "Six weeks ago I would have hesitated taking such action. But after what I've been through my attitude has changed. I can't help it."

Sonia sobered up, realizing that it was Elijah who needed comforting. She hugged him tighter and patted his back.

Aiyasha, seeing Sonia's turmoil started crying too. Ishmael sat with his body bent forward, his head in his hands.

"You poor dear," said Sonia to Elijah, her emotions changing gears. "You have always put our safety ahead of yours. I'm sorry. But we're not soldiers, this is not part of my world."

"Neither has it been part of mine until now," Elijah muttered into her hair. He gently released her. She dabbed at her eyes with her handkerchief.

They sat for a while quietly. Elijah moved back to his position behind the wheel. He just sat there, staring into the distance. It must have been about ten minutes before he checked traffic once again and moved out. They drove in silence.

        *   *   *

Rehman and his party continued westwards. Towards evening they pulled off into a well-known campsite and spent the night there. Rehman sat on a block of wood and stared into the fire his men had built. "Let's go back east one more time in the morning," he said.

        *   *   *

Elijah's mood brightened as he saw the approach to the Khyber Pass. A huge bronze plaque near a turn off, with parking slots stated the engineering marvels of its time when the British had improved the road through the pass as it is today, about a hundred years ago. They all got out and read the metal engraving before continuing on their way. But further down, a large sign, saying "Khyber Pass," was riddled with bullet holes. Target practice for the bandit snipers.

Serpentine roads cut into the side of the mountains like terraced farming. They wound gradually from one elevation to the next in a series of steps. They reached the highest point along the sloping road with a grade of six to one. The road at this point became wider, cut deeper into the mountain to allow trucks, SUVs and buses to make a hundred and eighty-degree 'U' turn and start up the second step in a series of Zs. On and on it went. They saw the lines of traffic down below as the van reached the higher zones. The sound of traffic from below filled the air.

There were three levels. The lowest was for motorized vehicles, the second was for a rail line and the third was for pedestrians and camel caravans.

"Those British," Elijah said, nodding to the scenery before them, trying to change their brooding to something lighter. "Those British," he repeated, "they thought of everything. From a distance this serpentine roadway must look like a pyramid."

Elijah looked with awe at the scenes unfolding before him. He saw deep into the misty valleys below dappled in sunshine in some areas and dark in others where clouds hid the sun. He had missed all of this in his trip to Afghanistan, because he had been pre-occupied as a prisoner in a crowded truck. He did remember Peshawar though.

He regarded Sonia with an inquiring look. "You drove through all this in your SUV, didn't you?"

"Yes," said Sonia, "but I wasn't paying attention to the scenery then. I'm more relaxed now, and am able to enjoy these magnificent mountains." She was mentally emerging out of the mists of the darkness of recent events. "Besides now I have you by my side." She slid closer to him and put her hand on his shoulder.

He turned his head and took a deep breath. "I love that perfume. Where did you get it? I think I'll name it 'Sonia.'"

She laughed. "It already has a name."

Trucks and buses passed them going in the opposite direction. Not many vehicles were going their way. An impatient BMW tailgated them for a while. Elijah accelerated up a bit and the car went around them in a burst of speed. They were on the outskirts of Peshawar. They had driven out of the mountains and the roads became four lanes. Small 'Chai khanas' – teashops – sprung up on the sidewalks. Large concrete buildings took the place of pine trees. Pedestrians and bicycles crowded the streets. It eased the tension they had been under, to see all these people, hurrying about their businesses. No one felt threatened in a place like this. They crossed into Pakistan and went through a customs checkpoint.

"I think we should stop for *Chai*," Ishmael said, indicating the shops.

"That sounds like a good idea," said Sonia.

Darkness approached in the late evening and lights came on in the various buildings. Elijah pulled over to what looked like a respectable hotel. He said, "Maybe we can find some comfortable beds for a change."

They walked into a restaurant with glaring fluorescent lights. Business appeared good. Waiters hurried to and fro and shouted orders to the kitchen. They found a vacant table and four chairs. The smell of spices and meat cooking filled the air.

Ishmael told the waiter, "I'll have my *Chai* with cardamom and ginger please." The waiter nodded.

Sonia said, "I think I'll try that too'"

"I'll have the same," said Aiyasha.

"Make it four," said Elijah.

The waiter hurried off shouting, "Four *Masala Chai*."

Sonia smiled at Elijah; "We're back home."

Soon four tumblers of hot tea sat before them.

"Would you like something to eat?" asked the waiter, pointing to a board with a menu written in Urdu. He rattled off a series of dishes. Elijah caught the name biriyani. They decided they would come back for dinner after washing up.

Elijah took a sip of his tea and let the taste swirl around his tongue, tasting the pungency of the ginger, the flavor of the cardamoms and the tang of the tea. "I like it," he said. They enjoyed the relaxed atmosphere while drinking their tea.

They left the restaurant reluctantly, wanting to prolong the friendly ambience and went looking for rooms for the night. Sonia kept glancing at Elijah. He looked sober and depressed. She wondered if this is what they called 'battle fatigue.' She shook her head to get rid of the train her thoughts were taking. She still worried about where Rehman and his men were. She knew Elijah was under the same uneasiness of not knowing when and where an attack would surface.

They reached the motel with the neon sign they had seen from afar. The manager was most apologetic. He only had one large room left, with four beds. After sleeping in the van in makeshift beds, this was luxury. "We'll take it," said Elijah, with enthusiasm. The manager walked them through the suite. The room had two common bathrooms down the hall with showers. Another bonus, they all agreed. They moved into the room with all their worldly possessions. Ishmael and Elijah left the rifles hidden in the van.

Everyone took turns in the showers. Washing away the dust of what they felt were countless days. Elijah and Ishmael went out into the lobby so that the ladies could have some privacy. Elijah found a newspaper, *The Times of India*, weeks old. He glanced through it giving his world a sense of realism after the isolation they had been thrust into for the past few weeks. Ishmael could read English too. He was flipping through the pages of *Time* magazine.

After about half an hour the ladies looking refreshed joined them. Aiyasha looked so different. She had her hair tied at the back. Her green almond shaped eyes, dark eyelashes and curved eyebrows gave her the look of elegance. She had silver earrings and lips red like cherries. Her youth showed in a healthy glow to her face. Her fine features were typical of her Afghani heritage. She wore a shalwar. Next to her Sonia looked equally beautiful. She had her hair in a chignon. Her wide and even cheekbones and long slender nose and full lips were what had made Elijah's heart skip a beat when he first saw her. She wore a blue sari. Looking at her Elijah's heart skipped several beats this time. Having two beautiful women under the same roof was a delight to watch.

The sight also stunned Ishmael. He had never seen Aiyasha in this light before. He stared at her wondering where he had seen her before. He looked at Sonia and then back again to Aiyasha. "You are very beautiful Aiyasha," he said in Pushtu stretching out his hand, "You have been a worthy friend."

Aiyasha couldn't hold back her amusement, bubbled over with giggles and took his hand, "I am grateful for all you have done," she replied also in Pushtu. Ishmael held her hand then covered it with his left hand, still looking at her. Aiyasha smiled. Then they both withdrew their hands looking embarrassed. This was not a Muslim custom.

Ishmael recovered fast and turned to Sonia. "Mrs. Davenport you look very beautiful too."

"Thank you Ishmael," said Sonia and gave him a hug.

Elijah waited. She walked into his arms and gave him a long embrace. "Love you," she whispered. They broke out of their hug slowly. Elijah touched her face with his fingers and took her hand. He looked at Aiyasha and said, "You look lovely Aiyasha."

"Thank you," said Aiyasha rather shyly.

"Let's have some biriyani," he said

Elijah asked the manager if there was a restaurant he would recommend. He suggested an excellent place further down the street called "The Taj."

They found it to be a quieter place with lights not so glaring. The waiters looked dashing, dressed in seventeenth century costumes of the Mughal period. They had red turbans with folds in front that moved upwards like an opened fan, red jackets with gold embroidery. They bowed to the visitors.

On a small raised stage sat a group of musicians composed of a tabla, a virtuoso on a sitar, a keyboard, a violin and a man singing gazals in a soft dusky voice. The smell of incense floated in the air. The ambiance was soothing. They felt relaxed.

After they were seated a waiter brought them menus. There was lamb biriyani. Elijah looked at the wine list, but in deference to both Ishmael and Aiyasha decided not to order any for him and Sonia. They made their selections and waited enjoying the music and the décor. Elijah casually glanced around. Several tables were occupied with customers. They were well dressed and appeared to be Indians on vacation. The place must be popular with Indians and foreigners, thought Elijah. He saw several foreign men and women. They must be Brits on holiday, he thought. "The Khyber Pass has seen countless invasions in the past," said Elijah, sounding like a professor. "The latest invasion has been by tourists like us."

"We are not tourists, saab," said Ishmael. "We're just passing through."

The smell of a variety of spices and the aroma of meat being cooked drifted through from the kitchen within. It presaged the handiwork of an excellent chef. While waiting they toasted each other with soft drinks in glasses. "To Peshawar," said Ishmael and raised his glass. All of them raised their glasses and clinked them together with a chorus of, "To Peshawar."

Their dishes arrived. First came plates with Naan bread, then the condiments and sauces and the main dishes. The *biriyani* with the chunks of lamb that was soft and the yellow, aromatic basmati rice, spiced and flavored by saffron tasted as good as it looked. The meat curry called *Nihari*, its taste accentuated with a few drops of lemon juice, was tender and sparked certain taste buds. "This is heavenly," said Elijah, at a loss for words. *Aloo ki bhaji*, diced potatoes cooked with sautéed mustard seed and turmeric and a little cayenne pepper. They both went well with the *naan* bread. Then came the lamb korma that had its own taste and flavor. It was cooked in a sauce of yogurt and a paste of unsalted ground cashew nuts.

There was more. The waiter placed *Moghlai* style spinach and scallions, spicy yet delicious platters on the table. After a diet of kebabs and roti for so long, the four weary travelers did justice to them all.

Ishmael listened to the music. "*Gazals* are poetry set to music," he said.

"Yes," said Elijah, "I understand a few words here and there."

"I like it too," said Sonia

"If more people listened to *Gazals* they would not go to war," said Aiyasha

"You do have dreams for this world, don't you Aiyasha," said Sonia.

*   *   *

While Elijah and his group for once had the comforts of luxury, miles away Rehman and his men shared their meal and slept in a tent. We are used to it, thought Rehman. This is the path to *Jihad*. The morrow will bring satisfaction when we capture Elijah.

Chapter Twenty-Five

Elijah and his group sat in the Pakistani restaurant enjoying the food and listening to *Gazals* performed live by a trio of musicians on a stage. The discussion had turned to, "If the effects of music could influence those at the helms of power to avoid wars." Good luck, thought Elijah.

"How I wish there was a way to stop all wars," said Aiyasha.

"So do I, Aiyasha," said Sonia.

The sitarist strummed a beautiful solo, weaving a melody that captured the imagination lifting them on the colorful wings of a butterfly. The tabla and violin joined in the melody, the violin harmonizing at certain intervals. Elijah listened impressed. He normally liked classical music by Beethoven and Mozart.

When they filed out of the restaurant the night air felt cool. The lights had come on in the streets and shops and buildings around. Ishmael and Aiyasha walked ahead talking to each other, Elijah and Sonia followed behind. Elijah took Sonia's hand as they walked side by side. He gently squeezed her hand. "I wonder how everything is back at the factory in Jullundur," he said as though talking to himself.

"We've been away, for how long?" asked Sonia.

"About three weeks," said Elijah.

"What a lot has happened in that short a time." She paused. "I can't believe it."

"Thanks to you Sonia, who knows how long I would have been held captive if you hadn't come to my rescue."

Sonia smiled up at him. Elijah squeezed her hand again and turned and looked at her. "If I kissed you right now, everyone on this street will stop and stare."

"Don't you dare," said Sonia looking around.

They reached their lodgings and went up to their room. The four beds were all made with pillows, sheets and blankets. A gap of three or four feet between each bed. It was a lot more comfortable than sleeping in the van. Ishmael took the bed at the far end, then Aiyasha, then Sonia and Elijah.

The next morning after a leisurely breakfast, they were on the road again. They were heading east to Islamabad, the capital of Pakistan. From there to Lahore and finally cross the border to Jullundur. Elijah looked at the map and asked, "Does anyone know what river we are going to cross next?"

"I do," said Sonia.

Elijah gave her the map and she studied it for a while. She thought she would get Aiyasha involved. "Aiyasha," said Sonia, "why don't you look at this and tell us."

She gave the map to Aiyasha who scanned it from side to side.

"Oh, I know," said Aiyasha. "It's the Indus river. The main river of the Punjab, now in Pakistan. It has four tributaries that meet the Indus further north. If we continue on this road we should be crossing the river Jhelum, the Chenab, the Ravi and the Sutlej. This is fascinating. I only read about these, now I'm actually going to see them. Do we have a camera?"

"Yes," said Sonia, "I have one."

"Can we take a picture of all of us on the banks of the river?"

"Of course," said Sonia.

They could see the bridge coming up a mile away. It was spectacular, an engineering marvel of its time when it had been built – so said the bronze plaque – built by the British Raj years ago. The river itself was impressive in its size. It looked like a sea with choppy waves. A mile wide and very deep fed by the glaciers of the Himalayas.

"Do you know," said Aiyasha, "hundreds of years ago, the people who lived here used to inflate their water-skins with air and use it as a float to cross these rivers."

Elijah could well imagine them doing that. Humayun and Akbar the Moghul kings among them.

When they reached the bridge, they all got out and posed with the massive structure in the background. A tourist obliged by taking their picture.

A train rumbled through on the upper deck of the bridge. The noise drowned out all conversation.

*   *   *

Rehman and his crew reached the Afghan border by noon the next day. The guard on duty recognized them. "Your party of four finally did go through here last evening," he said, smiling at them.

"Was one of them an American?"shouted Rehman in an excited voice.

"He could be," said the guard, "but they were all dressed as Afghans, except for one woman who I think was an Indian."

"It's them," said Rehman with undisguised elation. "*Shrukia*," he said, to the guard. "*Salaam Alekoum*."

He and his men ran back to the Jeeps and roared off. "Now we ask at all the hotels in Peshawar, if they have been there," said Rehman. "We should hurry, they may have left this morning."

*   *   *

Sonia drove the van giving Elijah a respite. They were not far from Islamabad. "You know I called the American Consulate in Delhi when you were captured and taken to Afghanistan," said Sonia. "I think I'll call again and tell them that you're not a hostage anymore."

"Let me know if they want to talk to me," said Elijah, sleepily.

Later when Elijah took the wheel again Sonia made the call and explained where they were and confirmed that the American citizen, Elijah Davenport was no longer a hostage of the Fundamentalist Muslims.

"Since you're on your way to Islamabad," said the aide to the ambassador in Delhi, "why don't you stop at the American Ambassador's residence in Islamabad and be our guests for a day or two? I will call them and inform them. Especially if you still need protection."

"Thank you," said Sonia. "We will stop and meet with the ambassador in Islamabad."

"Oh," he said, hesitating. "I forgot to mention that they are having a May Ball tomorrow, the day you will be there. I will tell them that you'll join the party. They will like that."

"You think so?" said Sonia. "Well thank you."

She hung up and said to Elijah, "We've been invited to stay at the American Ambassador's place in Islamabad for a couple of days."

"Why?" asked Elijah.

"In case we need protection from the guys who captured you. They feel obligated to one of their citizens in a foreign country."

"They said that?" asked Elijah.

"They implied it," said Sonia. "Oh, they did mention that the ambassador is having a party on the day we arrive there. Something called a May Ball, whatever that is."

"You know they have dancing at these parties," said Elijah, smiling.

"Yes," said Sonia. "I know how to dance."

"I can't dance," said Aiyasha, who was closely following the discussion.

"And neither can I," said Ishmael.

"That's all right," said Elijah, "you both can sit and watch us, all night long. When you can't dance, that's a lot of fun too."

"Why do you people do it?" asked Ishmael. "Can't you stay home and hold your own wife, instead of trying to hold everyone else's wife?"

Elijah and Sonia laughed. "Most of the time we do dance with our own wife or partner," said Elijah, "because we are used to each other's style. But sometimes, it is courteous to dance with another couple, especially if asked. There is no hanky panky."

"What is this hanky panky?" asked Aiyasha.

Both Sonia and Elijah laughed again. Sonia was hard pressed how to explain this. "There is no sexual attraction," she said, "we just dance the steps to the rhythm of the music."

"Aah," said Aiyasha, like she understood, but she hadn't.

*   *   *

It was late when Elijah and his party reached Islamabad. The city sparkled with lights. Victorian style buildings dominated the area. But there were also structures whose architecture had a definite Mughal influence. Large gardens abounded on the outskirts of the city with water fountains and reflecting pools. But as they entered the city, it gave way to multi-storied concrete housing projects and more traffic.

"There it is," shouted Ishmael, suddenly pointing to the spires that could be seen from several blocks away. "It's the Shah Faisal Mosque. I have heard about and dreamed of seeing it someday. Elijah Saab, could we make a detour to see it?"

"Of course," said Elijah, making a note of the direction he should be taking. He pulled up in a large parking lot. The mosque was enormous. It had a roof made of concrete, which ended in four peaked gables. Devotees flowed in and out in a continuous cascade of color. There were no fixed hours for worship.

Ishmael and Aiyasha walked together, Elijah and Sonia followed them into the massive concrete structure. All four of them spread their prayer rugs and knelt down.

After their devotions, Ishmael took them on a tour of the mosque explaining the various features and Arabic motifs.

They finally made it to the parking lot and climbed into the van.

"That was impressive, Ishmael," said Elijah. "I've never seen anything like it. Now let's try and find the ambassador's residence before everything shuts down for the night."

They made inquires as to where the American Ambassador lived, and soon found themselves back in the suburbs of the city. The Ambassador's home was a large Victorian edifice, more like a palace, surrounded by green gardens and protected by walls. A Marine guard at the locked gate took their individual names and ID and called someone on the phone in his cubicle of an office, at the guardhouse. Ishmael and Aiyasha had no IDs, but had been vouched for by the Delhi American Consulate. The Marine took pictures on his iPod and made ID tags for Ishmael and Aiyasha. When he was done he handed them over to the two of them. He also fingerprinted them. He explained that all these were normal security procedures. He then opened the gate with the push of a button and waved them in.

Elijah parked in front of the entrance to the mansion. Another Marine stepped forward and took his keys. A third Marine opened the doors of the mansion for them and the four of them walked in. Inside a well-lighted hall, with crystal chandlers everywhere, a maitre d' greeted them. He led them to comfortable looking ornate chairs. "Please be seated," he said. "The ambassador's wife, Mrs. Rorke, will be with you shortly."

They sat and waited. Elijah couldn't help noticing all the British heirlooms and paintings of past Viceroys and maharajas on the walls. This had to be from the time before the partition, when the British Raj governed the whole of India, which included what was now Pakistan.

The Ambassador's wife walked in. She was in her early sixties; trim and good looking nicely dressed in a red Cashmere suit. Her hair was blonde and medium length. Her eyes were ice blue. The scent of jasmine floated around her. She extended her hand towards Elijah with a kindly smile. "Mister Elijah Davenport, I presume. I've heard so much about you in the last hour. I'm Julia Rorke. Nice to make your acquaintance." Then looking over at Sonia and Aiyasha, "And look at these beautiful young ladies." She extended her hand to Sonia. "How are you my dear? You must have had a very trying time." She put her arms around Sonia and gave her a hug.

"I'm Sonia Davenport," said Sonia, "and this is Aiyasha Shalhoub."

Mrs. Rorke turned towards Aiyasha and held her hand. "You are so young and beautiful." She gave Aiyasha a big hug too.

She turned to Ishmael and Elijah was there by his side, saying, "And this is Ishmael Khan, who has been a great help to us."

Mrs. Rorke shook his hand saying, "How do you do." Then looking at Aiyasha, "Is she your sister?"

"No," said Ishmael, "we are not related. Her name is Shalhoub."

Mrs. Rorke put her hands together and said, "Well, you do know about the May Ball we're having tonight?"

"Yes," said Sonia.

"Good. Let me show you your rooms, where you can freshen up for tonight." She led the way. Elijah and Sonia were given one room, Aiyasha the one next to them and Ishmael got the one at the far end.

"We'll meet in the hall downstairs at seven p.m.," she said, "all right?" Then thinking of something she turned to Sonia, "My daughter is back in the States. She has a wardrobe full of gowns that are just about your size and Aiyashas. Come with me dear, I'll show you where they are and you can make your own choices."

Sonia and Aiyasha followed her, while Elijah and Ishmael went into their rooms and closed their doors. Elijah sat on the bed and looked down. He smiled to himself; it would be good to be alone with Sonia, after such a long time. He couldn't wait for her to return but must have dozed off. There was a knock on the door and it took him a minute to remember where he was. He opened the door and Sonia walked in with a red gown in her hands, holding it high, so that it didn't drag on the floor. She laid it upon the bed and looked at him. He walked over and put his arms around her. She looked up and put her hands around his head and they kissed like two people in the desert who had finally found an oasis. They nuzzled each other's neck.

"Oh, Eli," she whispered.

"Love you," Elijah said softly. He held her tight against him. They moved apart and Sonia undid the buttons on her blouse and let it drop. She next undid her bra and it joined her blouse on the floor.

The sight of her breasts brought a sigh from Elijah, "Oh, my God." He reached out to touch them. Sonia smiled. Soon the rest of their clothing lay on the floor and they were on the bed. They kissed again, a long kiss. Elijah moved his lips to her nipples, first one then the other. They turned hard between his lips. He moved his head down kissing her stomach and he lingered there nibbling.

Sometime later, they lay exhausted in each other's arms. After a while they made love again.

"Oh, I love you, I love you," whispered Sonia. Elijah just held her.

After maybe a half-hour, Sonia got off the bed. She paused and looked down at the floor. "Oh, look at this. My dress got knocked to the floor." She picked it up and looked at it. "No damage done." She smiled at Elijah and placed it on an armchair.

She looked at Elijah and said. "We have a party to attend. I need to shower."

"Yes," said Elijah, "you go first." He loved to watch her walk naked, her hair down, her breasts shaking and the curve of her hips and her rear. She turned her head and looked back at him and smiled and struck a pose, then another, with her arms above her head. Then she giggled and ran into the bathroom. Soon he could hear the shower running. After a while she stepped out, in a bathrobe with her hair tied up with a towel, like a turban.

When Elijah got out of the shower and had dried himself and combed his hair, he walked into the bedroom to find Sonia with the red gown on. She looked gorgeous. Her hair was up in a chignon and the gown hugged her in all the right places. It had straps over her shoulders and she had a diamond choker necklace around her throat. He had always seen her in a sari, but she looked just as elegant in this ballroom gown.

"Oh! My God," said Elijah, "I need a suit to escort you, looking like that." Then he stopped in his tracks. "You brought that along with you?" he asked, pointing to the diamond choker.

"Yes, I did," said Sonia, "I think there is a suit in your size right here in this closet." She took the hanger with the suit and handed it to him.

"Well I'll be," said Elijah. He laid it on the bed and started to put it on. There was a black tie that went with it. Now he looked equally elegant. "Wait," said Elijah, as he walked to the dresser and retrieved a small box he had placed there. This was something he had bought at the jewelers a few days ago. He brought it to where Sonia stood and dropping down on one knee opened it. The most perfect eight carat diamond sparkled in its setting on a ring.

"Will you marry me?" he asked, holding it up.

Sonia put both her hands to her face to hide her laughter. She sobered up and lowered her hands to hold Elijah's face.

"Yes," said Sonia, with her wide smile.

Elijah took her left hand and placed the ring on her finger. She put her arms around him and they held each other for a long time.

She pushed herself away and looking at him said, "Yes, I'll marry you. But I want four children and I don't want you kidnapped anymore. Tell them you're married if they come for you again."

"It's going to be fun being married to you."

"How old are you, Elijah?"

"I'm thirty and you?"

"I thought you knew my age. I'm twenty-eight."

"I kind of guessed, but you look much younger."

"Thank you, Elijah, you are most gallant." There was that twinkle in her eye again.

They both sat on the edge of the bed. Elijah was in deep thought for a while. "As marketing manager, you may consider exporting your product to the US. You could use my office in Oregon as a base to get started. That would give us a chance to be together without disrupting your job."

"That's a good suggestion. You think of everything don't you."

"It's something to put before the Board of Directors."

"You are going back to Portland and leaving me back here?" She was close to tears.

He put his arms around her. "Sonia, it's only for a short time. I have to check up on my business, get Ishmael started, while you are still working for Jullundur Machines and helping Aiyasha for the next three months."

"Well if that's all you care about me, the wedding is off."

Chapter Twenty-Six

Elijah was devastated when Sonia said that the wedding was off. His face paled and he gasped like he had taken an unexpected blow. He took a deep breath and wondered, how could she be so unreasonable?

He stopped what he was doing and bent down and looked at her face. She was smiling with mock hurt on the pulled down corners of her lips. Even those made her look cute.

She gave him a hug and kissed him on the lips. "I know, I was just kidding. But I shall hurt being away from you. Three months is a long time."

He held her close. Neither said anything and the minutes ticked by. Elijah finally spoke.

"And the marriage ceremony," said Elijah. "What do I have to do?"

"You will have to ride a white Arabian horse to the wedding palanquin. Remember the wedding procession we saw on our trip with Leela and Roy?"

"Oh, yes I do. Well I can ride a horse, as long as I don't have to ride it at a gallop."

"And you'll have to wear a special turban and a white suit with gold embroidery."

"I can do that. And remember you will have to wear a white gown with a train and a veil."

"Why? That's not part of our custom."

"Well, we want to make a melding of east meets west. A compromise," said Elijah, smiling.

"If you say so," said Sonia, standing and straightening her dress. " I'll go help Aiyasha, while you go see how Ishmael is doing."

Ishmael and Aiyasha had been given separate rooms adjacent to each other. Elijah walked to Ishmael's door and knocked, and waited.

Sonia knocked on Aiyasha's door which opened and Aiyasha let her in, to many gasps and squeals of delight.

Aiyasha had chosen a black dress with very short sleeves and a high neckline. With youth on her side, she looked striking, with the contrast in color of her light skin and the dark dress.

She had a chain of silver around the top of her forehead, just below her brown hair. A diamond gleamed in the center of the chain. That was the only piece of jewelry her mother had given her. She wore it like a princess. Sonia brushed her hair to make it fall to its full length, almost to her waist. Sonia adjusted the diamond so it lay just right in the center. They were both now ready to meet the men.

Ishmael also had a suit on. Elijah helped him with his black tie. "You look like a young and handsome Count," said Elijah. "Let's go meet our host and have some fun." They closed the door behind them and knocked on Aiyasha's door. Sonia opened it and the two ladies stepped out.

Ishmael couldn't control his enthusiasm. " *Aap donome bahuth koobsurath lagthi hi* (You both look very beautiful)," he blurted out. They bowed to him amidst soft laughter.

Elijah took Sonia's arm and led the way. Ishmael and Aiyasha followed, not daring to touch each other. They felt strangely on parade.

It was seven p.m. They walked down to the hall. Liveried attendants walked quickly past them, going in both directions. The sound of music floated from the rear of the hall where an orchestra was assembled.

The hall had been transformed into a well-lit ballroom. Several crystal chandlers shone their light down on about forty or fifty couples below. The couples had drinks in their hands and were talking in small groups. Sonia noted chairs in a row along the periphery of the hall where several older couples sat chatting.

The Ambassador and his wife saw them approach. Elijah walked over to them, "Mister Ambassador, I'm Elijah Davenport," he said, holding out his hand.

"John Rorke," he smiled and shook Elijah's hand. "Pleased to meet you, Mister Davenport."

"And this is my wife Sonia."

"How are you my dear? He smiled at Sonia, extending his hand. "You look lovely."

Sonia shook his hand. "How do you do," she said, then, "thank you." She smiled.

Elijah introduced Ishmael and Aiyasha, "Mister Ishmael Khan."

Ambassador Rorke shook his hand, "How do you do."

"And Aiyasha Shalhoub," said Elijah.

The Ambassador shook Aiyasha's hand, "How do you do my dear?"

Mrs. Rorke was beaming. She took Elijah and Sonia by the arm and said, "Come let me introduce you to some more people."

Soon they found themselves mingling with the other guests. Everyone had a drink in his or her hand. Elijah got Sonia a glass of red wine and one for himself. The bandleader announced, "Ladies and gentlemen, your partners for a waltz."

Elijah looked at Sonia and she smiled and nodded. He set his glass on a nearby table and so did Sonia. He held her hand and walked towards the center of the hall where others who intended to dance were gathering. The band struck up a Viennese waltz and Elijah and Sonia made a few tentative steps until they got a feel for the motion. Soon they were twirling around, like they had been dancing together all their lives. Elijah loved the feeling. Sonia seemed confident.

During a break, they sat next to Ishmael and Aiyasha, who seemed a bit concerned. She gave Sonia a worried look. "What if someone asks me to dance?" she asked.

"Well," said Sonia, "tell them, I don't know how to dance and they will say, don't worry, just follow me."

"So I should dance, if they ask me?" asked Aiyasha again, her eyes going wide in alarm.

"Yes," said Sonia, "you'll get used to it and maybe later, we'll teach you."

"Will you teach me too?" asked Ishmael.

"Yes," said Sonia, putting her arm on Ishmael's shoulder.

It wasn't long before a young man came over and asked Aiyasha for a dance. It was a slow foxtrot. "I don't know how to dance," she said, looking up at him.

Just like Sonia predicted, the young man smiled, and said, "I've just learned to dance myself. I can show you."

"All right," said Aiyasha, "but don't make me fall." She stood up and Ishmael was absolutely astounded.

"You are going to dance with him?" asked Ishmael.

"Yes, I'm going to try."

The young man held her right hand and his other arm went around her waist.

"When I move forward with my left foot," he said, "you move back with your right foot, All right?"

"Yes," said Aiyasha, timidly.

The young man moved forward with Aiyasha backing off.

"Wait till I tell her mother about this," said Ishmael to himself. "Dancing with strangers."

Elijah was preparing for another two step and walked up to Sonia and held out his hand. He hadn't seen Ishmael coming up behind him. Ishmael held out his hand to Aiyasha.

Aiyasha looked at Ishmael in amazement. "But you don't know how to dance," she said.

"I'll just follow you," said Ishmael. "You teach me."

She held his hand and put the other on his shoulder. "With your left foot forward, slow, slow, quick, quick," she said.

Sonia and Elijah found it hard to stifle their laughter. They just kept dancing with smiles on their faces.

The night was young and Ishmael and Aiyasha spent many hours trying to keep up with Elijah and Sonia.

Soon in the wee hours of the morning Aiyasha, just when she thought she had the hang of it, was surprised when the MC announced, "As all good things must come to an end, we have come to the last dance for the evening. Ladies and Gentlemen, your partners for a slow Foxtrot."

Later when they were walking back to their rooms, Sonia said, "I'll never forget this night for the rest of my life. I'm so happy."

Aiyasha who was walking by her side, nodded emphatically "And I shall never forget this night, either," she said. "I learned to dance."

Ishmael who was walking by the side of Elijah said, "And I too shall never forget this night, for the rest of my life. Aiyasha taught me how to dance."

Elijah laughed and the three of them laughed with him. They were happy. They were going home.

*   *   *

Rehman stopped at the nearest hotel, once they crossed into the city of Peshawar. He found the manager and made discreet enquiries. He came out and joined his men. "They are on their way to Islamabad," he said. "Let's go."

After reaching Islamabad late in the evening, they spread out seeking information on the van and its four occupants. They soon gleaned enough word of mouth to know that their quarry was inside the American Ambassador's place of residence.

"They're probably partying right now," said Rehman. "The damn infidels and their drinking and their women. We will give them a party when they leave in the morning." They had no problem finding a place for the night.

*   *   *

The next morning after expressing their deep gratitude to their hosts for their gracious hospitality, Elijah and his group bid Mister and Mrs. John Rorke a fond farewell. Mrs. Rorke was loath to let them go. But finally they were in the van headed eastward.

The marine at the gate to the Ambassador's palace saluted Elijah who was at the wheel of the van. The soldier walked over and Elijah lowered the window pane. "You might want to be on the alert," said the marine. "I saw a couple of Jeeps with suspicious characters in them. I'm sure they had weapons with them."

"Thank you," said Elijah. "We'll be on the lookout."

They drove through the outskirts of Islamabad. New concrete and red-brick buildings lined both sides of the road. Pedestrians ambled slowly, stopping at wayside vendors.

Elijah turned to Sonia and Ishmael. "Looks like Rehman and his men are nearby. Keep a lookout and have your guns ready. Also, Ishmael, give me two of the boxes with the explosive and detonators."

Ishmael shook his head. "We used the last units on the Jeeps at the bandits camp," he said. Elijah stared back at him letting that piece of information sink in.

Elijah switched his gaze to the rearview mirror and froze in fear. Two Jeeps had turned a corner in the distance and followed him. He accelerated and so did the lead Jeep. They were in a less populated part of the city now with a few abandoned buildings.

He made up his mind and pulled up in front of a closed gate leading to a courtyard of a two-storied building, hoping there weren't any inhabitants. "Open the gate Ishmael," he shouted.

Ishmael jumped out and unlatched it pushing it open. Elijah drove in and Ishmael closed the gate and shoved the latch on top. Elijah parked close to the front steps of the building. He looked back. The two Jeeps were a hundred meters away.

"Let's take cover in here," shouted Elijah, turning off the ignition . He hit the ground running with his rifle. Sonia did the same on her side of the van, running ahead of him to the front of the house pushing at the closed door. It was locked. Elijah hit the door handle with the butt of his gun and it flew apart. He pushed on the massive door but it remained locked. He turned to look if Rehman's Jeeps were in sight, then stepped back and heaved a mighty kick at the spot where the lock used to be. The door held.

Ishmael and Aiyasha were right behind them. "Let's kick at the center of the door together," shouted Elijah.

"Jee," shouted Ishmael, raising his right foot.

On the count of three Ishmael and Elijah's legs struck together and the door gave way with a rasping sound.

They crowded in onto a landing. A stairway led upwards. The rest of the room lay in darkness. No time to explore. They ran up the steps. Looking out from the first floor windows they saw the two Jeeps pull up outside the walled compound and the men jump out and take cover behind the vehicles. Several of the men fired their rifles and the windows in front of Elijah and Ishmael shattered. They were lucky not to be hit by the flying shards. Aiyasha let out a scream taken by surprise at the sound of the exploding glass. She screamed again. This time in pain as a bullet grazed her right upper arm. Sonia pulled her away from the window. With the dim light available she could make out a gouge deep enough to bleed.

"Give me your knife, Ishmael," said Sonia, like she was getting used to dressing wounds in the field.

Ishmael handed her his long knife drawn from his scabbard on his thigh.

Sonia inserted the tip of the blade between Aiyasha's arm and the fabric of her shirt and cut away the sleeve. She cut the cloth salvaged further into strips and bound the wound.

"*Shukria*," said Aiyasha.

Elijah and Ishmael were stationed at the two windows, five meters apart and firing their rifles when a target came into sight. They had a limited amount of ammunition and had to be careful.

*   *   *

One of Rehman's men made a dash for the gate from the safety provided by the Jeeps. Elijah shot him just as he pushed the iron frame, which squealed on its rusty hinges, and moved but a few inches. He fell to the ground blocking the entrance but it also held the gate open by six inches.

Rehman was furious. "Two of you aim your guns on the windows. At my signal you start firing. Iqbal, you run through the open gate and into the building. Wait there until one or more of us can join you. *Sumja*?"

"*Jee,*" said the three.

He looked up at the building and shouted, "Now!"

The two opened up a chatter of bullets raining towards Elijah and Ishmael who ducked down. Iqbal sprinted, pushed his way through the opening and made it to the open door. He stepped into the dark room and could see the stairway leading up. He waited in the gloomy room that stank of mildew and thought he heard mice scurrying around.

*   *   *

When the firing stopped Elijah and Ishmael slowly raised their heads and peered out. Elijah did a quick head count. "I think one of them is in the house below," he said. "Sonia, you and Aiyasha stand guard at the top of the stairs." He and Ishmael pushed a bureau away from a wall and into the hall to command a view of the stairway.

"Hide behind this barricade and watch," said Elijah, moving back to his position by the window.

Elijah looked out at the gate. The two Jeeps were parked close to the now open gate. "Try to hit the gas tank of the nearest Jeep," he said to Ishmael.

They both fired and the taillights of the Jeep flew into pieces with a clatter. They could see Rehman and his three men move closer to the brick wall.

"Try again," said Elijah.

Ishmael paused, aimed and fired. The rear of the Jeep blossomed into an orange ball of flame followed by a loud explosion. The whole vehicle lifted into the air in a fiery mass and fell back in pieces near and around the steel gate.

"What was that?" asked Sonia, distracted from her watch at the top of the stairs.

"We just destroyed one of their Jeeps," said Elijah. "But Rehman and his men are still out there."

Sonia turned her attention back to the immediate threat down the stairs. "Whoever is down there has to reach the landing before we can see him," whispered Sonia, noticing the stairway broke up into two flights. "Shall I call the ambassador's office for help?" continued Sonia, addressing Elijah.

He turned around and said, "I don't have his number."

*   *   *

All the gunfire had attracted the attention of the people living nearby and a crowd was gathering, though they stood a hundred meters back.

"What's going on?" asked one young man in Hindi. He had a large mustache.

"Looks like those are Muslim militants," said his neighbor.

"Should we join in and throw stones at them?" said yet another.

"Are you crazy?" said Mustache. "They'll turn those guns on us."

"Who are the people in the building?"

"Maybe another gang. That's Mr. Pandit's house. He's not going to like that when he gets back."

*   *   *

Rehman was getting ready to send his next man into action when the Jeep blew up. He and his men hugged the wall for protection and waited. When the debris stopped falling he looked around. "We're running low on ammunition," he said. "Try to make each shot count from now on."

*   *   *

Elijah tapped Ishmael on the shoulder. "Let's see if we can get a better shot from upstairs," he said. He ran up the stairs with Ishmael following. As he opened the door to the room he was shocked to see an elderly lady sitting in an armchair with a light turned on at a table. The room smelled of stale food. The woman stared at him crinkling her wizened eyebrows. "What are you doing in my house?" she asked.

Chapter Twenty-Seven

Elijah was stunned to find an elderly woman in a room in the house they had so invasively intruded in. The woman had demanded what he was doing in her house. She now continued, "And what is all that noise? My caretaker will be here shortly. She will make you get out." She spoke in English.

"I'm terribly sorry," stammered Elijah, completely taken aback by the fact that someone lived in the house. "But we were only seeking shelter from some men who wish to kill us."

"Now you'll have me killed also. Get out and leave me alone." The woman was seventy or eighty years old. She had a shawl covering her head and the skin on her face and hands were wrinkled. She wore glasses and had a book lying in her lap.

"This is awful," said Elijah. "Ishmael, keep an eye on the men outside."

Ishmael moved to a window. Two shots rang out and the lower floor windows exploded with the sound of breaking glass.

Ishmael saw a man run into the building. "That makes two men downstairs," shouted Ishmael so Sonia and Aiyasha could hear him.

Elijah once again addressed the lady. "How come the lights are off downstairs and yet you have power?"

"The breakers were turned off by my son. Since I don't move around he left just these on. Now get out."

When the old lady told Elijah to get out of her house, he sighed and looked away. She definitely has the right to tell me that, he thought. I'm the one who broke into her house. But it isn't easy to just get out. The men downstairs were the immediate threat.

"Those men who want to kill us are downstairs," said Elijah. "They could mean you harm too."

"But I wouldn't be in this position if it weren't for you," said the old lady with spirit.

"I know," said Elijah. "But I didn't know the building was occupied." He looked at her with a great sense of guilt. "However I could get rid of those men if there is a way down to the ground floor other than these stairs."

The Hunt for the Rajput Princess

The old lady considered his request for a moment then said, "The next room will lead you to the rear of the house and there's a balcony outside that bedroom. You look like a strapping fellow. You can swing down from there to the ground. The outside doors are locked, but you can use these keys." She dangled a bunch on a cord tied to her waist and as Elijah watched, she unclipped them and handed the lot to him.

With the keys in one hand and the machine gun in the other, Elijah spoke to Ishmael, "You keep the two men outside occupied, but don't waste any bullets. I'm going down and shall try to enter from the back doors."

Ishmael turned back to the window while Elijah opened the door to the next room. He didn't turn on any lights but walked in the semi-darkness through a carpeted bedroom that had a large bed and an armoire and a couple of armchairs. He opened the next door and stood on the balcony, which had iron rails all around, and a few flowerpots on the floor. The sun shone in the evening sky, cloudless and bright. People had gathered in the neighboring buildings at their windows and balconies to see what the commotion was about. Smoke and the smell of gasoline from the burning Jeep still lingered in the air.

He shoved the keys into his pocket and climbed over the railing. Then with the gun slung around his neck, he bent down and grasped the uprights of the metal railings and lowered his body to hang from the balcony, his feet about two meters from the ground. He dropped and landed on his feet and recovered with a bounce. He carefully selected a key and inserted it into the lock on the door. Wrong one. He tried another and yet another before he heard a click. Slowly he pushed the door open. The room was dark but for the light flooding in from the open door. He closed the door returning the room to darkness and felt his way to the connecting door to the rest of the lower floor where the two men waited with their guns. He could hear them moving around. They seemed unsure of what to do next without Rehman's directions. If there were some way of distracting them, thought Elijah. He unlatched the door carefully. This one wasn't locked. He took out his phone and dialed Sonia's number. In a second he could hear it ring on the upper floor.

*   *   *

Sonia and Aiyasha crouched behind the dresser, peering above the piece of furniture. After some tense waiting they saw a sandaled foot tentatively placed on the landing. Aiyasha nodded and they both stood, shouldered their guns and fired. Their bullets chipped the nosing of the wooden stair and the foot disappeared with a yell and a few curses.

They both hunkered back down, their eyes gleaming with fear and uneasiness. "What if they rush up firing their weapons?" whispered Sonia.

"We'll have to look from the sides of this wooden barricade, instead of above it," whispered Aiyasha. "Let's get a table on this side. That will give me more protection. I'll ask Ishmael to help me."

She got Ishmael's attention and she noticed Elijah missing. "Where's Elijah?" she asked.

"He's trying to go to the lower floor from the back of the house."

Together they moved a table onto its side, the round top facing the stairs and Aiyasha crawled in between its legs. This protected her, while she could see past the edge and Sonia did the same on the farther side of the dresser. Ishmael went back to his window.

It happened exactly as Sonia had predicted. Bullets thudded into their barricade and impacted the walls behind them, raining chips from the ceiling. around them.

Sonia looked at Aiyasha and said as loud as she could, "Wait till they show themselves."

The two men rushed up the stairs and Sonia and Aiyasha fired. The man in front was hit in the shoulder and dropped his gun to clutch at his arm and sit down. The second man fell heavily and slid down the steps out of sight. The first man crawled away.

Sonia saw that the table protecting Aiyasha lay in pieces and she was bleeding from cuts on her face made by the flying wood splinters.

Sonia felt the dresser had done a better job. She was temporarily blinded as dust from the ceiling fell in her eyes. We seem to have survived the onslaught, she thought. What will happen next, she wondered in fear.

With her pulse running high, Sonia slouched on the floor. She gave a start when her phone started to ring. Who would be calling me now? she wondered, not bothering to take it out of her gown. It rang again and they heard more shooting down below. They waited not knowing what to expect.

*　　　　*　　　　*

Elijah hoped the two men would react to the sound of the phone and focus their attention towards the head of the stairs away from the door where he was hiding. On the second ring he swung his gun into position and eased the door open. He saw the two men pointing their rifles upwards ready to fire. The door behind Elijah creaked and the men jumped turning around in unison and started firing. Elijah squeezed the trigger and fell to the floor keeping his machine-gun aligned and still belching flame. A bullet hit him in the shoulder and he felt a searing pain. He rolled and came to rest on his stomach. Both men had been hit and lay crumpled at the foot of the stairs, moaning.

Just as Elijah raised his knee to pick his way up, the front door crashed open and a bearded man with a turban and *patoo* opened fire into the dark room not taking pains to determine if he were shooting at friend or foe. Elijah fell back flattening himself to the floor. He could hear and feel the bullets whizz above him. The firing suddenly ceased and Elijah heard an empty click. The man had emptied his magazine. Elijah raised his gun and shot the man in the leg and he went down. Elijah ran to him and kicked away the smoking weapon. "You guys OK up there?" he called before he stepped out of the lower floor through the damaged door.

Sonia and Aiyasha heard him and moved the dresser, pushing and pulling. It was heavy and took an effort to move a few inches. They squeezed through the gap and slowly walked down with their guns ready. The room smelled of cordite.

*　　　　*　　　　*

Rehman seethed in anger when he saw his last man fall in the doorway of the building. As he stared in frustration, the door opened and Elijah fired at him from the cover of the door.

"You damn American," screamed Rehman. "You will not live to see another day." He raised his machine-gun and let loose a barrage of fire that made splinters fly off the door.

Elijah moved away. The door no longer afforded much protection. The firing stopped and Elijah peered from a window to see Rehman squeezing the trigger on an empty magazine.

Elijah stepped over the man lying in the threshold and into the open, pointing his rifle at Rehman. They stared at each other. Rehman with all the hate of a lifetime towards a people who had destroyed his way of life and all that was near and dear to him. Elijah advanced one measured step at a time, slow and sure.

Rehman stood his feet braced apart, the useless smoking rifle in his hands. They were now ten meters apart. With an oath Rehman flung the gun away and in a fluid motion drew the Mauser from his belt and pointed it at Elijah. Rehman couldn't miss at this distance. He was a crack shot at a hundred meters. Elijah stopped in his tracks, his gun still pointed at Rehman's chest.

"Go ahead," said Rehman, "pull the trigger and we'll see who is the better marksman." His hand holding the Mauser was steady and he held it at arm's length like he did at target practice.

"Your people killed my parents," snarled Rehman, with hate in his voice and his face contorted with the memory of his loss. "But you did help the village." He nodded and his hand wavered and lowered to his side.

Elijah relaxed his finger on the trigger.

Then with a change of heart, Rehman's arm swung in a sharp arc and the gun roared. Elijah spun around hit in the left shoulder. "I shall kill you piece by piece," said Rehman, raising his gun again.

Elijah was in pain and though he still held the gun his arm had dropped. He knelt down then raised his knee and supported the weapon on his thigh.

Rehman held his gun at arm's length for the final shot.

Two shots rang out and both men remained in their respective positions. Then ever so slowly Rehman's arm dropped to his side and a bright spot of crimson appeared on his left chest and another on his right and yet another on his sternum. His body folded to the ground.

The strength left Elijah's fingers and he dropped his gun. His mind whirled. Of all the things he could think of, he kept wondering that he had heard only two shots. He looked back at the building and saw Ishmael's smoking rifle at the window and lower down at the broken entrance door stood Sonia and Aiyasha, their rifles still at their shoulders. His knee buckled and he sat on the ground and put his head in his hands, thoughts still flickering vaguely in his mind. He was thinking about Sonia and Aiyasha, how just two weeks ago they hadn't handled a rifle ever in their lives. Good Lord, he thought. We've become a bunch of guerrillas. Will we ever be able to live a normal life after this?

Two trucks with Pakistani army personnel drew up at the scene. About fifty soldiers deployed rushing past the smoldering Jeep to the perimeter of the battered building. The officer in charge talked to Elijah and ordered his men to check out the lower floor.

The Army Medic examined Elijah's injured arm and found no bones broken, but an entry and exit wound in his deltoid muscle. The Medic sutured the wound as a field professional would, applied a dressing and immobilized the arm with a sling.

Aiyasha too got her wounds taken care of. She had a few lesions on her face, which the doctor assured her wouldn't leave a permanent scar.

They carried the two dead men on stretchers and helped the wounded into the trucks. Elijah looked at the body of Rehman being carried away on a stretcher.

You captured me for no reason at all, he thought. Then hounded me all the way to Hell. You had your reasons and I had mine to survive.

He thanked the Pakistani major for their help and moved towards the building. He had to make his peace with the lady of the house. Her caretaker had arrived after she found it safe to enter the building. She was an older woman who seemed at a loss at the sudden changes in what used to be her normal routine. She moved tentatively around all these people in her employer's house. However the first thing she had to do was prepare a meal for her mistress. She was busy in the kitchen and the smell of cooking floated in the air.

Her name was Lakshmi. Elijah interrupted her in the kitchen and talked to her. "The front door will be boarded up while they make repairs."

"Yes, sir," said Lakshmi.

Elijah now had the formidable task of facing the old lady. Sonia and Aiyasha stood in the background not wanting to interfere. Elijah apologized profusely and said, "I will make arrangements with a local carpenter to repair the damaged windows and to replace the front door."

"That's the least you can do," said the lady, with a twinkle in her eyes. "I see you hurt your wing. Hope you feel better soon."

"Thank you. I must take your leave now," said Elijah, taking her wizened hand in his.

"Where are you going?" she asked.

"To Jullundur in India," said Elijah.

Chapter Twenty-Eight

They made it back to Jullundur without further incident. Soon after Elijah had checked that all was well with the factory he left for the US to take care of business back home. Aiyasha sat for her entrance exams at the Christian Medical College. After a harrowing week of waiting they found out she had not made it. Reviewing the details of her test, Sonia found out Aiyasha's lack of a good grasp of English had played a prominent part in her failure.

"I've assigned a private tutor to coach you in English," said Sonia. "She will help you with understanding the terms and make the test easier to take next time."

Ishmael needed coaching too. Elijah, with Sonia's help found a High School Equivalency course. Ishmael brushed up on many subjects that had fallen by the wayside in his education at his village in Afghanistan.

While living with Sonia and occasionally with Leela and her husband, Roy, Ishmael worked diligently and in three months passed the test and got a High School diploma. He was now ready for college.

Elijah was still in Portland. Sonia concentrated on Aiyasha's education. After two months of intense training, Aiyasha took the test again with a lot of trepidation during the last week and butterflies in her stomach on the final day. Sonia could feel the agony Aiyasha was going through and empathized and encouraged her as best she could. When the results were announced that she had passed the test this time, the feeling of relief for both of them was immeasurable.

The relief expressed itself when Aiyasha jumped around screaming in delight while Sonia looked on, beaming like a proud mother.

"I knew you could do it," said Sonia, giving Aiyasha a warm hug.

Three months later, after taking care of business in Portland, Elijah arrived back in Jullundur. He and Sonia were married in a civil court and later in a lavish Rajput wedding ceremony, attended by her parents and brother and a host of Sonia's friends.

Elijah did indeed ride a white Arabian stallion to the wedding palanquin. He felt silly and could well imagine Sonia chuckling behind her composed smiling face. After the many farewell parties, Sonia settled down and joined Elijah on the flight back to Portland, Oregon. She now had the title of Manager of the Overseas Branch of Jullundur Machines Limited. Aiyasha was a freshman at the Christian Medical College at Ludhiana. Ishmael had entered the Engineering Program at Jullundur University. They both lived on campus, with Elijah taking care of the expenses involved.

*   *   *

Aiyasha packed up all her books and put them in her knapsack. She walked to a knoll on the campus of Christian Medical College and found a bench and sat down. It was late in the evening but the sun still shone. An Asian Koel called plaintively in the distance. "Koo-Ooo," it sang. A few white clouds floated lazily in a blue sky. To the north were the Himalayas, but all she could see was a white haze. To the south, was the campus sports arena. A soccer field stood in the center surrounded by an official Olympic size track. Many a prominent track star in India had taken advantage of the higher altitude and the cooler climate to practice in this arena. Ishmael had played soccer here and soon glowed as a star forward. He had spent one semester at the University, before immigrating to the US to attend the Electrical Engineering program at the University of Portland. A Mister Davenport had sponsored him, according to the Dean.

Aiyasha looked to the left. A month earlier, under that grove of dark leafed Beech trees, she and Ishmael had talked of the future.

"We will keep in touch," said Ishmael.

"Yes," nodded Aiyasha, feeling numb with pent up emotion. "I will email you every so often."

"Yes, so will I."

With tears in her eyes, she said plaintively, "But when I become a doctor I want to return to Afghanistan and my people."

"I will come with you," said Ishmael, putting his arms around her, forgetting all the conventions he had been raised in. That had been so long ago, thought Aiyasha.

The Hunt for the Rajput Princess

Coming back to the present, she picked up her knapsack and walked back to the dormitory where she lived with two other students. Since it wasn't time for dinner yet, she sat down at her desk and opened her laptop. She signed in and started, "My dear Ishmael, . .

*　　　　*　　　　*

In the hills of West Pakistan, a council was in session. The second in command for Fundamentalist Muslims made a comment. "We have lost a valuable member of our organization in Abdul Rehman. His methods were rather unorthodox, but we must avenge his death. I want a squad sent to Jullundur, in India, and matters taken care of."

There were several nods from the men around him.

"It will be done," said one of the men.

"They say a Rajput princess was involved. Find the princess and the rest will fall into place."

The hunt was on.

The End

Read Ralph Beaumont's and Laura Connelly's first adventure by author Oscar Z. Hutson

When terrorists snatch a surveillance robotic butterfly and kill the inventor, his friend Ralph vows those responsible will burn.

Ralph and his friend, Laura soon find their role reversed when the militants with a fanatic leader targets them for execution. Now they must run or stand and fight for their lives.

****

"Entertaining characters and cool gadgets. I want one of those Butterflies."

Cindy Hiday

Read Ralph Beaumont's and Laura Connelly's second adventure in the series, Mughal Gold by author Oscar Hutson

The Hunt for the Rajput Princess

In a historic battle in 1739, Nadir Shah, Emperor of Persia defeated the Mughal Emperor, Shah Jahan in Delhi. As the spoils of war he is forced to give up the famous Koh-hi-noor, the Peacock throne and two chests of diamonds and rubies. On their return journey through Afghanistan the Persian General entrusted with the chests of diamonds,

finds them large and cumbersome. He hides the diamonds in a cave on a cliff and draws a map on calfskin with details in Arabic.

In a surprise attack by Afghan Bandits, among those killed is the General with the calfskin still attached to his belt. An Afghan villager finds it and saves the map thinking it to be a prayer mat.

Fast forward to present day Istanbul, Turkey, where Ralph Beaumont and Laura Connelly are vacationing. On a visit to a famous mosque, they rescue a man with knife-wounds who has sought sanctuary in the holy place.

When the man, an Iranian recovers in the hospital, he mentions finding a map with an English archeologist Professor Oliver Goldsmith while exploring in the hills of Afghanistan. Oliver has translated the map and knows there's a fortune to be found.

When the Iranian disappears, Ralph and Laura take an interest in clues leading to the map and the treasure. With technical gadgets from the Robotic Institute in Berkeley, it looks like Ralph and Laura may beat Oliver in the quest for the richest collection of precious gems never before seen.

Oliver is not giving up. He intends to follow them to the ends of the earth and is willing to kill for what three nations may claim as theirs.

****

With meticulous research that makes you feel like you're making your way through the narrow streets of Istanbul or gaping at the brilliance of the Koh-hi-noor, Oscar Hutson takes you on a ride filled with twists and turns that will keep you turning pages until the very end.

Julie Clark

**Read Ralph Beaumont's and Laura Connelly's
third adventure in the Trilogy, The Flight of the
White Dove by author Oscar Hutson**

The Hunt for the Rajput Princess

With the millions made from the sale of one of their diamonds, Ralph Beaumont and his fiancè, Laura Connelly, succumb to the urge to help refugees from the embattled land of Syria.

Laura works as a nurse at the Tent City in Turkey near Aleppo on the borders of the two countries. Ralph joins the rebels with a leader named Akbar, against Bashar Assad in Syria. With the means and a strategy of his own, Ralph and Akbar's men wreck two platoons of Russian tanks and with the aid of his robotic Butterfly are able to break into Assad's high security prison and release thousands of rebels held for treason.

But when Ralph and Laura learn of the rebels being equally brutal with the execution of Assad's men taken as prisoners, Ralph is disheartened and decides to leave Syria.

Assad, however wants Ralph and Laura captured and returned to Syria for the damage they have caused to his regime.

With Akbar's help, they flee to France, only to be followed through the streets of Paris and the beaches of Nice by a hired assassin.

* * * * * * * *

"Oscar Hutson exquisitely blends intrigue, romance and espionage in this adventure that follows the amazing travels of Ralph and Laura on their dangerous mission to help Syrian rebels against Assad's forces. I loved the robotic Butterfly."

Erin Lehn Floresca